In My
Time
Of
Dying

Published by Long Midnight Publishing, 2020

copyright © 2020 Douglas Lindsay

ISBN: 979-8689844817

www.douglaslindsay.com

IN MY TIME OF DYING

DOUGLAS LINDSAY

1

There's some shitty line in the book *Jaws*, when the Richard Dreyfus character's taking a piss, and Chief Brody's wife's fantasising about him – they skipped this narrative thread in the movie – and she wonders at the amazing size of his man-bladder, and how he can just keep peeing and peeing, as though this was some epic, Herculean ability, bestowed upon men by the Gods.

Aside from the questionable, eye-rolling absurdity of having a grown woman impressed by this shit, it's also complete bollocks. Nevertheless, I read that book when I was a kid, and that always stuck with me, and for decades I imagined there was this significant difference between gigantic man-bladders, and those dainty little female bladders that need emptying every fifteen minutes or so.

Somewhere along the way I realised the truth of it. Men either have to constantly plan ahead, or else spend large chunks of their life searching for the toilet, while women can last literally days not giving a fuck. Next time you're on a commuter train, look around. You'll be able to spot the guy who should've gone before he got on board. His legs'll be jiggling like a bastard, and he'll be looking incredibly uncomfortable. Meanwhile, even if there are seven or eight women in the carriage who need to go, you'll never know. They'll just be sitting there, like a boss. For women, needing to pee is a thing that happens. For men, it's an event horizon.

I think about Chief Brody's wife every time I find myself caught short. Happened at the weekend. Ended up in a bar in the centre of town. One of those things, one of those evenings. Drank vodka for four and a half hours. Embarrassingly, pathetically drunk at the end of it.

Tried it on with four women. The first one humoured me, out of pity, for fifteen minutes or so. Then she blew me off. But not in a good way. The next completely ignored me. Probably just as well. She may, *may* your honour, not have been twenty yet. It's not like I need any more reasons to hate myself as soon as I wake up in the morning. The third introduced her boyfriend to the party, not long after I'd complimented her breasts, and that could have gone badly until I showed him my ID card, and he backed the fuck off. The effectiveness of the ID card isn't exactly a given, but on this occasion it did the trick. And then there was the fourth, near the end of the night, when she was as drunk as I was. Holy shit. She was no oil painting, I'll give her that. She, I'm sure, could have said the same for me. So that might all have worked out, until she sicked up a little into her mouth while we were slobbering at each other, then she ran off to the toilet and I never saw her again.

Beautiful night out. Clear sky, crisp and fresh. Decided to walk home from the middle of town. What is it? Four miles, maybe. Saved me worrying about throwing up in a taxi. At some point, inevitably, I needed to take a piss. I thought of Ellen Brody, and how disappointed she would've been in my inability to walk home without having to use the toilet.

I stopped and peed against a fence. Two-fifteen in the morning, somewhere in Dalmarnock, on a cold night in early October. A car pulled up just behind me as I was in the act. I turned round to tell them to fuck off, and was confronted by a plod, approaching, while sensibly keeping enough distance in case I turned out to be one of those wankers who'd try to piss on the copper.

We had a chat. During the chat it emerged that I too was a police officer, and senior to him as well.

Perhaps I could have handled it better. Perhaps I was a bit of a dick about it. I was drunk after all. In the end, he of course let me on my way, but my dickery has had its inevitable consequence, and so here I am, standing in front of the new Chief Inspector, getting my arse handed to me.

* * *

'How long have I been here?' she asks.

Chief Inspector Hawkins. Sophie Hawkins. St Andrews alumna, fast track police career, doubt she's ever looked a criminal in the eye, several years younger than me, dyes her hair a weird grey, though it kind of looks purple in some lights, and exactly the kind of woman I'd hit on, drunk in a bar, at one in the morning.

Yeah, all right, there's not a woman alive I wouldn't hit on,

—

2

drunk in a bar, at one in the morning.

'Two weeks,' I say, playing along, as though this is some kind of expositional opening scene in a new TV series.

'Two weeks,' she says, nodding, as virtually anyone would've scripted.

Way too early to get the handle on her. Promoted above her ability? Got where she is because she's banging the Chief Constable's nephew? Bureaucrat? Paper pusher? Petty, pill-popping ladder climber? Vindictive chip on her shoulder about us proper coppers on the front line?

Says more about me than her – a lot more – that all the potential character types I invest her with are pejorative.

Maybe she's good. Maybe she got where she is because she can run shit, she's good with people, she has an eye for police work. Nevertheless, all I see is the attractive younger woman, stepping on the balls of the workers in the trenches, as she makes her way to the top.

'Can I be honest?'

We look at each other across the desk. I don't bother with the *you're in charge, you can say whatever you like* line.

'No point in being anything else, is there?' she says, answering her own question. 'I'd heard about you, of course. I presumed you'd've been long gone when I was given this station. Couldn't believe they brought you back.'

'Needs must…'

'They must have needed a lot. Well, here we are, you and me… It's a small station, cut to the bone, and we're going to have to make the best of it.'

Another one of those stares. The one where I stare blankly at her, and she looks inside me, and reads me like the cheap headline on the front of a hack newspaper.

'I understand you've had sex with most of the women at the station,' she says.

'Not any more,' I toss back quickly, deciding to engage in the conversation, rather than invoke mock offense that she's enquiring about my sex life.

'What does that mean?'

'That's old news. The old days. I went away for a while, and when I came back, things had changed. The constables had changed.' A beat. 'I haven't had sex with anyone at this station in, I don't know, three years maybe. Most of them call me granddad.'

—

3

'Well, that's a start.'

Finally shake my head. Can't really be doing with the telling off. There's work to be done. People to interview. Criminals to crush.

'Can I get on?'

'I'm going to need you to go on some courses.'

Jesus suffering holy fuck, what new madness is this?

'What?'

'Courses.'

'What courses?'

'There are a variety of health and safety courses, there's diversity and inclusion, there's the manager's toolkit. There are a variety of BAME issues…'

'Really? That's never been a prob –'

'And I know there's an AA meeting in French Street, you might –'

'I've been.'

A beat.

'You might want to consider re-attending. There's also the more general addiction meeting, which you might also want to…'

'I've been to that too.'

'And I see here you've been to counselling before, perhaps that's –'

'I had sex with the counsellor.'

'I'm sure we could find you a male counsellor, or a woman you don't find attractive.'

'I find all women attractive.'

She stares blankly across the table. She swallows.

'I'll send you a list of the courses I'd like you to attend, then we can talk about it.'

'Can I get on?' I repeat. The same words as a minute ago, the other side of this conversation where the young chief inspector decided she would try to shape me.

I have not contempt, just sorrow.

'Don't be getting ideas,' she says. Must still be thinking about that casual line I threw out about finding all women attractive. And really, is that true? Nah, of course not. Although, there's something there, you know. Take the physically most unattractive woman, and imagine her on the point of orgasm, her face alive with passion. Whole different ball game. Or the coldest, meanest bitch, the one you can't stand, the one who

—

4

makes your life miserable, the woman you hate with every ounce of your being, and do the same. Stripped bare, all the artifice and the malice gone, lost to the moment, in the throes of orgasm. Phew… Totally different picture.

And yes, this just applies to women. Even attractive men look brutish in orgasm. I know this, because I've seen them in porn movies.

'You're glazing over,' she says, and she snaps her fingers, albeit, she's not quite close enough to me to do it in front of my face.

'Sorry.'

'Look, I know about… it's all over your file, that you had an affair with the previous female head of the station. I expect you have a grid you tick off, or something. Just… I'm just warning you, don't even go there.'

I stare blankly across the desk. I can feel myself shutting down.

How small we all are. How trivial. How inconsequential. Me. Her. All of us.

She continues talking. She changes subject. Well, the subject is still me and my deficiencies, but she does at least move on from the possibility of her and I ending up in bed. Which, if I can just be fair to myself for a moment, was not something that had even crossed my mind.

Now, though… Now it's crossed my mind.

—

2

Her eyes open.

Lying on her back, mouth dry. She licks her lips, swallows. Wonders if she's been snoring.

Thinks about Harry. Can't sense him next to her. Moves her hand to the right, the sheets are cold.

She blinks, lifts her phone, checks the time. The light of it illuminates the room. 2:25. No messages.

Clicks the light off, settles her head back on the pillow. Her eyes are wide now, and she feels a twist in her stomach.

Harry.

Working late was one thing. He often worked late. Midnight wasn't out of the question. But he'd messaged at eleven, said he wouldn't be too much longer. What time had she turned out the light? 11:15?

A noise beside her right ear. A tap on the pillow. She turns her head, lifting it slightly. What was that?

It's dark, she sees nothing. Maybe a fly? She hadn't noticed a fly in the room, nor heard the sound of it.

She holds her head just above the pillow, listening. Listening. Waiting.

Nothing.

She settles back, eyes still wide open staring straight up. Strange shadows on the ceiling, cast by the street lights through the gap in the curtains.

What was casting the shadow? Her brain not working properly. It's sensing something is wrong, but it's not functioning alertly enough to identify the cause of the ill feeling in the pit of her stomach.

Something, something cool and liquid and heavy, drops onto her forehead. Her heart pounds, she bolts upright, she fumbles for the light…

3

Can't sleep. Some time in the middle of the night. Feeling stupid and useless and wasted and pointless, at the worst end of inadequate. Like inadequate has a good end.

I had some time off a while ago. Paid leave while my behaviour during my previous case was examined by the appropriate internal police authorities. I was found wanting, but since my existence had come to the attention of the press during the course of that investigation, my superiors chose to represent my actions as those of a hero. So the police wouldn't look bad, I guess. I was praised for not shooting the suspect when I had him in front of me, a gun in my hand.

Seemed slim heroic pickings, given he was unarmed at the time. Anyway, that was the narrative they went with, and since there was a certain amount of redemption involved, the press went along with it. Apparently on Twitter, that happy blend of art, music, wonder and total dumbfuckery, I was vilified by the American Right for not popping a bullet in the guy's head. I deserve, so many of them opined, to die for my pusillanimity.

If only.

Nevertheless, despite being cast as the hero of my own story, it didn't mean the police actually wanted me back. Quietly put out to grass was their plan, although it never actually got to a stage of being fully formulated. Paid leave while under investigation, became unpaid leave.

Then, somewhere along the way, Covid-19 came along and bit everyone on the arse. The police were already struggling for numbers, and then when the lockdown was lifted and crime got an uptick – *It's back! And it's bigger and better than ever!* – they started calling in the random strays, recent retirees, and ne'er-do-well police outcasts.

It was a different station I got called back to. They'd sold up the building, moving back to smaller premises, where we used to be, in Cambuslang precinct, that shithole of a 1960s building project. The superintendent had taken early retirement, and been replaced with a Chief Inspector. Our resident DCI, Dan Taylor, was still here when I got back, but he didn't last much longer. I still talk to him every now and again. Shorn of work discussions and shared senior officer resentment, neither of us has properly adjusted to the new dynamic. Perhaps it'll come. DC Morrow's also gone. Passed his sergeant's exam, and they moved him to Baillieston. Good on him. Decent kid, has way more going for him than I've ever had.

There's a new Detective Inspector. Kadri Kallas. Estonian. Long, light brown hair, attractive, slim, early forties, blunt as fuck. Been in Scotland fifteen years. I'd be lying if I said I hadn't thought about sleeping with her, but she's married, she has three children, I have zero chance, and so far, thank fuck, I've been fortunate enough not to be drunk in her presence, and therefore haven't done anything stupid. Our working relationship is fine, helped by her quickly adopting Taylor's attitude towards me. That of the slightly concerned, slightly troubled, slightly baffled parent.

Given she's about ten years younger than me, that's pretty fucking embarrassing.

The constables have changed, or if they haven't, I don't remember them. Sgt Harrison's still here, thank God, so I've got someone to sit with at lunch. Not that the new place has a canteen. Now we eat at our desks, or we muddle out into the precinct and sit on a bench, trying not to overhear other peoples' conversations.

When I think of all the coming and going, the ripping up and barely reassembling of the station collective, I hear the words *All change!* cried out in the background in the middle of *Supper's Ready*. Haven't listened to that song in years, but it's still in my head, somewhere.

All change!

Except nothing changes. And this is what we do when we're unhappy, when life gives us nothing to hang our hats on. We regress, and cling to the certainties of youth. Nothing can happen to them. Set in stone. Me and my mates listening to early Genesis, when everyone else had moved on. Reading *Jaws*. Long hot summer of '76. The ruination of Ally MacLeod in Argentina. Playing down by the river. Spangles and Marathon and a finger of fucking fudge, and that impatient little cunt with the conker.

Can't sleep. Think of doing various things, but they all threaten to extend the wakefulness into early morning – get up and drink, watch TV, listen to music, read a book, masturbate –

but I don't want to do any of it, so I lie with my eyes determinedly shut, occasionally shifting position. Mind all over the place, but the only time it seems to settle is on some uncomfortable embarrassment, all those occasions that lurk in amongst the certainties, emerging from the fog of the past.

My phone wakes me up at one minute past three. The last I looked at the time it was two-fifty-one, yet the sleep feels deep, like my head was completely buried in another world.

'What?' is all I can manage.

'Probable murder,' says Ramsay, from the front desk.

Of course, Ramsay's still there. Guy's a rock. He's been the sergeant on the front desk at Cambuslang police station since some time in the 1880s. Also seems to work twenty-four hour shifts, seven days a week. Maybe he's just avoiding his wife.

Squeeze my eyes shut, open them wide.

'Address?'

'Far end of Hunterfield. Hundred and forty-eight.'

Take a moment as I emerge from the sleep. Head clearing quickly. Up that way doesn't sound like the kind of place they'd have been having a party that went awry.

'Domestic?'

I put the phone on speaker, get up, head into the bathroom to throw cold water on my face, guzzle mouthwash.

'Doesn't sound like it. Body in the loft, blood dripping through the ceiling. Wife called it in. She lost her shit. Ablett and Milburn just got there. Husband's dead, cut to ribbons.' A beat. I don't fill it. 'That's all I've got.'

'You call Kallas?'

'Yep.'

'K. Tell them I'll be there in ten minutes.'

We hang up.

This sounds ugly, but it's barely worth thinking about at the moment. Not enough information.

Still, we've all got gut instinct in this job, that's one of the things that allows you do to it for so long, even when you're as much of a fuck-up as I am.

A body cut to ribbons in the loft is not normal. It's not domestic. It's not alcohol-related. It transcends a regular case of revenge.

I don't know yet what it is, but my guts are screaming.

—

9

4

Half an hour later. The single loft light has been augmented by several others brought in by CSI. There are currently just three of those guys in the house. Two in the bedroom, and one of them up here in the loft, along with the pathologist, Dr Fforbes, DI Kallas and me. A small loft space for the four of us, not a huge amount of it floored.

Kallas and I are standing back on the floored area, watching Fforbes, bent low over the body, supporting herself on two beams, one hand pressed against a diagonal strut. The SOCO – white suited and beyond my recognition – has his legs stretched between two beams, shining a torch into the far corners beneath the eaves.

Kallas, as ever, looks like she got out of bed an hour ago, spending most of that time putting herself together. A little make up, hair tied back, a simple white surgical mask, the same suit she wears to the office, her permanent air of cold, northern-European efficiency.

'Did you see the wife?' she says, after we've been standing quietly for a few moments.

I arrived with a blue non-surgical face-covering stuffed in my pocket, only pulling it on when I saw that everyone else was wearing one.

'I glanced into the room. She was sobbing. Sounded like she could barely breathe.'

'She needs to pull herself together,' says Kallas.

Brutal.

I give her a look, which she picks up, even though she's watching Fforbes.

'Her husband is late home from work. Very late. She does not seem bothered. It gets to two in the morning, and she's fast asleep. Most wives will notice. Some would be worried. She never called him. There's a text on her phone that he sent, though we may well find it was not him who sent it. But I wonder…'

She lets the thought drift away.

'You think she's crying for effect?'

10

'One must always question strong displays of emotion in a northern European.'

I smile at that, behind my blue mask.

'There's also the shock of it,' I say, surprising myself with a defence of the weeping widow. 'I mean, it's one thing not giving a shit your husband's having sex with his PA, or his boss, or some random woman he picked up in a bar. But slashed to death in the loft, so that the blood runs through the ceiling?'

Kallas does not respond. Kallas joined the station, on promotion, about two months after I returned, and in these past few weeks we've been working together, there's been very little that's required both of us to be on the same case. Nevertheless, I've already got used to those silences. If she has nothing useful to say, she won't say anything.

I wish I knew such restraint. Can't keep my damn mouth shut most of the time. Thing is, with her, it's not restraint. It's who she is. She doesn't have to stop herself.

'You were drunk last night?' she asks.

I give her the benefit of an eyebrow, though it's wasted, as she doesn't look at me. Not as though I can blame her for the assumption.

'Haven't had anything to drink since Saturday,' I say, hating the defensiveness of it. Could just have said no. And yet, here I go, the talker saying too much. 'I don't still smell of drink?'

'Mouthwash,' she says. 'Listerine Cool Mint. I presumed you were masking something.'

'Oh.' A beat. Hmm. Now we're just getting into the small print of a gentleman's toilet. Sleep, even just for ten minutes, makes me want to wash my mouth out, drink freezing cold water, clean myself through. Too much information for standing over a bloody corpse in the middle of the night. 'Just waking myself up,' I say.

'That's good,' she says. 'We should talk about your drinking.'

Her voice is not soft, the exchange conducted for the benefit of the pathologist and the unknown CSI guy.

'Sure,' I say, drily. 'We can livestream the conversation.'

A moment, then she turns and looks at me curiously.

'Why would we do that?'

'I was kidding.'

She nods, as though we've just had a worthwhile chat, and

11

then turns away and looks back at the doctor leaning over the corpse.

The body is covered in blood. The victim was bound, possibly sedated, we don't yet know. But if the murder was carried out *in situ*, which presumably it was, then immobilisation by some means beyond tying his wrists and ankles seems likely, as presumably not a thump was heard below. He is naked, bar a mask that has been placed over his face. Full-face, plain white, cannot tell the substance it's made of from back here. Blood has welled up, and out of the eyeholes. It doesn't look as though the mask has been crying tears of blood, however. It looks like the blood has exploded out of the eyes, there's so much of it.

'You have initial impressions, Dr Fforbes?'

The doc stays bent over the corpse, leaving us hanging for a few seconds before answering.

'At first sight, there's nothing to indicate cause of death as anything other than bleeding out. Obviously that may change. But this looks, on the face of it, like your classic *death of a thousand cuts* affair.' A beat. Another. Kallas waits for it. Finally, Fforbes turns, looks at Kallas, and then chooses to direct the comment at me. 'Perhaps you could run a book on how many cuts there'll actually be.'

'Why?' asks Kallas.

Fforbes smiles at me, then turns to Kallas.

'The victim has not been dead long. You've got the issue of how the killer got the body up into the attic without the wife knowing, but equally, how did they get out of here without disturbing her?'

'Expensive loft ladder,' I say, nodding behind me. 'Not that I've heard it being lowered and raised, but it didn't creak, at all, walking up here.'

'Yep, I noticed,' says Fforbes. 'Still, you might want to check in the far corners in case someone's hiding.'

Can't help looking over my shoulder, as Kallas says, 'I looked already. It is clear.'

'Impossible to tell for now how he was kept still. Hopefully I'll have that when I get the body on a slab. Other than that…' and she shrugs in the glare of the intense lights illuminating the neat and orderly loft.

'You can't tell us anything about the mask?'

'Not at the moment,' says Fforbes. 'I've had a quick look beneath it. The blood that soaked up through the eyeholes was

---

12

from cuts in the face, rather than the eyes themselves being stabbed or cut. But that's all I have for now.'

'Thank you, Doctor,' says Kallas. 'Perhaps you could also check if Mr Lord had ever been infected with Covid.'

'Will do.'

'We will speak to the widow now,' says Kallas to the room. 'If she can speak.'

Fforbes smiles at me, I return the look – there's something guiltily naughty in it, like we're quietly and Britishly amused by the blunt foreigner in our midst – and then I follow Kallas back down the steps.

5

One of those kitchens, given the same level of expenditure as the loft ladder. Sleek and expensive; bespoke design; an island, a KitchenAid, an Aga; utensils and pots hanging from the ceiling, double doors out to a garden, herbs in the window; everything reeking of order and convention, as though the room was only two days removed from a Country Life photoshoot.

Lady Trumpington-Dumpington loves to pluck pheasants at her Versace-designed kitchen peninsular, while drinking home-brewed gin, flavoured with limes grown in the family's 19th century orangery, where once King George IV banged three housemaids and a goat in a debauched, animalistic orgy.

The widow has, thankfully, calmed the fuck down. She was still with heaving chest when we got in here, but Kallas has a calming effect on everyone. She herself is so calm, she exudes reserved chill like she's made of it, that everyone else in her vicinity is quickly infected.

I wonder what would happen if she walked into a riotous bar fight at eleven at night in the middle of Glasgow, Old Firm weekend, both sides going at it full pelt. She probably wouldn't have to even speak.

I don't know any other Estonians, but they can't all be like this. If they were, at the start of WWII, both the Russians and the Germans would have got to the border, there would have been a few thousand Kallas's standing there looking stern, and Stalin and Hitler would have been like, yeah, all right, it's cool, just leave us alone and we'll leave you alone.

But Estonia got fucked, same as everywhere else. I guess a stern look only gets you so far.

We have coffee. Kallas and I, at the widow's bidding, have removed our masks. One minute past four in the morning, dawn still some way off. Me, Kallas, and the widow, Victoria Lord, with Constable Bateman standing by the door. Bateman didn't get coffee. Above her pay grade.

Lord is wearing expensive-ass, silk pyjamas. Dark blue. One button undone at the neck. Hair down over her shoulders. Face devoid of makeup, but she's going to have scrubbed that face to the bone after a drop of her husband's blood landed on it.

The circumstances might be completely different, but she's going to be pulling that Lady Macbeth shit every time she looks in the mirror, never quite removing the bloody stain from her forehead.

'Tell me about your husband,' says Kallas.

Kallas's coffee sits untouched. She made three coffees, instinctively knowing how the widow and I would take ours – actually, she may have completely fucked the widow's coffee, who knows, but she's drinking it – but if she's going to drink the one she made for herself, it will likely be at some perfectly timed moment.

'He's dead,' says Lord, bluntly. She doesn't lift her eyes.

'We need to accept what we all know, and get onto information that you know and we don't. Information that will help us identify his killer as quickly as possible.'

Lord lifts a hand, a sad, desultory hand, and lets it flop back onto the table.

'OK,' she says, the voice heavy, the words forced. She takes a drink of coffee, a deep breath, takes another drink, sets the mug back down. The actions of preparation. 'He made his money in the City. London, I mean. Hedge fund manager. I don't need to tell you anything else about that. Then we came here when we had a family, and he's been running his portfolios out of a small office in St Vincent Street. Small-time stuff compared to the old days, but given how things are now, or at least, were before the lockdown, he was still making more money than he was when he was working at Goldsborough.'

That's all very interesting, and raises a question or two, but I can't help the obvious question that springs unbidden from my mouth.

'You came back to Cambuslang to raise your family? Who does *that*?'

She raises her eyes at last. This is a lovely house, but really, location, location, location and all that. I suppose, once dawn crawls upon the land, we'll see they have a view out over the city to the Campsie Fells, which will be nice enough when the sun shines, and when the snow lies on the hills.

'He grew up here. Had a connection to the place. I was ready to come back to Scotland, I didn't mind where.'

'Had the lockdown and the recession had a negative impact on the finances of his company?'

The sensible, and relevant question, from Kallas.

'Of course,' says Lord. Still doesn't look at her. I'm obviously the easier one to talk to. Always simpler to engage the fool.

Kallas gives her a moment to expand, and when she doesn't, she says, 'What effect did that have on him? On his business? On your life here?'

'The business overheads were low, he wasn't in debt. Still isn't in debt. There are only five staff in the office, and he kept them all going throughout, working from home. The house is paid off, we have a holiday house outside Ballater, and an apartment in London. We were safe from the...' she tosses words around in her head, then says, '... the ravages of the downturn.'

'Do you have any idea who killed him?'

A tortured sound escapes her lips, her face briefly looks like it might crumple, then she steels herself, her shoulders straighten a little more, the British stiff upper lip gets an outing.

'No.'

'Had he fallen out with anyone over work in recent weeks or months?'

'No.'

'What else did he have going on in his life, outside of family and business?'

Deep breath, she holds it together.

'We go to church on Sundays, he plays golf down at Troon.'

'There are no closer golf courses?'

A beat. Her fingers tap together.

'It suited who he was. The moneyed executive. And look, I don't mean... Golf on an Open Championship course worked for him. He'd have clients arrive at Prestwick in private jets. Troon's right on the doorstep.'

'How long had he been a member?' I toss in from the sidelines.

'Since Trump bought Turnberry. There was something of an exodus, and Troon's much closer to the airport in any case.'

'Wasn't there a queue to get in?'

She rubs her thumb and second and third fingers together, doesn't bother looking at me.

'How the world turns,' she says.

She lifts the cup, she takes another drink. And now, for

—

whatever reason, Kallas judges it's time to have a sip of coffee. Finally the widow lifts her eyes, and the two women engage each other for the first time.

The widow's shoulders straighten a little more. One look from Kallas, and a saint would be considering themselves guilty of something.

Of course, the saint's probably banging a choirboy, so that fucker deserves his guilt.

'Did your husband catch the virus?' asks Kallas.

A moment, the wife looks as though she has to think about it, then she says, 'Covid?' as though there might have been some other virus on the front page of every newspaper in the world, every single day for the last eight months.

'Of course.'

'No. Harry did go down with something at one point. Me too. Early July some time. We both got tested, but it was negative.'

'There were false negatives.'

'What does Covid have to do with anything?'

Kallas leaves it a moment, pausing with the finesse of Tendulkar waiting to late cut a short delivery down to third man.

'The killer, for reasons we cannot yet know, placed a mask over your husband's face. While it is obviously a different type of mask from the ones we've seen all year, it is not unreasonable to think there might be a connection.'

The widow stares across the table, as though not quite understanding.

'It has been mask season, Mrs Lord,' says Kallas, not letting the silence endure. 'Now your husband is dead in a mask.'

'We all wear masks, detective,' says the widow, when she finally finds the words.

6

Morning upon the land. Crisp and fresh. One of those autumn mornings you remember happening when you were a kid, but only because the thought of a crisp morning sticks in the mind, not necessarily because they were any more prevalent.

The leaves are yellow and red and brown, there's a clear blue sky, a few clouds on what we can see of the horizon between city buildings. Car parked, and now Kallas and I are walking along deserted hospital corridors, going to conduct the regulation interview with the pathologist, over the body of the stiff, in the morgue.

'The Chief spoke to you about your incident from the weekend?' Kallas throws in unexpectedly.

My incident. Those damned uniforms. They could've been cool about it, they could have let it the fuck go, but they had to punt it up the chain. Like *I* was the bad guy.

Yeah, all right, I *was* the bad guy.

'She did.'

'Everything is OK?'

'I got the speech. You know the one, the *don't do anything else stupid or you're finished around here* speech.'

'No one has ever given me that speech,' says Kallas.

'I suppose not.'

A beat. We walk along a disinfected white corridor, the walls dressed with public information notices and the remembrances of illness and death.

'And she told me not to even think about getting her into bed.'

Kallas stops dead, like I've just grabbed her by the shoulders as she's about to stand on a land mine.

'She said that?'

She looks curious, her brow furrowed. That's about as much expression as I've yet seen on her face.

'She did.'

'Had you been thinking about getting her into bed?'

I smile behind my blue mask. Didn't see this conversation coming. I expected to have that particular piece of information

---

18

ignored, or at best, to be granted the sceptical eyebrow.

'Not yet,' I say.

'I do not understand.'

'I have a reputation.'

'For getting women into bed?'

'Yes.'

'Including Chief Inspectors?'

'I number one superintendent amongst my kills,' I say. I mean, I say it drily, so that it's delivered with immaculate self-deprecation, but who knows if that comes across?

'And people say something about a sex video,' she says, continuing with the blunt force trauma conversational approach, 'though I have not seen it.'

'Sex with a witness, filmed by the guy who... you know, it was just something that happened. There was a thing, and then... yeah, not much else to be said about it.'

'Hmm,' she says, the look of curiosity not yet leaving her face. 'Why is it women want to sleep with you? I do not understand.'

Well, there we are. I probably ought to strike cuckolding her husband off my to-do list.

'We should get on,' I say, indicating the far end of the corridor.

'Yes, of course.'

She walks on quickly, although she's not done with the subject.

'That seems unprofessional of the chief inspector to say that to you.' A beat. 'She is young,' she adds, explaining it to herself.

* * *

'Well,' says Fforbes, 'this is impressive, but what we have here is literally, literally and precisely, one thousand cuts. *Lingchi*, to give it its Sunday name.'

We're looking down at the corpse, every bare inch cut and scarred. In three places pieces of skin have been pulled off, the torso flayed; in another, a large chunk of flesh has been removed.

'He'd been injected with GHB,' Fforbes continues. 'So, he could've been awake, aware, but completely unable to do anything about it.'

'Paralyzed,' chips in Kallas.

'Exactly. You can work out the chances of someone, an individual, being able to haul that kind of dead weight up into an attic. Seems unlikely.'

'There was more than one killer, or Mr Lord was ordered up there under threat,' says Kallas.

'Or he went willingly.'

'Yes. We do not have enough information at the moment. Speculation is useless.'

'He had an average evening's meal in there,' continues Fforbes. 'Steak and chips.'

'Your chips, or frites?'

Your chips.

'Frites. Good quality steak, too. So, if he didn't eat at home, you'll want to find one of the better quality eating establishments in the city. Unless he went to someone's house, of course. Anyway, that's for you people, and I'll leave you to it... What else have we got? The man was healthy. I noticed that small gym set up next to the bedroom.'

'Wife says he worked out at five-thirty every morning,' I chip in.

'It was working for him,' says Fforbes. 'As fit and healthy a fifty-seven year-old as you'll find, outside of an ex-professional athlete. So, he ate dinner at some time between eight and nine pm. He drank maybe half a bottle of red wine. The drug was administered a little later. His wife was at home all evening?'

'Out until just after ten,' I say. 'She thought he'd be in when she got home.'

'There's someone to vouch for her whereabouts?'

'She says she was at the cinema, on her own. If it's an alibi, it's thin. We're checking it out. When he wasn't home, she texted, there were a few back and forth texts until just after eleven, and she went to bed.'

'Hmm,' says Fforbes. 'Possibly he ate elsewhere, and then went home with his killer, and went up to the loft. Then the killer administered the drug. The first cut was made around about eleven pm, approximately two and a half hours before the final cut. It was a slow process. The cuts themselves, as you can see, come in a variety of sizes, depths, different methods of wielding the blade.'

'The same blade?' asks Kallas.

'Yes.'

'Any idea what kind of blade?'

'A straight-bladed kitchen knife. That's all I can do for you. Giving you the brand is out of the question. The blade, maybe six inches, narrow and sharp, very sharp. Could've cut a free-falling strand of hair.'

'At what point would he have died?' asks Kallas.

'Haven't pinned that down yet, but you know, close to the end. Maybe right at the end. The smallest cuts are the oldest. Many of them would have started to heal up long before the end came. The killer started out causing pain. Small cuts that wouldn't necessarily have resulted in much blood loss, but which would've hurt. A lot of pain.' Fforbes nods to herself. 'Then he began… I'm saying he, but obviously…' and she looks at Kallas, and together they silently agree that it's all right for the moment to refer to the killer as male, while there will be no presumptions made, 'he began to mix up blood-letting with pain, and on and on. This large chunk of flesh here, that's from near the end. The three sites where the skin has been flayed, they vary in time. That's obviously going to be very, very painful. Our killer made the most of these.'

'A tortured, drawn out, excruciating death,' says Kallas.

'I'm afraid so. Our man was made to suffer, something that was obviously done with a lot of premeditation.'

Kallas nods, now reaches out as though she's going to touch the body, instead running her hand the length of it, her fingers a couple of inches above the decimated skin.

'Had he had the Covid infection?'

'Yes, he had. Can't put a timescale on it.'

'Would he have shown symptoms?'

'Possibly, but…' and she finishes the sentence with her hands held apart.

'OK, that is good,' says Kallas, then she gives me a quick look. 'You have anything else, Tom?'

Had kind of switched off, and it takes a moment for the words to reach me. A snap of the fingers, and I pluck them out of the air, where they'd been waiting for me. Lost briefly in the horror.

How mundane it seems, how ordinary, how quietly we stand here, looking at a body with this done to it, as though we're discussing a dental patient with an abscess.

'I'm good,' I say.

'Thank you, Dr Fforbes. You will keep us informed of any further findings.'

Fforbes smiles at the instruction/request, we share the familiar glance, and off Kallas and I go, back out into the antiseptic corridor.

'You want to go home and get some sleep?' says Kallas, as we're halfway back to the car.

She's been up the same length of time as I have, and looks completely fresh. Of course, she possibly slept for a few hours before she had to get up.

'I'm good, thanks,' I say. 'I'll just make sure I get an early night.'

And that's it for conversation, until we're back at the station.

7

God, I'm knackered.

1:17. Lunch. Sgt Harrison and I sitting on a bench in the middle of the precinct. There aren't many people around, but there are a couple of pigeons, and several seagulls looking at our sandwiches with some optimism.

There are only so many times it's worthwhile telling a seagull to get to fuck. Eventually, you have to progress to drawing it in, then kicking it in the face, and if you're not prepared to do that – and I'm not – you might as well accept you're eating your lunch under the hungry gaze of a greedy-ass bird. Your only weapons are a firm grip on the sandwich, and a watchful eye.

'The Chief told you not to even think about sleeping with her?' says Harrison, smiling.

'Yep.'

'Holy shit.' She laughs now. She's got a great laugh. Light. Sexy as fuck. 'I mean, this might seem like a stupid question given your history, but *had* you been thinking about sleeping with her?'

'Surprisingly no.'

'But you are now?'

My turn to laugh.

'Yeah, sure. Top of the list.'

'She's pretty fit, by the way,' says Harrison. 'I mean, does she have a pole surgically rammed up her arse? Why yes, she does. But she's got something. Nice lips. Have you seen her lips?'

I smile.

'I've seen her lips.'

'They would be nice lips to kiss. Nice lips to feel on your neck, and down across your chest, small kisses across your stomach…'

She shivers.

'Well, look at you,' I say.

'A girl can dream.'

'My gaydar's off,' I say.

23

'You don't have a gaydar.'

'Yeah, whatever. You think she's gay?'

'Ah, I don't know,' says Harrison, her voice almost wistful for a moment. 'But she's my type, I'm afraid, despite the pole/arse arrangement.'

We go quiet, and stare ahead, across the precinct. There's no one about. Early afternoon, not another single person in the square. To our right, the thirteen stories of a residential tower block; straight ahead, up a level, Main Street, running through the heart of this end of town.

She glances at me, she rolls her eyes.

'What?'

'You're imagining me and her together, aren't you?'

'Yep. You make a very attractive couple. When it happens, any chance there'll be video?'

She elbows me.

'Hey, at least she hasn't already told you it's not happening,' I say. 'So, you're still in with a shout.'

'The very fact she told you it's not happening, means you're in with more of a shout than me, my friend.'

We look at each other, two feet apart on the bench. A silent conversation, leading to a quick agreement. We lift our respective cans of Coke Zero and tinnily clink.

'What are the stakes?' she asks.

'Just the glory.'

'You're on,' says Harrison. 'I don't know that I'll be trying desperately hard, I have to admit. Might have to wait until office Christmas night out. See what she's like when she's drunk.'

'Doesn't look like the kind of boss to get drunk at the office Christmas night out.'

'Wait, what if she sleeps with someone else at the station before either of us?'

We look at each other, we turn and glance back at the station, we turn back, heads shaking at the absurdity of the conversation, and start laughing.

'Fuck,' I say quietly, as the laughter goes.

The silence of a lovely October afternoon settles upon us, for now no cars on Main Street. Blue sky up above, a moment's reprieve before having to return to the fray.

We enjoy it while it lasts, and then a car appears, and another, as the lights up the road have changed, and then the

---

24

silence is gone, and maybe we notice the silence wasn't punctuated by birdsong, and maybe we don't, and the return of the cars is enough to start the conversation off again.

'How's your murder case looking?' asks Harrison.

'You know. Brutal, bloody, violent, painful, horrific. Pick your adjective. A grotesque business, whatever it was.'

'You all right?'

A beat. I smile, without looking at her.

'Tickety-boo,' I say.

'Sure you are, cowboy. It's perfectly all right not to be OK, you know.'

'You're right. Too early to say. Kind of on autopilot for the moment. Didn't sleep last night anyway, had just dropped off when the phone rang. So, I'm operating off ten minutes' sleep in the last thirty hours.'

'That explains it. So you weren't drinking last night?'

I give her a side-eye. I can hardly blame them, can I, the concerned women of the station? I brought this upon myself with my previous conduct. And by previous conduct, obviously I don't just mean last Saturday.

'No,' I say finally. A moment. Try to recall what it was we were talking about before I stupidly turned the conversation onto myself, like some narcissistic man-baby. 'This afternoon I'm just making calls. Got the wife's alibi to check out, do a little bit of digging into her life. And the boss is in at St Vincent Street at the moment, talking to the victim's colleagues. He was a member at Royal Troon, we're going down there in the morning.'

'Sounds like a one-man job,' says Harrison, smiling.

'Just doing what I'm told. Playing it straight down the line, this time, Sergeant, straight down the line.'

She smiles, pats me on the leg.

A seagull takes a step closer. I pop the last of the sandwich into my mouth and it looks at me the way my dad did when I got my 'O' level results.

8

Heading back to Cambuslang from the Vue cinema at Coatbridge.

Mrs Lord checked out. Was seen entering the cinema in time for *Tenet*, caught on camera leaving at the end. No sign of her nipping out in between. Not out of the question she tossed on a disguise and left, tossed on another one and came back, mask on the whole time, of course.

You never know how elaborate people are going to want to make it. Generally, of course, in real life people aren't so elaborate. All the convoluted plotting usually comes in fiction. Real life murders are spur of the moment, or cases of fairly basic planning. Elaboration tends to come on the hoof, as a reaction to an unexpected twist. The cases of genuine, intricate, labyrinthine plotting are rare. If you're thinking of an example right now, then we'll call it the exception to prove the rule.

Still, I'll give the CCTV to one of the constables whose name I will try to recall, and they can scan it more closely for any sign of our bereaved widow.

And now, always one of my favourite parts of an investigation, going to speak to the local minister. As good a place to start as any. Not as much fun as talking to a priest, of course. For a kick-off, priests are liable to know a lot more secrets they can't tell. And they certainly act like it, even if the secret they're protecting doesn't amount to anything more than some guy pulling his pudding thinking about his best mate's wife, or, I don't know, one of those completely trivial pieces of emotional luggage Catholics find to toss to the Gods during confession.

Church of Scotland ministers just have church gossip, which they may or may not choose to share.

This one is relatively new, not long ensconced at St Stephen's. It's the 1950s shit-tip on Main Street, and, as it happens, a drunken piss up a wall away from the police station.

She's waiting for me in the nave, sitting in the second row from the front, leaning forward on the back of the front pew, looking up at the muddy stained glass windows behind the altar.

Excellent. This conversation is going to be straight out *The Untouchables*. Might struggle to get some *he pullsh a knife* shtick into it, but I can give it a go.

God, I'm so moronic sometimes.

She turns as I walk down the aisle.

'Reverend Goodbody?'

'Detective Sergeant Hutton,' she says, and we nod and I sit down a few feet away.

No unnecessary hand shaking these days, and for some time to come.

'Thanks for making the time.'

She nods again. She looks grim. Tired, unhappy. Whatever solace she was searching for there, sitting in her church, communing with her God, it wasn't working.

I guess she wasn't seeking solace. Just waiting for her next appointment, while considering the awfulness of being a minister in twenty-first century Scotland, when more or less no one under seventy cares anymore.

'What's going through your head?' she asks, though there's little compassion in her tone, and I realise I'd been staring at her.

'I've just got a few questions about Mr Lord,' I say. 'Shouldn't keep you.'

'It's fine,' she says. 'Got all afternoon.'

The word *fine* may have crossed her lips, but it was not well meant. Her tone is short, business-like, as though she's had fifteen of these discussions already today.

'Mr Lord was a regular?'

'Every Sunday.'

First tick in the confirmation box with what his wife said. That one was pretty straightforward though.

'And Mrs Lord?'

She makes the kind of disinterested face people make when you ask them if they like anal sex.

'Not so much. She comes when… I don't know what she thinks. Sometimes she comes, sometimes she doesn't, that's all. Maybe she has other things going on in her life.'

'You don't know them well?'

She holds my gaze. I know that look. There are things to tell, and maybe she'll tell them and maybe she won't. Sometimes people think these things through before the police interview, the getting the story straight of it, and sometimes they wing it. The Rev Goodbody is winging it. The plus side of that it

---

27

she's unlikely to be hiding anything.

'Harry was good to us. The church, I mean, he was good to the church. He had the largest standing order, weekly donation I mean, amongst the congregation. If there were any supplemental things, I don't know, the roof, the kitchen, the whatever, he was always willing to help out. Didn't *do* much, didn't get involved, but was always happy to provide funds.'

'And what was the other thing?' I ask.

'What other thing?'

'The thing you weren't sure whether you should tell me or not. I don't think it's just that he was incredibly generous.'

Her face sours a little bit more, perhaps at the revelation she's more transparent than she would like to be. She holds my gaze for a second, maybe two, then looks away.

Her eyes are dead, but she doesn't look upset as such. Whatever it is that ails her, I'd say it's ingrained, long-lasting. Not something that just cropped up today, like her lover turning up dead, body laid waste in his attic.

'I shouldn't tell you this, because I'd rather Victoria didn't know, not that I really care. Really, it's that I'd rather the parishioners didn't know. But I realise in telling you anything, I can't ask that you keep it to yourself.'

'I won't gossip unnecessarily. If it's relevant, you should tell me.'

'Well, I don't know if it's relevant.'

'Then best let me decide.'

She nods ruefully, but there's no smile on her lips.

'God, it's so predictable,' she says. 'I might as well say it. We had a brief thing, Harry and I. Didn't amount to much, but it happened.' Staring at the floor. Wallowing in her regrets. I recognise that look. Here I am, a fellow liver in the past, a regreter of rash things, a rememberer of every act of stupidity.

'You ever tell anyone about it?'

'Nope.'

'Did Harry?'

'I don't know. However, it's possible he told Victoria, or somebody somewhere, so it's possible they tell you, and so here I am, telling you first, in case you find out from someone else.'

'How did it end?'

'Ha. Usually with him ejaculating inside me,' she says bitterly, 'though he did cum over my face that once, which was a bit unnecessary.'

28

I do one of those sideways glances to the camera. Like I'm being filmed for a day-in-the-life type docudrama. Even though there's no camera. But I give that invisible camera a look that says, *no one saw that coming from the vicar's mouth…*

'How did it end?' I repeat. Deadpan. No judgement. I'd hardly be one to judge, after all.

'Much as it started. No announcement, no declaration of intent, no fanfare, no objections, no remorse, no complaints. We were here one night, in the vestry, going over the church finances. He wasn't the treasurer, didn't want the official position, but he knew money and financing in a way our dear treasurer doesn't, so… he was the *de facto* treasurer. And there was a look across the table. That was it. Out of nowhere, and suddenly there we were, having sex on the desk.' A pause, then, 'Happened another couple of times, then it didn't happen anymore. That was all.'

'When was the last time?'

'A year and… a year and a half ago, something like that. We'd been having sex, then we weren't. It was always here, always after discussing church financing. Neither of us seemed happy about it. Then that last time… I don't know, it went a bit further. Lasted a little longer. We had oral sex for the first time, and then…' She grimaces, shakes her head. I glance at her, so that I can share in her feeling of self-loathing, then she continues, her voice now soft and low and bitter, 'then there I was, on my knees, the penitent believer, kneeling before God, with Harry's cock in my mouth. And I couldn't stop, and he couldn't stop, and he came on my face. And that, I think we both knew, was that. It wasn't like we had love or affection to retreat to.

'He continued in his unofficial capacity, but the next time he came it was like it'd never happened. There were no looks across the table. I was disgusted with myself.'

'And Harry?'

'No idea.' She turns and looks resentfully at me. I recognise that look. You're a man, you ejaculate, you can bear the burden of all your sex. 'Would it disgust you to do that to someone?'

Unavoidably, the couple of times I've done that in my life appear in my head. And when I say *couple of times…* Alison, my brief third wife, very, very unimpressed. A hooker I originally busted in Buchanan Street, who was being paid to enjoy it. A vague memory of a drunken party a few years ago, one of those nights that gets lost in the swirl, where the woman – about whom I recall nothing – seemed to like it, though that may be alcohol remembrance. There were others.

'It didn't matter,' she says, when I don't answer. I can feel her contempt, reading my thoughts. 'That was all there was. Maybe he'd had enough. Added me to the list. Screwed the minister. Tick that box, move along, find a nurse or a doctor or an astronaut, or whatever uniform was next in the catalogue.'

'When was the last time you saw him?'

'Sunday, of course. He came every week. Services started back up again in August. For what they're worth, given the attendance.'

'I mean, the two of you alone in the vestry?'

'Oh.' Voice dead, the sound of someone who hates herself. It's always heart-warming when you can bring an interviewee the gift of bitter introspection. 'March, before the lockdown. During the summer we chatted briefly over FaceTime, once or twice. We were going to meet later this week, maybe next week. That would have been the first time.'

She finishes that sentence with a small head twitch, and I know that look, that involuntary spasm, the build-up of remorse and repugnance.

'OK,' I say, trying to keep my head straight. Unavoidably thinking myself into a depressive state as I sit here. Hating everything in this bloody church, dark and bleak and grim, nothing about it inspiring devotion or awe or compassion for one's fellows.

'I should get on,' I say. 'Sorry,' I add, which might be odd, because I have to be here, but I feel bad for blessing her with guilt and revulsion.

She doesn't look at me. Doesn't ask why I'm apologising. She knows. Doesn't accept the apology.

'You drink?' I ask.

'More and more,' she says. A beat. 'And you, Sergeant? You wreak of it.'

'I haven't had a drink in three days.'

'That's not what I meant.'

'I'm good, thanks.' I don't want this to be about me. 'Can you think of any reason why anyone would want to kill Harry?'

'No. I mean…' The pause, the lowered head. 'I don't want to think about it, that's all. He was sharp with money, knew

---

what he was doing. Maybe he annoyed people. And, as we have illustrated here today, he slept around behind Victoria's back. Maybe he annoyed someone by doing that. The way he picked me up and dropped me, I could've been annoyed.'

'Enough to kill him?'

The contempt flashes across her face.

'Everyone's different, Sergeant. I was too busy hating myself to hate him.'

I nod, though she's not looking at me to see it, then I straighten a little, detaching myself from the inquisition. Eyes straight ahead, running over the usual suspects of a nave, and an altar, the stained glass windows behind. Here, disciples or angels or saints, kneeling at the feet of the exalted Christ. Whatever.

'How'd the congregation hold up over the summer?'

'You need to ask?' she says.

'How bad?'

'Thirty-one members of the congregation died.' A beat. She lets the number sit there, old and ugly and unrepentant. 'Thirty-one. Maybe they weren't all Covid-related. Must be the same all over. Church congregations more or less hit the demographic of the illness head on. Now... now, a lot of those thirty-one didn't come here anymore anyway, or at least, not regularly, but what...' Heavy sigh. 'It made a dent on our Sunday morning, either way, and worse, there were far more people who just found something else to do on a Sunday. As the lockdown lifted, people might have raced back to pubs, and raced back to the airports, and raced back to the beach, but they seem to have rather enjoyed whatever else it was they were doing on a Sunday morning. I mean, can you blame them? Here we are, still constrained. No singing, no joyousness, nothing.'

She looks at me, and holy shit, that is a wonderful look of loathing, as though the entire thing has been my fault – and I've been looked at loathingly by *a lot* of women, so I know what I'm talking about – and then she continues her look around the nave.

'Now we could seat our entire congregation in here about twenty times over,' she says, turning back to the altar, sharing that contemptuous look with her Lord. 'Thank you, God.'

'Maybe they'll come back,' I say, finding common cause with her misanthropy. 'The ones who found something better to do,' I add, to clarify I didn't mean those who had died.

She doesn't look at me. It wasn't worth turning her head.

'They never come back,' she says, after a while.

9

I lie in bed at just after ten-thirty. Been a long day.

Got home at some time after eight. Moved a ready meal from the freezer to the oven. M&S, lasagne for two. Took the bottle of white wine from the fridge, opened it, hesitated for all the world like I was in some shitty TV drama, then poured it down the sink. A £7.99 Tesco Finest Pinot Grigio. Yeah, I know, it would've been wrong to mix supermarket brands like that in any case.

But there it went, down the sink. The only bottle of wine in the house. How bold of me, how brave. What a statement.

Bollocks. I had as much contempt for myself pouring it down the sink, as I would've had drinking the fucker. Might as well have. The only point in pouring it away, is when you don't buy any more, ever, and for that you need commitment and determination and balls.

I don't have any balls. I'll hold off a day or two, and then I'll crumble, because that's what happens. That's what always happens.

I had the same damn bottle of wine in the fridge for the past couple of days and managed not to drink it, but somehow tonight, with murder back on the agenda, and after talking to the cloven soul of the wasted minister, sitting in that desolate building, I wanted to pour myself the biggest glass of wine anyone ever drank down in a oner. And once I'd had that, I'd've finished the bottle before the lasagne had defrosted in the oven, never mind cooked, and I'd have been taking that six and a half minute walk to the off licence on Reynolds Street, and no amount of mouthwash would've been disguising the smell when I'm sitting in the car with Kallas tomorrow morning.

We have a nine a.m. appointment with the club secretary down at Troon. I've to pick the DI up at her house at eight.

I just can't turn up there reeking of mint-covered, stale drink, the stench of it leaking from my skin. And so the wine went down the plughole, and I stood over it as it collected in the sink before draining away, clutching at vapours, embarrassing enough that a small moan escaped my lips at the scent of the

---

wine in my nostrils, and then it was gone, and I was standing above a sink, breathing in fumes, stopping myself bending down and licking the basin.

A steel sink. That kind of basic steel sink you get in houses the world over.

And I didn't manage to stop myself bending down and licking it.

It wasn't the highlight of my career, though, let's be honest. If Channel 5 ever made one of those Top 100 Embarrassing Moments shows about my life, it wouldn't even be close to making the cut.

The sink, at least, was relatively clean. I didn't taste anything other than wine, so there's that. When I licked the rim of the plug, I was reminded of too much else, and finally pulled myself away, shrouded in even more disgust than I'd found earlier.

And now it's ten-thirty and I'm in bed. Long since dark outside, curtains closed, orange of the streetlights creeping around the edges, casting an eerie light across the room.

I should be asleep. I was exhausted five minutes before getting in to bed. I could barely brush my teeth, barely change out of my clothes, or throw on those pyjama shorts I wear, falling into bed was the easiest thing in the world. And then my brain was like, *fucking get in, we're in bed, let's start thinking about stuff!*

Round and round it goes, buzzing industrially, so many things to think about, all of them terrible.

I don't know how people like that idiot Trump do it. I don't know how you continually make an arse of yourself, I don't know how you continually say stuff that's proved to be unbelievably stupid, and not want to go and shut yourself in a room and never speak to anyone again for the rest of your life. What's the mental process that allows brazen, constant fuckwitted stupidity? How is it that that brand of fool manages to not give a fuck?

Yeah, I know, Trump is literally a psychopath. No self-awareness whatsoever.

I lie in bed, my brain plagued by the past, a smörgåsbord of embarrassment, a neverending series of incidents and accidents and missteps and long drives in the clown car, seemingly long forgotten, that are just waiting to latch on to some random thought. A humiliation for every occasion.

33

So here I lie, in the same position as yesterday evening. A little earlier this time, as I never learn. I thought perhaps the ten minutes sleep in the last thirty-six hours thing might have had a part to play. But my brain's having none of it.

I give in to it, as much as I gave in to leaning over the sink and licking up my shame, and I start thinking about the conversation I had with Eileen – and thinking about Eileen always gets me excited, even though it shouldn't – and then I'm thinking about fucking Chief Inspector Hawkins on her desk. An easy, cheap thought, that needn't ever trouble me in real life. It's never going to happen, the idea of it so remote and absurd and ridiculous it's worthy of a throwaway moment like this one. A cheap fantasy, based on nothing. An image easily conjured up, easily forgotten. So I imagine her lying on her immaculately clear desk, her short skirt bunched at her waist, her blouse and her bra thrown aside, and me leaning over her, hands grasping her hips, licking her pussy, and she's soaking and moaning and as loud as you want someone that cold to be in passion, and she's pushing back at me, demanding more, desperate for my tongue on her clitoris, and then she's gasping, and grabbing at my hair, and coming loudly, and while she's still shuddering, her eyes closed and mouth open, I stand up and thrust my erection inside her, and she cries out and looks at me with so much lust, and says something both mundane and exciting like, 'Fuck me! Fuck me! Come on!' and I fuck her, and her small tits are moving back and forward, looking absolutely amazing, and I lean over her and take her tits into my mouth – *and try not to think about leaning over the sink, lapping desperately at the wine* – and the noise of my cock slapping into her soaking pussy is as glorious as the noises she makes, and then my cock is shuddering in my hand, and I ejaculate, lying on my side, semen shooting out over the sheets.

I lie there, cock still twitching, a moment, another, in the dark, feeling the tiredness, and then I wipe the end on the sheets, and move to the other side of the bed, and settle my head into the pillow and let the tiredness wash over me, and then my brain says, you'd better make sure you wash those sheets before you go to work in the morning, and then I start to calculate what time I'll need to get up in order to wash sheets and get them out the machine before I head off, and that seems incredibly early, and then I wish I'd figured out how to use the timer on the machine, because I could just do that, but I've never worked it out, though, really, it can't be that hard, and I wish I'd just got up and gone into the bathroom to ejaculate, or just come in my hand, or something, something, something, anything, and now I'm thinking of all the other small things that need doing around the house, and my brain is whirring, and all I've got for my sexual fantasy about the chief inspector, is messy sheets, an adrenalin buzz and several more hours of wakefulness.

Fucking chief inspector.

Like it's her fault.

10

In the car, sitting outside Kallas's house. 07:53. Got here ten minutes early. Texted from the car, rather than ringing the bell. What was I doing, other than seeking the new DI's approval? *Look, I may be an alcoholic, borderline suicidal, useless wreck of a messed-up wastrel, but I'M EARLY! I'm up. I'm risen!*

Showered. Shaved. Sheets washed. Teeth cleaned. Coffee, toast and eggs for breakfast. And water. We all have to drink water these days, even though we didn't have to drink water in the seventies and eighties when our bodies were made of exactly the same shit they're made of now.

Had a look at the news online, what everyone's saying about our murder victim in the loft. We didn't give them all the details, so at the moment, they're not saying much. For now it's just a guy dead in his loft under suspicious circumstances. Didn't make a single front page, which it would've done, had they known about the mask and the thousand cuts. The press like Statement Murders, and this was a murder that made a pretty big fucking statement. It's just too early for us to know exactly what the statement was.

I wondered if Kallas would invite me in for coffee. Not that I wanted her to, and it's certainly not why I turned up ten minutes early, but it wouldn't have been the weirdest thing to have happened. Fortunately, she said she'd be out in seven minutes, which means I don't have to make uncomfortable conversation with the husband and the children, whoever he is, whatever age they are. Or maybe there's a child minder or a mother-in-law, or a whoever. I know nothing about her life, and now, sitting outside a detached house, with broad bay windows either side of the elegant front door, a driveway that swings round with an entry and an exit, a perfectly sculpted hedge, and a magnificent monkey puzzle tree emerging from a small planted area in the middle of the central lawn, I feel I'm all caught up as much as I'd like to be.

And I know that when she emerges from the house, it will be exactly seven minutes since she texted. That's who she is.

Windows open letting in the chill October air, Dylan low

36

and soft on the CD player. This morning, *"Love and Theft"*, early 00's classic. Come for *Mississippi*, stay for the blues and the folk and the jazz and the rock 'n' roll and the lyrics that rip your heart out. Or something. I like it, that's all. That'll do, that's all that matters.

All my wives so far have hated it.

As with anyone these days waiting in a car, I look at my phone. Who doesn't?

No messages. Nothing on WhatsApp. No personal e-mails. *Nobody loves you when you're down and out…*

Look at the news, what sport there is, then a quick look at work e-mails. I already looked at them, cleared them while sitting at breakfast. There are three more, including one from Chief Inspector Hawkins, entitled 'Courses.'

Deep breath, glance at the house to see if Kallas is about to emerge, although I know she's not due for another three and a half minutes, and then open the e-mail.

There are some words at the start that I skip. I'm not really interested in what she has to say, just curious at the courses she thinks I need to attend.

Unconscious bias in the workplace
Mental health at work
LGBT+ awareness
Becoming disability confident
Resilience and well-being
Understanding the menopause

I click my phone off and place it in the side pocket.

What was that about being *borderline* suicidal?

I'm still sitting in position, staring straight ahead, that creeping, growing, festering, ugly ball of resentment churning in my stomach, when the door opens and DI Kallas gets into the car.

She's carrying two thermos mugs of coffee, and places them in the cup holders in front of the gear stick.

'Good morning,' she says.

'Hey,' is all I manage back, then, 'thanks,' with a nod at the coffee.

'You did not sleep at all,' she says. 'Are you all right to drive?' A beat, while I look at her, then she says, 'You will be fine on the way down. Perhaps later you will be tired. Perhaps I will drive home. Nevertheless, I am glad I brought coffee. You should drink.'

—

37

I lay in bed until four-thirty. Didn't come close to falling asleep. Mind all over the place. Finally dragged my sad ass out of bed. Stripped it – the bed, not my ass – stuck the wash on. Did the getting up routine. Had time to do some stretching – stopping well short of actual exercise – and even cleaned the bathroom. Stayed awake through the night, and by the time I was walking out the door, I was balls out, full of beans, chalking things off the to-do list like a hyperactive Mary fucking Poppins. I know that at some point I'll crash, but I walked out that door and drove my car and was sitting here reading bullshit e-mails from the chief inspector, looking like I slept for Scotland, then Kallas sees right through me, as though my skin is pulled taught across my bones like a desiccated corpse in the desert.

I look at her, my resentment likely shows on my face, then I take a drink of coffee and start the car.

'You were unlikely to have been able to get enough sleep to catch up on all that you missed the previous evening, so even if you had slept well, you would have looked, and felt, tired. The study by Doctors Rubenstein and Klutz, Harvard University, published in the New England Journal of Medicine in 2011, showed that total sleep deprivation can conversely lead to energy, alertness and an enhanced mood in the morning, due to an increase in serotonin, tryptophan and taurine. It is apparent from your bright eyes and more exuberant than normal demeanour that this is what you're experiencing.'

End of the road, slow, stop, cars go by, pull out into traffic, and now we're turning onto the bridge across the motorway, and heading south-west. Cross country, hit the East Kilbride Road, then turn up towards Eaglesham, and likely go over the Fenwick moor for old times' sake, before joining the M77.

'Nothing like some in-depth psychoanalysis to crush a guy's mood,' I mutter.

She drinks coffee, staring straight ahead. She'll have heard that, but obviously has no rational, obvious comment to add.

'Sorry I did not invite you in.'

'It's fine,' I say, aware that already the vim has begun to seep away, the enthusiasm for the day, such as it was, duly lanced.

'Things are not good in my home at the moment,' says Kallas. 'My husband lost his job in the lockdown, and has not been re-employed. He is drinking too much.'

'I know all about that,' I say, again at a mutter.

———

38

'You, as far as I know, are a melancholic drunk. There is something of the poet in the melancholic drunk.' She pauses, allows those words to hang there in the car, mixing in with Bob crooning – such as he does – his way through *Moonlight*. I'll take that, of course. The poetic drunk. An illustration that she doesn't know me, at all, but I'll take it. 'My husband is an angry drunk. It is not pleasant. The children do not like it. I do not like it.'

Can't help myself, and the words, 'Too much information,' are coming out my mouth, and I feel bad about them before they've touched my lips, but it's too late to stop them.

'Yes, you are correct. We should talk about the case. It is one of the reasons we are both travelling to the golf club. It is good to talk over the details of the investigation.'

She takes a drink, I take a drink, we pass a golf club, trees shedding leaves in the wind as we go by.

'I went to speak to Mrs Lord again yesterday evening,' says Kallas. 'I thought a little distance would be positive. One of her children has already arrived home. I managed to speak to her without the child in the room, though the child is not a child any longer. She said that her husband was a serial adulterer, and that she too was a serial adulterer.'

'Did you tell her about the minister?'

'I didn't need to, so no, I did not. I suspect, however, that she already knows about the minister.'

'Was he seeing anyone in particular at the moment?'

'He did not see people as such. He slept with women, generally on a one-off basis. He had a way with them, that was how she described it. He talked smoothly and easily, made women feel comfortable. She said he would flirt with women and they would be won over before they had even realised he was flirting in the first place.'

'And Mrs Lord? What about her serial adultery?'

'She refused to give details, insisting it is not important. It could mean she is hiding something, but it could also mean she is protecting someone, or quite possibly, that she is lying. Perhaps she is not an adulterer. Perhaps she is making such claims so that she herself does not look weak and cheated upon. A marriage of equals.'

'Why didn't she give us any of this last night?'

Kallas makes a small gesture, and it's fair enough. There are a variety of mundane answers to that, but the most basic is, why should she have done?

'Some people live lives of secrecy. Once one starts down that road, it is not necessarily addictive, it does not necessarily become second nature, but it happens again. It becomes a part of who you are. If you have one thing in your life you do not share, then where is the line drawn? Yes, she knew who he was, but these people hid things from each other. Therefore, what he did, and she did not know about, is a bottomless pit.' A pause, then she pedantically adds, 'Or a shallow one. It is too early to speculate.'

'How about the Covid infection?'

'She stuck to what she said last night. They had mild symptoms and a negative test. That is all.'

'Did they isolate?'

'They chose not to. That is who they are. Or were, in his case. We can make, for now, an assumption he was infected in July. Perhaps she is not hiding anything but let us not forget about it.'

'You went into his office yesterday?' I ask.

'Yes. There are four women and one man, though two of the women had gone home when they heard the news. There was a feeling of shock with the other three. It seemed genuine.'

'You think the women had been his lovers?'

'I do not have sufficient information.'

Can't help smiling. I wonder if that'll be a catchphrase. Might start using it myself.

'What did your gut say?' I ask, more out of curiosity as to how the theoretician will view the whims of the gut, something on which most of us rely.

'I thought the older of the two women had a little more reserve. My guess, and it is nothing more than that, is that she has had romantic liaisons with Mr Lord some time in the past, and they had moved on. The younger woman held him in some awe, and therefore possibly had not yet slept with him. She is nineteen. We do not yet know enough about Mr Lord to understand if he is the kind of man in his fifties who would sleep with a teenager.'

Haven't we all?

Stop it!

'The man in the office was young, though not quite so young. He seemed more shocked than the women. I would say he held Mr Lord in some kind of elevated respect.' A beat.

Another. 'A fanboy,' she finally says, as though hesitating before using such a colloquialism. 'Whenever one deals with issues related to hedge fund managers, or the stock market, anything that involves the transfer of money, one is inclined to invoke *The Wolf Of Wall Street*. In money trading, Glasgow might be a very small pond compared to Wall Street, and Canary Wharf, and Frankfurt, and Tokyo, but Mr Lord was a big fish in this very small pond. We will find out there is a lot of money in Mr Lord's past, that much was evident from his house, and that there is a lot of money passing through that very small company in a small office on St Vincent Street. Now we have money and sex, and so the story begins to take shape.'

'You've had a look at company records?'

'I directed Detective Constable Ritter to look into it while we make this trip.' A beat. There's something about those little pauses, a cue that allows one to know she hasn't finished. 'What do you know of Constable Ritter?'

'Nothing.'

'You have not worked with her?'

'Nope. Only been together at the station for a few months. We face each other across the desk, but we're both there so infrequently…' I pause for a moment, try to think if Ritter and I have had any conversations of note, any at all, but there's nothing. We're not even on *would you like a coffee* terms. We say hello, that's it. I believe Ritter is the kind of young officer who views people like me as dinosaurs. A moribund generation, both feet out the door, hanging on by the dead skin on the end of our fingers. I may have been a kid in the seventies, but in her eyes, I'm one of the asshole cops from *Life On Mars*. Sure, I've never even caught her looking at me disdainfully or anything, but she thinks she has nothing to learn from me.

She may be right.

Tell you what, though, once I've been on my hysterectomy awareness course, I'll be teaching those young 'uns all kinds of shit. Wait, not hysterectomy, the other one. Menopause. That was it.

'Haven't really talked to her,' I add, finally. 'Seems like a decent kid.'

We drive on. Silence takes over. Up beyond Cambuslang, country lanes, then past Eaglesham, the golf course down on our right, and up over the Fenwick moor. Takes me back, but I don't want to wallow in it. And it's changed anyway, of course, with wind farms and the looming presence of the motorway, inexorably closing in from the north.

* * *

'We didn't talk about your alcoholism,' she says out of the blue, sometime after a long silence.

Sitting at seventy in the inside lane, about to have to move out to pass a Tesco lorry.

Alcoholism? I prefer the term drinking. In fact, I prefer the term silence.

'I poured a bottle of wine down the sink last night,' I say, and I almost look curiously at myself in the mirror. Where did that come from?

She's using her powers. That's it. She has powers. She's so clinical and sensible and straightforward, one can't help oneself. She says something, and it's like Waterboy, or whatever the fuck he's called in *Justice League*, when he touches Wonder Woman's whip and can't stop himself being truthful.

Kallas is literally Wonder Woman.

Ha!

'You bought a bottle of wine and then poured it down the sink?'

A beat. Having begun to open up, I instantly question my sanity. But she's got the whip.

'It was in the house.'

'You said you hadn't had alcohol since Saturday.'

'No.'

'So, you didn't feel the need to pour it down the sink on Sunday or Monday, but you did last night.'

A beat.

'Yes.'

Fuck it. I never had this kind of conversation with Taylor. This woman is opening me up like Fforbes with a murder victim.

'This is because there has been a brutal murder and you are stressed. You had the urge to drink, but knew that once you started, you would continue, and you would be sitting here, in the car with me this morning, and you would have the stench of stale alcohol about you.'

She's not even asking questions, just rhyming off every thought that goes through my head. She can only be one step away from asking which one of my colleagues I masturbated

---

42

over last night, while already knowing the answer.

'Was it difficult?'

Fuck me. Please, just leave me alone.

'Yes.'

Silence, but not for along. There's another question there, the continuation of the inquisition, poised, as though the words have already been formed, but haven't made any sound yet.

'Did you try to recover any of it?'

'Were you filming me?'

'I know about addiction, that is all.'

I don't answer. Not straight away. Wait to see if she's going to say something else. But if she doesn't, I will. I'll crack. The Wonder Woman whip of hers is more or less inserted in my arse.

'It's OK,' she says, letting me off the hook, who knows how many seconds before I would've caved.

I drive on, easing back into the inside lane, having not really been aware of the last mile or two of road, driving on automatic.

We pass the sign that says **Troon 5**, and we both notice it, and it's like a switch. Time to get back to the case in hand.

11

Standing by a window, looking out on the first tee, the beach barely more than fifty yards away, the blue-grey of the sea stretching away from behind the gorse bushes.

There's little more therapeutic in life than looking at the sea, and I wonder if Kallas will allow us a few minutes to wander down to the beach. Perhaps if she sounds keen to get back to the station, I can casually bring up licking the sink, and she'll be like, *Holy shit, Sergeant, you're right, I forgot, you really need to stand on the beach, let's get ice cream.*

'How was Mr Lord's game?' I ask, by way of an opener.

We've been given time with the acting Assistant Club Secretary, Anderson. Hmm. Acting assistant club secretary doesn't sound so far up the food chain, but this guy knows how to play the part of an asshole guy at a posh golf club, I'll give him that.

He nods at the question. Always good to start with the basics. Don't come in here with questions about ego and money and expect anyone to open up about a fellow club member. Information will be given reluctantly, or not at all.

We're standing in formation by the window, the three of us in a line, mugs of coffee in hand. Kallas, as we entered the old place, casually informed me I'd be doing the questioning, on the cold, analytical basis that I would know more about golf than she would, and I would get further as a result. In such circumstances, the detective sergeant awaits the interfering questions from the detective inspector, when she feels he's not pursuing the right course of interrogation.

'He was good,' says Anderson. 'Very good. And look, I know how it is with clubs like ours, we have a waiting list of however long, a lot of names, an indeterminate number of years to work through it, and then we had the sheer hell of Trump buying Turnberry, and the knock-on effect on all the other old courses in Ayrshire.'

'People were upset that someone like Harry Lord was just allowed to join straight off the bat?'

'Exactly.'

'How many Turnberry refugees did you accept?'

Anderson smiles, takes some coffee. Always significant when the interviewee pauses to take coffee.

We're in the Smoke Room. God knows what happens in the Smoke Room, now that the fuckers can't smoke in it. Maybe they smoke anyway, because they have the connections to not give a fuck. Maybe this is where they have their rich white man orgies.

Keep that smile off your face, you cheeky bastard!

Thick red drapes, wooden tables and chairs, rich carpet, black and white picture of some crusty old bearded fucker on the wall, large windows to our left, looking down the length of the course.

Wonder who won the Open the last time it was here. I have no idea. I don't follow golf. Don't mind hacking my way around a course, but watching other people do it is like drinking a bottle of wine, popping a Xanax and settling yourself down in front of *Britain's Lost Masterpieces* in a warm room at eleven pm. Asleep in seconds.

Maybe I should try that tonight.

Wouldn't work without the wine.

Maybe I should just watch golf.

Who am I kidding?

'Straight off the bat, members like Mr Lord, only seven or eight. Another few have been fast-tracked since, a few others still waiting, but perhaps a little further up the list than they might have been.'

'So, there was a hierarchy, and Mr Lord was in the elite?'

A moment, and then he says, 'Yes,' because what else could he say?

'And that was because of his money or because of his golf?'

A small nod, as though giving his blessing to the question, then he says, 'We're all practical men, Sergeant Hutton. His golf was good. We always said he could be a scratch golfer if he had a little more time. As it was, he played off seven. I think he might have been five when he got here… However, it was, of course, his money that got him in.'

'He bought his way in?'

'Good grief, certainly not.' I get the glance, the genuine outrage, quickly dismissed from his face, because really, I'm hardly worthwhile being outraged at. 'We valued his connections, the quality he brought to the club. Every golf club wants members such as Harry. We were lucky to get him, and gosh, we weren't going to let Prestwick get hold of him.'

'So, what about these other six or seven who got in straight off the bat?'

'What about them?' he asks, tone a little tetchy.

I look at him, and we share the unspoken glance. Kallas is standing on the other side of him, not a player, as yet, in the conversation. I must be behaving.

'No,' he says, picking up the gist, 'none of them have been murdered.'

'Are they all still members?'

'Are you really implying that Mr Lord was murdered by someone at the club, or not yet at the club, with a vendetta against those who were given priority membership status? Apart from the utter preposterousness of the suggestion, it's been six years, for goodness sake. Six.'

'Do you know anyone who would want to kill Mr Lord?'

'No!'

'Do you know who *did* kill Mr Lord?'

'Of course not!'

'Guess what? We don't either. So, we have to investigate every aspect of Mr Lord's life until we find out who did kill him. And this is us, investigating his life, because you may be outraged at the suggestion anyone would want to kill him, but he's dead, slashed to death, every inch of his body covered in cuts, chunks of skin cleaved off, so much blood it pooled beneath his body, so much blood it poured through the ceiling and dripped onto his wife's face.'

His eyes are wide, he swallows, he backs off a moment, a look of panic crosses his face, and then Acting Assistant Secretary Anderson vomits into his mug of coffee.

Coffee and vomit splash over the floor. Kallas, having seen it coming because she's more or less Wonder Woman, had already taken a pre-emptive step away, and so avoids getting either coffee or vomit on her clothes. Me, I'm not so quick thinking. I mean, what kind of lame-ass fuck vomits at the mention of blood and chunks of flesh?

The second heave just sends vomit over the carpet, but from the point of view that this is entirely about me, there's already vomit all over my trousers.

Jesus.

46

12

'I do not think Mr Anderson vomited to avoid answering any more questions.'

Kallas and I are standing on the beach. Bright day, chill in the air, yet barely a breath of wind, looking out over a flat calm to Arran, the hill of the Holy Isle before it. The tide is high, the beach at its narrowest.

No wind? In Ayrshire. In October.

How can this be?

My life is a lie.

'Yep,' I say. 'We can look into those other names he gave us, the quick entry club, but I don't get any particular feeling about it. Feels more likely we'll get something from the list of Lord's playing and dining partners.'

'I believe so too. You did well not getting out of the way of his sick,' she continues. 'He was embarrassed that he vomited on you, it made him more agreeable to giving up information.'

'I didn't do it intentionally.'

'I know.'

She nods, then she turns and starts walking away from where we parked the car. I wondered if she might allow me a quick breath of air, but she seems happy to embrace the sea for a little longer. Obviously not anticipating anyone else getting murdered in the next couple of hours.

She slips her shoes off, and suddenly, out of nowhere, she's walking barefoot in the sand, which seems utterly incongruous. Here I am, in a suit and shoes, dull as ever, except I no longer have my suit trousers on, because they're washed through and damp in a bag in the boot, while I'm wearing a pair of random breeks a steward at the club dug out of lost property.

'I miss the beach,' she says.

'You grew up by the coast?'

'We lived on the outskirts of Tallinn. Every weekend we would go to Pirita beach. In the winter the sea froze, not so far out as it used to, and they say it barely freezes at all anymore, but you could walk on the ice.' A moment, then she adds, 'You had to walk quite a way on the ice sometimes before you could

---

47

go swimming,' as though that's a normal thing to say.

I give her a glance.

'You used to swim in the Baltic in the middle of winter?'

'It is not really the Baltic. Tallinn Bay. Very shallow by the beach, a very different sea climate.'

'But there was ice.'

'Yes.'

'So, it was freezing. Literally.'

'When you go swimming every weekend, your body is used to it.' She walks on. Her sergeant looks at her like she's mental. 'I miss that. And the feel of sand on my feet. I swim in the Clyde every weekend, but it is not the same.'

I give her the appropriate look. Who, in the name of all fuck, swims in the Clyde *every weekend*?

She stops, staring out to sea. There's snow on the top of the Arran hills, just a dusting, no more, but beautiful nevertheless. And so I stop beside her, and we stand there long enough in silence, that I finally switch my brain off, and I stop thinking about the case, and I stop thinking about swimming in ice water, I stop thinking about being thrown up on and pouring wine down the sink, I stop judging other people, and I stop judging myself.

High clouds going nowhere, blue sky, the sun glinting off the flat sea, the sound of waves treading lightly upon the beach, and every now and again the cry of a gull, the ululation travelling far in the still air, bringing tales of lands beyond Arran and Kintyre and Islay, away across the ocean, far beyond the horizon.

The sounds of the sea blend with the stoppage of time, that impossible concept, to create a vacuum. Everything slows to nothing.

Maybe it's just for a minute. Maybe it's half an hour. I lose track, and then it's gone. Time is gone. Like falling into a deep sleep, and waking up at what the clock says is only twenty minutes later, but what feels like an hour, a day, a lifetime later. Who decided that interval was twenty minutes?

'The first day is always the worst in this kind of case,' says Kallas suddenly.

The words penetrate slowly, like the six a.m. alarm call, and from nowhere I'm dragged back to the beach, and the sea, and the cry of the gulls.

'This kind of case?'

—

48

'We usually know. Straight off, we know. But in this one, where we have little to go on, then we must first put together the pieces of the victim's life. So, here we have family, we have friends, we have business, we have money, we have golf, the church perhaps, and we have lovers. There are myriad roads, but we can only start discarding some of them when we know which ones we should be following.'

I nod. Nothing else to say to that. In fact, it seems kind of weird that she said it at all, because it didn't need to be said.

Hmm. It's like space-time was inverted or something while I was daydreaming. We've come out of that, and she's talking unnecessarily and I'm not responding, because there's nothing that needs saying.

'We shall divide calls when we get back to the station, and then later this afternoon we should get the team together. Maybe you could message them, let them know. Room C, five o'clock. Sorry, it is beneath your position, but could you check if the room is available?'

'Sure.'

Beneath my position. Jesus, Taylor never said *anything* was beneath my position. Kallas is beginning to sound like a keeper.

She glances at me, nods and almost smiles in that kind of confirmatory way of hers, then she looks past me along the beach, and back along in the other direction.

'The beach is deserted,' she says, and I can't help glance in either direction to confirm this assertion, another line that seems kind of pointless. I don't even know who she is anymore.

'I will go for a swim,' she says.

She places her shoes in the sand, takes off her jacket and lays it neatly down beside them, then she starts to unbutton her white blouse.

'You may want to look away, although I do not mind if you do not,' she says.

What is happening? I mean, is this what happens in Estonia normally? You're just walking along the beach with women, and suddenly they're whipping their clothes off and diving into the sea?

I can't stop looking at her. She did say she didn't mind, after all.

'I don't expect you to join me,' she says, as she removes her slim, calf-length trousers, 'that would be inappropriate. You will watch my clothes.'

—

49

Camisole off, now she's left wearing the smallest pair of knickers in the catalogue and a white bra. *I can hold them for you, if you like*, comes into my head, but really, I'm more or less struck dumb.

Then she removes her bra, slips the panties off, and places them neatly on top of the small pile.

Holy shit, she's gorgeous. Slim, small breasts, long hair tied up, pale pink lipstick. She smiles in an *I'll be off now, I think this has gone well* kind of a way, and I suddenly imagine her swimming out to sea, not stopping, cutting round the bottom of Arran and Kintyre, hoofing it out to the Atlantic and never being seen again.

She starts to walk naked into the water. The Clyde, sports fans, is not warm this time of year. That, to be honest, applies to all times of the year. From the back she looks stunning. That is as close to the most perfect naked body I've ever seen in my life.

And then, without fuss or screaming, short, loud, gasping breaths, or any palaver whatsoever, she eases herself into the sea, and swims away from shore with a smooth breaststroke, her head above the water.

No one, absolutely no one, saw *that* coming.

13

Kallas is by the whiteboard, and there are five of us around the table. Me and Eileen Harrison, dragged into the investigation because really this has the potential to throw so much shit at the fan, DC Ritter, and Constables Ablett and Milburn.

Kallas has drawn up the board with immaculate neatness. Two pictures of Harry Lord in the centre, the before and after, and around it the areas of his life which she identified previously as requiring investigation. Friends/family, work/money, lovers, outside interests including, but not necessarily limited to, golf and the church. There is already a line drawn from golf to work/money.

'Covid,' I say, as she pauses, her back turned to the room.

'Yes, of course,' says Kallas. 'Mask season,' she adds, as she's writing Covid. Neat, ordered words written as though placed by a computer's hand, then she turns to the room.

'You were investigating his family, Emma?' she says to DC Ritter.

Ritter has a slight build, shoulder-length dark hair tied back, pale, slender face. There's something insignificant about her, as though she could make herself invisible if she wanted. Perhaps she's in the room sometimes, sitting across from me at the desk, and I don't even notice.

I heard she was making an arrest at a pub a couple of months ago. Not breaking up a fight or anything, she's a detective not a beat copper after all. She was arresting the landlord, who'd been working some sort of scam selling under-the-counter booze and pocketing the cash. I don't know the details. The tough guy did a runner. Well, he tried to do a runner. Ritter rugby tackled him before he got to the door, he threw a punch, she took it on the cheek then broke his nose with the palm of her hand.

Her pale face was lit up by a bruise for a few weeks, but the arrest was witnessed by a couple of our guys, and the word was out. Insignificant? Not a bit of it. Ritter's tough as fuck.

'Yes. The eldest, Liam, is in his final year at Edinburgh, reading history. The daughter, Bethany, is a second-year

---

psychology student at Durham. Liam came home yesterday, Bethany came up this morning. I spoke to them both. They have that teenage reserve… I know, neither of them are teenagers, but they haven't moved on yet. The teenager is still inside them. I'd say they were largely brought up by the mother, a little more detached from the dad. He and the boy used to go to Ibrox, seven or eight times a year. They had sport in common, that was all. Went to Twickenham last year to watch American football, went to the Open a couple of times, Murrayfield a couple of times.

'The daughter seemed a little more distant. Tough to say what their relationship was. Nothing in common with the dad. She doesn't play sport, she's interested in K-pop, Buzzfeed Unsolved and Love Island.'

'Any hint they were unsurprised the dad had been murdered?'

'No.'

'Any sign of malice towards the dad?'

'No, not malice. They were both reserved, like I said. But you never can tell, perhaps the reserve was one of them nervously covering up complicity. Guilt. Though it would be possible to feel guilt about his death, while having had nothing to do with it.'

'Nothing brings home the pain of an incomplete relationship with a parent than the parent dying,' tosses in Harrison, and Ritter nods.

'Any other family members we should know about? Anyone resentful of Harry Lord's money?'

'There's a brother. I didn't get to talk to him today, meeting him after breakfast tomorrow. Lives in Hamilton, works from home. Writes some sort of romantic fiction. I don't know any more yet. Mrs Lord said that Harry had set him up in a house, you know, bought him a house. Beyond that, they don't appear to have had much of a relationship.

'The brother has no family. Harry's mother is dead, has been for some time, his father had been in a nursing home up the Clyde Valley. Not far from Garrion Bridge. He died in July. Suspected Covid, but one of those that never made the official statistics.'

'July? The same time as Harry and Victoria had symptoms?'

'Yes. And they did see him in the weeks before he died.'

52

Kallas nods. I can see her thinking, *and they still didn't isolate*.

'Perhaps that will be relevant. We should hang on to that information. That is good. Any other family connection of which we should be aware?'

'That's all I've got for the moment. I'll let you know in the morning how it goes with the brother.'

'Good.' And now she looks at Ablett, eyebrows raised. 'Constable?'

Ablett, tasked with trawling the Internet for all things Harry Lord, glances at her notes, takes a moment, nods to herself, and then starts speaking.

And so it goes, the round table, round and round, the investigation kicking in to gear.

* * *

Nine-thirty, Harrison and I still at the station, sharing a Domino's pizza, drinking Coke Zero. We're likely not going to do any more work, but we wanted the chat, and what were we going to do if we left here to get something to eat? Sit in a bar? Sit in a house? Sit in the presence of alcohol? With words unspoken, we stay at work to break bread and chew the fat of the day. And not for the first time.

'How are you coping?' she asks, with something of a mischievous look about her.

I sigh a little, take a bite of Extra Spicy Meat Feast Bonanza, or something like that. No idea what it's actually called. Give her the eyebrow as I look at her, take a drink of Coke.

'How d'you mean that, exactly?' I say, finally. She's smiled at me all the way through.

'All these women. The men of the station have gone, stage left, and in their place… women, everywhere. It's like you've been beamed onto the set of *First Wives Club*. Or *Mean Girls*.'

I'm still giving her the eyebrow. Take another bite of pizza, this time getting a nugget of kangaroo.

'I mean,' she continues, 'I hadn't even thought about it. People are just people, 'n' all. Then I was sitting at the round table, and there's me and you and the Inspector and three female constables. And the boss is a woman, and the pathologist. The victim might be a man, but that means there's a widow, and even

---

53

the minister you went to talk to is a woman.'

'And my mum,' I throw in, 'don't forget her.'

'You're surrounded by them,' she says, not letting me away with being glib. 'And weirdly, as if you've landed on your own personal fantasy planet, most of them are pretty attractive.' A beat, then she smiles. 'Not as nice as me, obviously, but there are some good looking women in your life now. Wide span of ages to choose from, too.'

'Are you finished?'

'I don't know,' she says, smiling, 'think I might run with this one for a while.'

'Really? The boss thinks I'm addicted to sex…'

'You are.'

'OK, so how is you taunting me with all these women any different from you whipping a bottle of vodka from your desk drawer and insisting on me having a swig?'

Well, there goes the smile, and she nods.

'Brutal, Sergeant,' she says. 'But effective.'

Can't help smiling, taking away any notion that I might actually have been serious about that, and she shakes her head.

'Anything to report from your romantic getaway to the seaside,' she asks. 'You two talk up a storm in the car?'

'Conversation was… sporadic.'

'I'm shocked. Did you get ice cream and walk barefoot in the sand after you'd been to the golf club?'

Can't help smiling again, and she perks up. 'Ooh, this sounds interesting. Go on.'

Take a moment, wondering how to frame it. Don't want to sound too gossipy, or judgy, or anything really. It was just a bit weird.

'The inspector said she missed living by the sea. Said she used to go swimming, every weekend, year round, in the Baltic.' Harrison shivers. 'And she says she goes swimming in the river every weekend now.'

'The river?'

'Clyde.'

'Where it runs through Uddingston?'

'Yes.'

She stares blankly across the desk.

'So, we're standing there for a while looking wistfully at the sea, then she takes her clothes off and goes for a swim. Just for a couple of minutes. Then she comes out again.'

———

Harrison is giving me the appropriate, *wait what?* look, then she says, 'Wait, what?'

'So, that happened.'

I shrug.

'She took *all* her clothes off?'

'All of them.'

'She went swimming naked, at Troon beach, in October?'

'Yes.'

'Did you?'

'No.'

'Were you tempted?'

'No. Even if I had been, she told me just before she got in that it would be inappropriate for us to swim naked together.'

'This is the weirdest thing I've ever heard. Was there anyone else around?'

'Beach was deserted. I think that was why she took the opportunity.'

A beat. The next hundred questions formulate on Harrison's face.

'Did you watch?'

'She said she didn't mind if I looked at her, it was of no concern.'

'So you looked at her?'

I shrug apologetically.

'I guess there was some part of me wanted not to, but…'

Another moment, then she says, 'And?'

'And what?'

'She's an attractive women. How's she look naked?'

Eileen, of course, likes the look of a naked woman as much as I do.

'Amazing.'

A beat.

'That's all your giving me?'

'She looks amazing.'

'In the unlikely event of our lives being made into a movie, who's playing her?'

'Vikander,' I say, nodding, having already given that a certain amount of thought.

'Vikander,' repeats Harrison, with just the right amount of awe, looking away across the office. 'Hmm, I can see that. Wow.'

'Yep,' I say, 'wow sums it up pretty well.'

—

55

She takes a bite of pizza, another drink of Coke, staring dreamily off across the office.

'That's a kind of weird thing to do,' she says.

'I'd say.'

'D'you think everyone in Estonia's like that?'

'Don't know any other Estonians.'

'Wow,' she says again, still with that same look on her face. 'Maybe Estonian beaches are filled with gorgeous naked women stepping boldly into the sea.'

Can't help laughing.

'That can be our next trip.'

'I'm free this weekend,' she says, and we both laugh. 'Oh my God. Maybe I can wangle a trip to some seaside town with her. I'll see if I can dig up a lead in Girvan or St Andrews.'

'You're shallow, Sergeant,' I say.

'You'd know about that.'

'Exactly.'

'Maybe we could switch our bet from the Chief to the Inspector,' she says, shoulders raised slowly, hopefully, looking for me to play along.

'Married, three kids,' I say. 'We really shouldn't try and fuck with that.'

'Yeah, all right.'

'I mean, I know we don't know anything about the Chief. Maybe she's engaged to some twat called Rupert, and they're getting married at Christmas, but there are no kids, and she is way more fair game. And anyway, we both know neither of us is going to play.'

'Speak for yourself, coward,' she says, and we smile, and we eat pizza, and we drink Coke, and soon enough we're wrapping up for the day, and heading out into another chill, October evening.

14

Sometimes it's the small things. The smallest things. The look in the eye, the turn of phrase, the glance cast over the shoulder. Never takes much to fall for someone.

I've been trying to be on autopilot. Easier that way. Clinging on to Eileen Harrison, the platonic friendship, the easy conversation. In some ways I've been clinging on to alcohol addiction. Which, by the way, is a fucking stupid thing to cling on to. To focus on.

By this means, I try not to think about women and sex.

And now, not even thinking about sex.

It wasn't the inspector getting undressed and walking naked into the sea. It wasn't the strangeness of it, it wasn't the easy acceptance of the intimacy, it wasn't those perfect, small breasts, the beautiful slim body, the strange little smile she gave me when she emerged from the water, like, I don't know, Ursula Andress times a thousand, taking a small cotton tissue from the pocket of her jacket, and somehow drying herself with it, not concerned that I couldn't stop watching her the entire time.

We were in the car on the way back up the road from Ayrshire. Another long silence, one which felt a little awkward, unlike the silences of the way down. Then, somewhere between the motorway and Eaglesham, it was me who broke it. One of those occasions when I was thinking about something, and from nowhere the words were in my mouth.

'Is he ever violent?' I asked, which was a follow-up to our conversation from two hours previously.

It was not impossible that she'd have had no idea what I was talking about, but of course she did. Perhaps she'd been thinking about it at the same time. Perhaps we'd been having some sort of telepathic conversation.

'No,' she said. The silence threatened to crawl back in, then she added, 'He is angry, and it is uncomfortable, but he is never violent.' Another long pause, then, 'You do not need to worry.'

It would have been the predictable thing to say that I wasn't worried, but then she would have known I was lying.

'He has two job interviews in the next week,' she said. 'Hopefully one of them will come off, and he can be himself again. He does not like that I am the breadwinner.'

Well, there's another tale as old as time.

I think I was ready to leave the conversation there. I'd checked in on her, expressed my concern, played my part – even though I wasn't thinking of it as playing a part – and I could have driven home in silence.

'I'm sorry,' she said, as we hit the East Kilbride Road, five minutes from the station. Another one of those long silences that pepper her conversation followed, then she said, 'I should not have gone swimming. I should not have undressed completely.'

'That's OK.'

'Thank you, but I should not have done it. It was unprofessional.' A beat. 'I did not want to get my underwear wet.'

Passing a BMW 320 on the outside, heading towards the turn-off down to Kirkhill golf club, I thought about Kallas removing her underwear on a cold autumn beach, goosebumps on her skin, her nipples hard.

I didn't bother with the *really, it was fine*. The concept of not saying everything that was going through my head must have been catching.

Down past the golf club, past the farms, to the top of the town, then on down Greenlees Road, past the Institute and the site of the old police station, down to the Main Street. Stopped at the lights by The Clock, and the building where I spent so many godawful hours of my youth at the dentist, she finally said what she wanted to say.

'Sometimes I miss home. That's all.'

* * *

And that was all. It didn't take much. But it was the delivery. The sadness. The years of melancholy and longing poured into four words. *Sometimes I miss home.*

I wanted to hug her. And weirdly for me, it was entirely about making her feel better. I wanted to hug her, and make her a cup of tea, and then take her back to Estonia.

We drove the final minute round the road in silence. I didn't ask why she doesn't go back, at least to visit. Maybe she visits, and the visits make the parting all the more painful.

—

58

Sometimes I miss home.

Lying in bed, those words mixing with the longing of the day, and the flat calm of the sea, and the strange, absurd, bizarre and beautiful sight of her walking out into the water naked, as though she would swim away and never be seen again.

Fifty-two. I'm fifty-two now. Too old for this shit. Too old for infatuations and fantasies, and dreams of hopeless, melancholic romance. I'm fucking wasted. Mentally wasted at least, and my body probably worse, though I haven't had a medical in three years to find out.

I don't want to fall for my boss. I don't want to think anything about my boss, other than vaguely wondering what she's going to tell me to do next. I don't want to fall for anyone. My longing for Eileen that will never come to anything is quite enough. I drink, I have random sex, I go to work, and sometimes I think about putting a gun in my mouth and pulling the trigger, and one day maybe I'll actually do it, and that's all there is. That's all there need be.

And now here I am, one a.m., once again unable to get to sleep, staring at the orange of the streetlights and the shadows they throw across the ceilings, wide a-fucking-wake. Thinking about Kallas, like some ridiculous nineteenth century poet, looking wistfully at an Italian lake, writing some shit about feeling as miserable as the next poetical cunt on the balcony two along.

Jesus.

15

Thursday morning, and the tentacles of the investigation go off in various directions, each of us dispatched to play our part. Quite relieved to get a mundane task, and not be doing anything in conjunction with Kallas. Will be happy to avoid her today.

I have no ideas, no dreams or ambitions, to crack the case, get a breakthrough, solve the crime, find the killer. I genuinely don't care. Look, it may not sound great, but what difference does it make to me? I'll still be doing this shit, one way or another, every day until I pluck up the guts to retire, or I finally go too far and get pushed, or I pull the trigger on the gun aimed at my head, the gun that I don't yet have in my possession. And all the while I'm doing it, crime will come and it will go, weaving in and out of the fabric of society, picking off victims as it winds its way, and there'll be someone sitting at the desk opposite Detective Constable Ritter, and maybe it'll be me, and maybe it'll be someone else.

All I have to do is make sure that when it's me who's at that desk, the job is getting done as well as it can be, and – with due consideration given to the fact I'm a messed up, alcoholic, sex addict – all in, I still believe I do a reasonable job.

But I don't *care*.

Maybe that helps.

Park my car in front of the large house set back from the Clyde, up past the Garrion Bridge. Haven't been up this way in a while. Don't really like to think about the last time.

This is care home and garden centre country. More or less every building up this way is given over to one or other of those pursuits. Looking after old people, or providing old people potting soil, and lunch in the God's waiting room of the garden centre restaurant. As soon as you come off the motorway, there should be a sign warning you to get the fuck out if you're under seventy. If you're over seventy, enter at your peril. You may never leave. Maybe when you hit seventy, there's a chip that gets inserted, and you suddenly aspire to spending all your time in these places.

Thank God I'll be dead by then. Cannot stand the thought

---

of it, me old and wizened and bitter and wrinkled – and with the amount of smoking and drinking I've done, there's no way I'm going to be one of those fit seventy year-olds you see – sitting in the corner of the café with my fish and chips or my bread and butter sandwich, with bread on the side, my wee, mini-arsed bottle of wine on the tray, struggling to keep my teeth in, eyeing up the women, desperately trying to imagine them in the midst of a screaming orgasm, in the forlorn hope I can find them attractive, even though there will be zero chance that any of them will find me attractive.

For now, here we are. A care home. The one where Harry Lord's father died. Might be a stretch, but there are so many strands here, who knows which one will lead to the pay off.

Living the dream.

Can hear the river as I get out the car, though the house is between it and me and I can't actually see the water at the moment. All around, the weeping branches of trees, shedding leaves as I stand, the day nothing like yesterday. Wind up, grey clouds covering the sky, rain in the air, coming our way, sometime, somewhere.

Up to the door. I press the intercom, give my name, the anonymous white doors swing open, and then I'm inside, into the reception area, a small unmanned desk, four armchairs, and a table with a coffee machine, a sliced sponge cake on a plate, a plate of biscuits, cups, a small jug of milk. Magnolia walls, a large, atmospheric black and white photograph of the Garrion Bridge in the mist behind reception, another couple of small black and white shots of the river on the side walls. Large windows either side give an enchanting view of the carpark.

However, like all care homes, the first thing that greets you is the smell of death.

OK, not death.

Piss.

A woman in a white uniform appears from the door behind reception and smiles.

'Sgt Hutton?'

I begin to extract my ID from my coat pocket, and she waves it away.

'That's OK. I'll show you through to see the day manager, Geraldine. If you'd like to follow me.'

Geraldine. That's the way it goes. No reason why the person on reception couldn't be a man, no reason why the day

—

61

manager couldn't be a man, but here we are, and as Harrison observed, I'm cursed to be surrounded by women on this case.

'Windy day,' says Karolina, easing straight into small talk.

'Blew in the clouds,' I answer mundanely.

'Just through here,' she says, holding the door open for me to follow her, then we're walking down a short corridor, everything about it painted and cleaned and scrubbed to make it depressing as fuck. Pictures of flowers on the walls, the kind of picture you would pick up at a car boot sale for fifty pence, with a couple of noticeboards covered in A4 posters proclaiming, *Pilates at 4 every Thursday*, and *Weekly movie night, Saturday at 6, this week* 633 Squadron, and *Wash Your Hands So You're Clean When You Die!*

An open door, a quick glance inside as we pass, the lounge, several occupied seats, old people in somnambulant repose, not a word being spoken, nor a word being read or listened to, behind them large picture windows looking out on the river, and then we're at the end of the corridor and Karolina is knocking on the door, and the voice, 'Just a minute,' comes from inside.

Karolina and I stare at each other, trapped in social awkwardness at the end of the corridor.

'It's OK,' I say, 'I can take it from here.'

'Geraldine likes guests to be escorted in,' says Karolina, and I nod, and we resume standing awkwardly outside the door.

'Where are you from?' I say. It's my job to ask questions, after all.

'Kaunus.' Then as she adds, 'Lithuania,' I'm saying, 'Lithuania,' at the same time, and we smile again like we're in some sitcom or other.

'Have you been here long?'

'Three years,' she says. 'I might have to leave after this year, I'll see.'

'How's it been over the spring and summer?'

Her face falls a little, and she shakes her head.

'We lost a lot of people. Residents. A couple of staff too. But then, the staff have not needed to be replaced, as the residents have not particularly been replaced.'

'You knew Mr Lord?'

'Yes, of course.'

'Did you know his –'

'Geraldine asked that I do not answer questions about them. She will tell you everything you need to know.'

———

62

We hold the stare in the confined space of the end of the corridor beside a print of a painting of a vase of flowers, and she smiles apologetically.

'You go swimming in the Baltic every week when you're in Lithuania?' I ask, and she says, 'Kaunus is two hours from the sea,' and I feel ignorant and stupid and British, and decide I'm just going to keep my mouth shut, then she says, 'We do swim in the lake sometimes, but not in the winter,' to make me feel better, and then, thank God, the voice comes from the room, and Karolina opens the door, announces me like I'm a guest at a ball hosted by Mr Darcy, and then I'm in the room, and Karolina has gone, the door closed behind me.

In a turn of events that surprises no one, the day manager's office does not smell of piss, and the art on the walls is of a vastly superior quality. Large windows looking out on to the river, the desk to the side, so that Geraldine can look out the window when the mood takes her, two armchairs on the other side of the desk, a small table with a similar drinks set-up to the one in reception, minus the cake, a large and immaculate ficus on the floor, and a vase of flowers on a small table opposite the desk. From them, or perhaps from Geraldine herself, comes a delicate floral scent, which is not at all old or sad, and really rather attractive.

'Sergeant Hutton,' she says, 'please come and sit down. Help yourself to coffee on the way.'

'I'm good, thanks,' I say, taking the seat.

Geraldine is haunted. Drawn thin, her existence stretched to nothingness, the scars of a long summer on her face. At some point she stopped dying her hair, grew it out, but she has yet to visit the salon, and her hair is a mix of greys, turning to the old blonde at the end. The collar on her turquoise blouse is a little loose, her cheeks are tight to her bones, as though her mouth were a vacuum.

'Thanks for making the time,' I say.

'These days we have all the time in the world.'

After the initial offer of coffee delivered in a familiar welcoming manner, her voice quickly takes on the quality of her face. Exhausted.

'Must've been a tough few months.'

She doesn't reply. Those eyes. Jesus. Just trying to do a minute or two of introductory, ice-breaking small talk, and she crucifies me from four feet for mansplaining the shittiest spring

—

and summer in seventy-five years.

'We should get to it,' I say, voice down in the resigned bin, and she makes a small papal gesture, indicating for me to get on with it, even though she started off by implying we literally had all day.

I'm probably over-thinking it. She's just miserable. Who isn't these days?

'You had a resident named Benjamin Lord, who died in the summer.'

'Yes. Benny. Lovely man. Died on 23rd of July.'

'You remember the date?' I can't stop myself saying, even though it's kind of obvious she remembers the date, and she looks at me like that's exactly what she's thinking, then I say, 'When did Covid get into the home?'

'July.'

Her voice now is sharp and cold, a slap across the face on a bitter day.

'That was late.'

'We managed to shut down before it arrived in the spring. We did everything we should. It was tough, tough on the residents, and the staff, and the families – some of them, anyway – and we got through it. Then, when the restrictions started to be relaxed, we managed to stay on top of things, played it a little tighter than was required. Kept it at bay. Then some of the families started complaining, insisted we relaxed things further. They went over our heads, went up the corporate ladder. Some people knew other people. Connections. Money. You know the score, how the world turns.'

That phrase again, the same words from Victoria Lord's lips two days ago.

'We asked that all visitors test themselves, but we could do little more than trust people. And, to the surprise of no one, the virus got in. Not with a dry, hacking cough, not with a sweating, tortured gasp, but invisibly, silently, on the breath of who knows?'

'Who was the first to get the illness?'

'Benny.'

'And he was the first to die?'

'Yes.'

'That's why you recall the date.'

'I recall all the dates, Sergeant. The first to the last.'

'When was the last?'

64

'Three weeks. Everyone, everyone here, has contracted the illness. Those of us, staff and residents who remain, have all survived it. As a result, we're more relaxed now. We're out the other side, you might say. Hallelujah. The great virus war of 2020, and here we are, the survivors, allowing people like you to just walk in off the street, untested, unmasked, while we laugh at Covid, that will not touch us.'

'People do get it again, people do d –'

'No one cares,' she says. 'They're either all ready to die, or they think they're invincible. Everyone was fed up with restrictions, everyone has been through hell, there's a signed letter from every resident and every power of attorney family member stating they wanted all restrictions on the home lifted.'

A beat. Another. The bitter pill they have all swallowed. How the war was won and where it got us.

'Fuck it,' she says, as a statement of intent from the inmates of Home 292.

'Did you ever have any idea who it was who brought the illness here?'

She laughs, the sour, rueful laugh with which we're familiar, and says, 'You're kidding me, right…? Pick one out of two hundred, Sergeant. What can I say? Benny was the first, so maybe it was someone who had contact with him. Maybe it was one of his sons, or his daughter-in-law, or his grandkids. You know if any of them ever had symptoms?'

I automatically shake my head.

July.

She doesn't need to know about Harry and Victoria Lord having symptoms in early July.

'But the paths of a virus are so labyrinthine, who can say? It could have been any visitor, passing it to any resident, or any other visitor, and on and on, through the passageways of innumerable human bodies, people being infected or not, showing symptoms or not, all at different rates and different stages. But Benny was the first to die, that's all we know for certain, and thereafter, the cataclysm. Just as the rest of the country was slowing down, and the graphs were flatlining, and people were starting to think of moving on, we were dying. Those random days when there was one death announced, or two deaths or whatever… those deaths were ours. Day after day. And now, now it picks back up everywhere else, and many more will feel our pain.'

She swallows, breaks the look, stares at the desk.

'Was Harry Lord one of the ones who used his influence and money to make sure the home lifted all its restrictions?'

She doesn't lift her eyes, the lips purse even more tightly, nothing flashes across her face, then she closes her eyes, lifts her head and stretches her neck. The physical attempt at releasing the tension, a pose held for a few moments, and then she looks coldly across the desk.

'Of course,' she says. 'Harry Lord more or less ran the home. When he wanted to, at any rate.'

'OK.'

And then, silence. We stare across the desk. The onus is obviously on me, as I was the one who came here.

What else is there to know? We wondered if Harry Lord's death might be Covid-related, and within a couple of minutes we have a connection. But if the home weren't aware that Lord might have had the virus, and therefore potentially was the person who infected his dad, and as a result, potentially infected all the other patients, why should it have any bearing on the investigation?

There are a fuck-load of potentials in there. Nevertheless, if someone, somewhere knew about it, then might they not consider killing Harry Lord a reasonable act of vengeance?

'Would you be able to give me the list of all the patients who died?' I ask, heart sinking at the question.

It makes sense, but Jesus, that is going to be a lot of people to follow up. That has phone calls and paperwork coming out its arse.

'Why?'

I don't answer. That, there, is a fairly regular question directed at the police, and there are two kinds of people who ask it. Idiots, and those who know well and good why we're asking. Those people then have to choose who they're going to be.

She sighs heavily, a sigh that will have crossed her lips a thousand times these past few months, then she says, 'You really suppose someone thinks Mr Lord brought the disease to the home, and now they've taken their revenge?'

'No, I don't think that. But, it wouldn't be the weirdest thing that ever happened. People kill for all sorts of reasons, and this has been one hell of a year. For everyone. We're in the early stages of our investigation into Mr Lord's murder, and so we need to pursue every avenue. This one is as likely as any other to

---

66

be a dead end.'

'Well, I suppose we can, but I'll need to speak to the Director first.'

'The Director's here?'

I'd've been better speaking to the Director.

'The Director hasn't been here since March. She got set up to work remotely, and has not darkened our doors since.'

No bitterness there, then.

'I'll need to speak to her too,' I say.

'Of course.'

And that might be it for the Day Manager. The conversation, such as it was, had been drawing to an end, and now we've added in the higher layer of authority, she can hand over the reins, and I wonder if she's thinking she should just have mentioned the Director right from the kick-off.

'There's one other thing,' she says. 'No idea if it's significant. Just kind of creepy, really. We wondered about calling the police, decided it wasn't worth the bother. Dial 111 and you can write off the rest of the day while you're waiting, right?'

I don't answer that, if for no other reason than I have absolutely no idea.

'What did you want to report?'

'There was a thing nailed to the door of the home a couple of mornings ago. Kind of sick, given everything that happened.'

She pauses, seemingly having to think about where this thing might be, and I get no sense of it, what's coming, and that it might be of the utmost significance.

And so, when she rolls her eyes at herself, opens the large desk drawer, takes out the item that was nailed to the door of the home and passes it across the desk, I'm completely taken aback, the words, 'Fucking Jesus,' unavoidably escaping my lips.

I take it from her, holding it gingerly by the edges, and then set it down on the desk in front of me. Empty eye sockets stare back at me from an identical white mask to the one placed over the face of Harry Lord.

16

We got the list quickly enough. The care home lost twenty-three residents in just under two months. Around half of their complement. That's Black Death levels. Add to that two members of staff. No wonder Geraldine the Day Manager looked as though she'd had the living shit kicked out of her. They did a nice job of making sure that didn't get into the press.

And so there are now a multitude of people to talk to, the investigation given a sudden, brutal kick up the arse. The family members of twenty-five Covid victims; the Director, continuing to self-isolate, as she has been doing since March, refusing to have the police at her house, and requiring interviewed by video; and there's Mrs Lord, who will know more than anyone about her husband's dealings with the care home, and with whom Kallas and I are now sitting.

'What?'

The crumpled brow, the crinkled nose. The bags beneath her eyes like bilious clouds. In her face, the confusion of the murder victim's wife. Or, as we all have to be cynical around here, the feigned bewilderment for the police audience.

'There was an identical mask to the one placed over Harry's face, nailed to the door of the home where his father died.'

'Why? Why would someone do that?'

'To make a connection.'

'Why?'

'We'll start with us asking you that, Mrs Lord,' I say. 'How involved was Harry in the home?'

'Involved? Not at all.'

The crease hasn't left her brow. She's found a prop, and she's clinging to it.

'He was a wealthy man. He provided funds to the church far in excess of what he might have been expected to, is it possible he did the same with the home?'

The furrow relaxes a little, she blinks. She holds my gaze for a moment, then looks at Kallas, then glances at the daughter, who's sitting next to her looking young and in over her head, unfamiliar with dealing with death and its aftermath.

'I don't know. I don't really know what Harry did with his money.'

'You knew about the church.'

'Yes. I was a member. The church was different.'

'So, you don't know if he gave additional funds to the home?'

'No.'

'When the home held onto restrictions into mid-July, was he one of those applying pressure to have those restrictions lifted?'

She hesitates, but only because she knows where this is going. This entire conversation is heading in a direction she doesn't want to think about. A direction Harry would not have wanted to think about, were he still alive. A direction they would both have been intending to ignore for the rest of their lives.

'Yes.'

'Did he speak to other families? Get a group together?'

'Yes.'

'Was he the first to visit?'

A beat. Finally, 'Harry and I and Liam went. Mandy was still in Durham. I don't know whether we were the first to visit or not. One of the first, I suppose.'

'And this was just after you and Harry had had symptoms of the virus.'

'We were tested.' Voice hard, lips thin, as defensive as a Walter Smith Rangers team playing Barcelona.

'Could've been false negatives.'

'Harry paid for good tests. The best.'

'It was done privately?'

'Yes.'

'Perhaps you could give us the details of that?'

'Why?' snaps the kid, and her mum squeezes her hand, gives her the *it's OK, just leave it* side-eye.

Mandy, undaunted – and what twenty year-old is ever daunted by a side-eye from a parent – removes her hand so she can lean forward.

'What do you want to prove? That my parents both had the virus? That they took it to the home, and they gave it to Granddad? They gave it to them all? What does that have to do with whoever killed dad?'

The connection is clear, and I don't bother making it for

—

69

her. The mum finds her daughter's hand again, entwines her fingers. They swallow with perfect synchronicity. The daughter looks as though she might be about to cry.

'I'll get those details for you,' says Mrs Lord.

'Thank you.'

'Is there anything else you'll need?'

'Everything you know about other families with whom he was in contact with regards to reopening the home.'

She looks a little lost at that, finally shakes her head, though more at the enormity of the task.

'I'll see what I can find.'

'D'you know if there was anyone who was dead against it? Against reopening?'

'I really…' and she shakes her head, and lets the answer drift off, hoping, more than likely, that it will take the question with it.

We already have at least one solid answer to that from Geraldine, the Day Manager, but there's rarely ever only one answer to any question.

Fuck me, that's deep, isn't it?

I glance at Kallas, the *have you anything you'd like to ask* look, and she shakes her head. Has been silent throughout, an invisible, yet focussing presence.

I can't help myself holding the look a little longer than necessary, then drag my eyes away and turn back to the widow.

'I think that might be all for the moment, Mrs Lord, thank you. There's nothing else you've thought of in the last day that might be significant?'

The head shake, the barely moving lips, the eyes dropping to the table, the fingers gripping more tightly the fingers of the girl.

'Thank you, Mrs Lord,' says Kallas, getting to her feet, and that's that one for the moment.

I watch the mum, the widow, waiting for the flicker, the look in the eye that speaks of relief, but there's nothing. She looks washed out, the look of these times, when so many have had their lives torn up and spat out.

She stares at the table, her daughter stares at the same spot, and Kallas and I see ourselves to the door.

* * *

'We have a lot of phone calls to make,' says Kallas. Heading to the mortuary to see Fforbes. 'If I could ask you to coordinate the team once we get back to the station.'

'Sure.'

'I will speak to the chief, see if we can get more resources. Human resources,' she adds, just to make sure I didn't think she meant coffee or toilet roll.

The phrase *human resources* always sounds a little too *Soylent Green* to me, even more so coming from Kallas's monotone.

'You want to be included in the roster of calls?' I ask.

'No. There are many things to consider. I'll stay at the operations room, try to fit everything in to place. We have too many different strands at the moment, it can be easy to get lost.'

'It was a bold statement,' I say, 'the mask nailed to the door, though weirdly, in its way, not an obvious one. There was no guarantee we'd make it public that there'd been a mask placed on the victim, and we hadn't; and there was no guarantee the home would tell the police about their mask. A connection was never definitely going to be made, and if it was, the killer had no control over the timing of the connection.' Take a moment, try to squeeze that thought into something more constructive, but there's nothing there.

'There are various ways in which the link could have been made,' says Kallas. 'One of those links happened. Perhaps the killer would have found some other way for it to have happened, if it had not.'

'How would he have known it didn't?'

'Good,' she says, I think meaning 'good point', but it's not entirely clear.

'It feels enough of a statement, however, that it might be the killer is not done,' I say. 'Leaving a calling card is not a good sign.'

'I agree. We can hope, perhaps, that the intention was to link Lord's death to the home, and leave it there. But if that were the case, why would the killer give us that clue to their identity? We are now interviewing everyone who had anything to do with the home, and in particular Mr Lord. So, was it to throw us off the scent, or is it just the beginning?' She pauses a moment, but I know she's not looking for an answer, her questions entirely rhetorical. 'We cannot focus on the end product of the investigation,' she continues. 'We must, for now, do what is right in front of us. That also means not losing sight of Mr Lord's many lovers.'

'You're on that?'

'Yes.'

'How many have you counted so far?'

She glances at me, wondering if it's a serious question, then she says, 'I'm not running a tally. I think six, though perhaps it is more.'

'Six this year, or six lifetime? I mean, the lifetime of his marriage.'

'Six this year. I do not think it will be the final number.'

Stare straight ahead. Lucky bastard.

I mean, he's dead, so let's not get carried away about him being *that* lucky, but still, six women and counting. I'm supposed to be a sex addict, and I haven't had that many women this year. Of course, he was fit as fuck, and much, much wealthier. He was probably turning women down, while I, for my sins, take anyone I can get.

On we go, round and round the investigation race track, regularly passing the same points, hoping the perspective is a little different, making our way to see Dr Fforbes, and to breathe in the Kool Aid of disinfectant.

* * *

Fforbes, Kallas and I sitting around a white table in the mortuary, drinking tea, eating Fox's biscuits. Or *bisqwits* as I can't help saying in my head, ever since the Sopranos panda was on TV.

Kallas initially refused, until it became obvious that the doc and I would be sitting here drinking a brew, and she was able then to shake off those Estonian shackles and go wild. Drinking tea and eating Fox's bisqwits in a mortuary is the Estonian equivalent of downing a bottle of gin, shooting LSD into your eyeballs and running naked onto the set of Captain Marvel looking to anally bang Brie Larson.

On the table are the two masks, side-by-side, identical, Lord's death mask identifiable as being marked with soaked-in blood.

'So, nice of you to come in 'n' all, but –'

'It is not a problem.'

'But these are both… you know, I think this second one

72

just confirms what we had from the first. These are made in a factory somewhere from a mould. Could be Bangladesh, could be Vietnam, could be anywhere. Putting them together then, yes, we have confirmation they are identical. Quite probably from the same batch. The one found at the home does not give up any further secrets, however.'

'Is there *anything* to be revealed from the mask at the home?'

'Zip. No DNA, no blood, no body matter of any description.'

Fforbes takes a drink of tea, then scoops up another chocolate biscuit.

Kallas runs a light finger over the mask that was attached to the door, the hole at the top of the forehead where the nail was hammered through. Then she takes a drink of tea, regarding the cup with shame, before placing it back on the table.

'You have the final report on the autopsy of Mr Lord?' she asks.

'I e-mailed it about ten minutes before you got here.'

'You didn't say.'

'No,' says Fforbes, and I get the conspiratorial glance again. 'I guess we got carried away talking about tea and biscuits.'

'Is there anything of note?'

'I've got the time of death down to between one-fifteen and one-thirty. There were only seventeen cuts carried out post-mortem, so our killer knew what he was doing. They kept him alive for a long time. There was also evidence of bruising of the testicles, so it looks as though there was some gratuitous pain delivered, along with the slashing.'

'A bruise from a sharp whack, like maybe a kick to incapacitate him at the beginning, or –'

'Nope, I'd say there was a slower process than that. There would have been plenty of pain, but it would have been drawn out.'

Let out a sigh, can't help squirming a little.

'Plus, there's further evidence of pain being delivered just for the hell of it. Several cuts through the jaw, right to the nerves of the teeth for example. It was never going to kill Mr Lord off any more quickly, but it would certainly have hurt. I think what we likely had was pain rotated around the body, so that he never quite became used to it in any one particular place.

—

73

'The killer, I think we can say without doubt, was exacting his or her revenge on Mr Lord, and it would have been a very, very painful one.'

She lifts her tea, she takes a bite of biscuit, then delicately licks a crumb off the side of her lips.

17

'Hi, this is Detective Sergeant Thomas Hutton calling from Police Scotland...'

'What d'you want?'

'We're investigating the murder of a Mr Harry Lord.'

Leave it the requisite couple of seconds to gauge if there's any reaction. In this instance, nothing.

'We believe there might be some connection between Mr Lord's death, and his relationship with the Garrion Bridge care home, where his father died in the summer. Did you have any dealings with Mr Lord at th –'

'Guy's a cunt.'

Manage to stop myself laughing. Like I said, I'm here to do a good job, but I don't particularly care either way how this pans out. On the one hand I find blunt statements like 'guy's a cunt' pretty funny; on the other, laughing out loud isn't too professional.

'You knew him at least.'

'Never met him, naw, but he phoned us up a few times. Always looking to get people jumping on whatever bandwagon he was pushing the fuck out of that week. He moaned about it taking too long to shut down, then the cunt moans about it taking too long to open back up again. And every time he wanted to make some change or other, he'd always try to rope in other people.'

'Did you disagree with him?'

'Usually not, to be honest. They bastards at the home did take too long to close down, then they'd fucking still be closed now, if they'd had their own way.'

By way of making the obvious point, I say, 'Your mother died in August?'

'Aye,' he says. 'They said she had this Covid crap, but I don't know. She was old, right? I mean, she wouldn't have been in there if she hadn't been. They say a lot of people would've died anyway, and I reckon she was one of them.'

I nod down the phone. The man isn't exactly inspiring sympathy, though neither is he looking for it. But there's nothing

---

to see here, one of those obvious ones. You don't leave the calling card, and then sound like this guy. Wrap up the phone call, put a red line through the name, no need for a visit, and on to the next on the list.

* * *

'He was a rat-faced twat.'

Nice. From what we know of Harry Lord so far, I'd say he sounds far more of a cunt than a twat, it not being a particularly fine distinction, though perhaps the wording is more to do with the messenger than the message.

'Go on.'

'There was some cocktail up at the home last year… Christmas, it was Christmas. You know, some families invited, just a bit of an event. Guy was hitting on my wife. I mean, what was he doing? He was at an old people's home, his own wife was there, I was there, and he was hitting on Abigail. What a twat.'

'Did he pull it off?'

Couldn't stop myself.

'What?'

Don't get much further with *that* phone call. Make a note that it'll likely need a follow-up.

* * *

'Called themselves the Carluke Cowboys,' says the woman, amused disdain in her voice. 'They'd golf once in a blue moon, send each other jokes on WhatsApp all the time. Really filthy stuff. They always had these plans to take over the world. Just an in-joke they'd had since university, all those plans that were never going to happen. Not that it mattered, as they were both so damn rich. It gave them freedom to dream, because it wasn't like they were failing in not pulling them off.'

'So they'd known each other since university?'

'Yep. Thirty-one years and counting. Well… no more counting.'

She swallows, I can see her pulling herself together at the other end of the phone.

Jennifer Royale, wife of one of Lord's oldest friends, Sebastian Royale. Her husband is dead now, a Covid victim with

—

no obvious underlying health conditions, early August this summer, when the deaths were low. Covid's mid-career slump, before the autumn reboot.

'That's the way it goes, isn't it?' she forces across her lips.

'So, how did it work with the home? Was it Sebastian or Harry who put the other onto it first?'

'It was always one of those places they'd known about. I don't think you could pin it to one or the other. But they egged each other on, or perhaps just encouraged each other gently when it came to their parents, and they put their fathers in there within about a month of each other a couple of years ago. I mean… well, I can't speak for Harry, but Seb could certainly have afforded to set up his father in his own place with live-in help, but he decided dad would be better off with other people his own age.'

'What did his dad think?'

'That didn't really matter with Seb, I'm afraid. I think Harry might've been the same.'

'Did Sebastian lobby the home as much as Harry?'

'Oh, Harry was always the leader. That was Harry. But Seb would go along, no question.'

The eleventh phone call. I have yet to make a mark against any as being truly worthy of a follow-up visit. It's hard to tell over the phone, but there's certainly no time to visit them all. Perhaps, as this drags on from one week to the next, we'll get around to that. But at the moment, trying to get a jump on the investigation, this will have to do it, and we have to be able to pick up on the slip of the tongue, the inconsistency, the wavering tone.

There's been nothing.

'How did Sebastian catch the illness?'

She shakes her head down the phone. I can feel it. Then, 'We never knew. Who did? Never knew, never will.'

'Is it possible…' and I naturally hesitate before planting my foot in it, but, for fuck's sake, I have to ask the question, and she gives me the space to do it anyway, and then I say, 'is it possible he caught it from the home?' which really means, is it possible he caught it from Harry, so in fact, it would sort of be Harry who killed your husband and therefore you, even more than some of these others, would have a motive to kill Harry.

'That, at least, is one thing that didn't happen,' she says. 'We hadn't been back there since before it was locked down. We joined in with the argument to get them to open up again, but Seb was travelling a lot at the time. You know, with everywhere opening up at the same time, and businesses not really knowing how long it'd be before they had to shut down again, he was always shooting off around the place. Hardly saw him the last few weeks, and then he was in hospital and… and I couldn't see him at all.'

'And you didn't go to the home?' I ask, sticking the knife in.

That one doesn't get an answer, which is all the guilty answer I need. She didn't go. The care home opened up, neither son nor daughter-in-law visited, then the dad died.

No getting rid of that memory, my sad and desperate witness. You're fucked. And just as you were coming to terms with your father-in-law dying, unvisited in several months, your husband died. Rather than making you forget how shitty you previously felt, it just added to it, coming on top, compounding the shit, and now you're buried beneath it.

* * *

And so it goes, one awful conversation after the next. Stupidly I blundered into it without much aforethought. But of course, here we are, us bold and uninvited police officers, calling up to open a wound, and to invoke the crime, murder. More than one of the recipients of a call was suspicious, naturally, and few were talkative.

I've been doing this shit for thirty years, and rather fancy I've got a well-developed grasp of the liar and the thief, the fool and bullshitter. The young 'uns, though, these constables with barely a year or two behind them, they came back with far more doubts, far more names they thought needed to be followed up, a lot more interviews requiring to be done.

Not surprised. No one wanted to have those conversations. Maybe I was slapdash, too willing to cast names aside, to put down someone's reticence to ill feeling and depression. But I don't think so. I'm not saying I'm not useless in all sorts of ways, but in this at least, I know what I'm doing.

18

End of the day. Harrison's gone, don't have my buddy to talk to. Domino's pizza again. I don't even like Domino's pizza, but here we are. Me and my desk and a tonne of work and a giant-ass pizza.

We had our end of the day wrap-up, and we all fed in where we'd got to, and the sum total of it is that there's a long way to go, a million people still to speak to. All we've got is a link to the home, but then it's a link that someone wants us to make, so maybe it shouldn't actually be a link we're making at all.

Be wary of shit handed to you on a plate, as some famous detective or philosopher or someone must've said at some point.

Ritter's still here, and Ablett, though they're both currently in the ops room. My new crush left half an hour ago. I can't say she looked tired, as she never looks anything. A beautiful portrait hanging in a gallery, the expression forever unchanging.

Kind of glad we didn't spend too much time together today. From now on, any day when I don't have to watch her get undressed on a beach will be a bonus. I mean, it was literally the most enjoyable thing that's happened to me *in my life*, but God, the whole Troon escapade has completely fucked with my head.

Uh-oh. Incoming.

The Chief leaves her office, light off, starts to head towards the exit, then notices me sitting at my desk. *Rats.* Same thing happened last night, but she chose not to interrupt Harrison and I. Now that I'm on my own, I'm easy prey. Like the baby elk that loses the back of the herd and gets picked off by wolves.

'Sergeant,' she says, by way of starting off the evisceration.

I genuinely haven't given the woman any thought whatsoever since I so easily dismissed that stupid list of courses she sent me.

'Everything all right?' she asks, when I substitute replying with staring dumbly across the desk.

'Yep.'

'I know we have a murder enquiry, but really, you should go home, eat at home, get an early night. I expect you'll be in early tomorrow.'

I have a piece of pizza in my hand, the sixth of the eight, already gone cold, a can of Coke Zero to my left. The pizza is poised. The only thing I can do at times such as this is be honest, which is one hell of a failing.

'If I eat here, I won't drink,' I say.

'Oh.'

She looks concerned, her brow furrows, I can see her contemplating whether or not she should recommend that I go for emergency counselling, and then she says, 'Well, that's a positive start, Sergeant. It's something. I do think we need to have a much longer conversation than we did the other day.'

'Oh, I don't think so,' leaves my mouth, like a fucking boss.

Slightly taken aback by that unexpected candour – and so, after all, am I – she says, 'Inspector Kallas is very impressed with your work on the case so far.'

I've got nothing to say to that. Just shocked silence, obviously.

She's not the best when talking to a brick wall, looks kind of awkward, then she adds, 'You never got back to me about the courses.'

'Haven't had a chance to look properly. I'll, eh… I'll take a look.'

'OK, thank you, Sergeant.' She nods, she runs her management-trained, heavily consulted brain through the past couple of minutes of conversation to see if there's anything she's missed, then she says, 'You shouldn't work too late. Maybe finish eating, then get on.'

'Yes, ma'am,' I say, and she smiles at that, as though I was trying to be funny, and off she goes, home to her new-build, one-bedroomed executive apartment, to have an avocado salad and one third of a glass of Muscadet.

I take a bite of pizza, there's hardly any of that slice left, so I cram it into my mouth, lick my fingers as I do it, then I'm just taking a napkin to my lips, my cheeks bulging, when she's standing next to me. We look at each other from two feet, her with that vaguely concerned look on her face, and me looking like Squirrel fucking Nutkin.

'Sorry,' she says.

I make a gesture to indicate it's fine, and that she can go ahead. Wary of swallowing too quickly, so I don't choke like a dick.

'That thing I said the other day…' I give her the wide eyes to indicate I probably know what she's talking about. 'It was unprofessional. It did not require to be spoken out loud, it was all about me attempting to impose myself, impose my will, some kind of alpha bullshit. Like I said, very unprofessional.'

I swallow. I make sure to have another elegant dab at my lips with the napkin. I stop myself saying something stupid, and instead go for the measured and respectful, 'Really, it's OK. I deserve everything I get.'

She smiles, she touches my shoulder – holy fuck, you're not allowed to do *that*! haven't you done the courses? – and then she turns and is gone, and I'm left to enjoy the last of my cold Domino's pizza in peace.

Constable Ritter pulls the seat away from the desk opposite and sits down. She stares across at me. Constable Ritter never stares across the desk. She looks tired.

'Bit of a day,' she says.

I smile. It didn't even make my top thousand *bit of a days*, but sure, it wasn't the best.

'Would you like a slice of cold pizza?'

'You're selling it,' she says, smiling. 'It's OK. Gina and I are just about to hit Yo-Yo's. Would you like to join us?'

Fucking hell, what a world. Hitting a bar with Ablett and Ritter. I mean, they're both the respectable side of thirty years younger than me, that's a positive, right? If one considers that Audrey Hepburn and Fred Astaire in *Funny Face* wasn't creepy as fuck, I'm doing better than that.

And Ablett, in particular, has a way about her. A look.

Stop it!

'I'm good, thanks, Emma. Just going to finish up here and head home.'

'Oakie doakie,' she says, and she smiles and turns away, and I know from the look that she really didn't want me coming anyway, and I'm so relieved I wasn't a dick about it.

19

This one struggled a bit more, the GHB not working so effectively from the start, and so the killer had had to employ rougher tactics. A disabling assault on the testicles was required much earlier in the process, a blow to the head, another dose of the drug administered. Naturally, having had to take such precautions in order to get the body safely into position, when it came to it, it proved much more difficult to revive the victim. No point in carrying out the execution, if he was to sleep through it.

In the end, he was roused by the deployment of extreme pain, his killer flaying the skin of his penis. Oh, he woke up then, all right. Eyes wide, consumed by terror. Didn't know where he was, the strange lighting in the church confusing him.

The killer would have liked it if the victim could have talked. The one-sided conversation was always a little disappointing. One needed a bit of give and take, one needed to know the customer truly understood why they were suffering this mind-fuck of pain. And, of course, if they could talk back, the killer would be better able to understand how much they believed they could talk themselves out of it. It would be funny to listen to their *let's call the whole thing off* speech. Once they'd decided that wasn't working, they might switch to threats. A classic of the genre. To be in a position of such weakness, absolute vulnerability, and yet, to act as though holding all the cards. They've seen James Bond do it, so it must work, right?

Maybe some time in the coming weeks, the killer thinks. There will be some venue where such a murder can be carried out, the victim given free rein to voice their supine self-pity. And it would be a fun to hear the screams. But not here, in this deserted church, illuminated only by the lights of the streets outside.

David Cowal is tied to the cross that was left behind the altar. It's not high, it's not, to be honest, really big enough for a crucifixion. But it serves its purpose, after all, it supports his weight, the blood runs, dark black in this ill light.

'How does it feel?'

The killer looks at him, standing back, staring at the blood

82

running from the latest cut.

Some of the cuts, many of them, are small by necessity. If one truly wants one thousand distinct cuts in the human body, there's no other option, particularly when the human body is slight, like this one.

The insignificance of David Cowal. Weak muscles, no fat on him, but not through exercise, not through diet or working out, just by a quirk of his genes. He'd got lucky, never having had to worry about weight. But Cowal never ran, he never lifted weights, he never sat on an exercise bike, he never went anywhere on foot when there was a car to hand, even if it was two hundred yards down the road.

'You're practically an American,' his wife used to say.

She liked the joke. Cowal not so much.

Dead now, Mrs Cowal, so there was no need to hear that joke anymore.

'I know,' says the killer, piercing the skin just beneath the right armpit with the pointed tip of the knife, enjoying the tensing of the muscle, the way the body reacted when the usual outlets were denied it. 'I'm like a dentist, chatting away with my fingers in your mouth, and you unable to answer. Did you have a nice weekend, and where are you going on holiday, and did you lose anyone in the pandemic…? Such mindless questions. But actually, wait…'

The killer stops, poised, the knife inserted in the skin, and now drives it in a little further, turning it slightly. Cowal's muscles strain, his eyes scream, even if his gagged mouth can't.

'Did you lose anyone in the pandemic? Did you, David?'

The killer looks curiously at him, trying to think what the tone of voice is reminiscent of. A smile, a shake of the head. Of course, the vicar at the end of *Four Weddings*.

Do you love someone else? Do you, Charles?

Maybe it's the setting.

'Oh, yes, you did, didn't you?'

The knife is jabbed in further, the pain sears across Cowal's face, his eyes widening. Then the killer presses the knife into the skin, drawing it down sharply as it's extracted from the flesh.

The killer stands back. *Don't talk to him anymore. It just gets you annoyed. Annoyance leads to mistakes.*

A deep breath, a quick survey of the work done so far, much of it now obscured behind the mask of dark red blood.

———

Still seven hundred and fifty-three cuts to go. There's no way Cowal will survive as long as Lord. Lord had been tough. David Cowal, however, is small and weak and sad and useless. Funny, then, how the GHB had not had quite the same effect on him. The mysterious ways of the human body.

There will likely be several hundred cuts administered to a corpse, so more pain will have to be inflicted earlier, even if it means the earlier death becomes something of a self-fulfilling prophecy.

'That's the way it crumbles, cookie-wise,' says the killer, the words not really aimed at Cowal, turning to the small stone altar, where a few implements of torture are laid out. The good ones are the ones that cause pain, but do not speed the descent to death.

Here lies the ninety-nine pence, plastic tub of table salt.

'Very simple. Crude. But you know what…?'

The killer pours an ample amount into their left hand, holds the hand over Cowal's flayed penis, and lets the salt pour over the raw flesh.

Cowal's body squirms with the pain, his face flushes with it, his eyes pop and he yells, the muffled scream pointlessly juddering to a stop in his mouth.

The killer watches him, eyes very accustomed now to the low light, no smile on the face, they rub the salt off their hands, and then the knife is lifted, to return once more to the fray.

'Onwards and downwards.'

20

Can't sleep, won't sleep. A fine attitude from any brain.

Maybe I just need something to help me switch off. One of those all-absorbing hobbies, where you can't really think about anything else while you're about it. I mean, sure, that description applies to masturbation, my usual night time sleep aid, but it never lasts long enough, and one never falls asleep while actually doing it.

Had a brief affair a while back with a sergeant I met at a thing. A group counselling thing, when they thought I might be suicidal. I mean, they were bang on, I *was* suicidal. Still am, in my dark moments, though I think we all know I'm probably not going to do it. Not yet. Maybe I just tell myself not yet, because I want to be some kind of edgy fucker, always on the point of putting a gun at my own head. Such a wanker sometimes.

The woman. We got an Airbnb near Aberfoyle. Three nights. I mean, it was decent enough, perfect in its way, in that we got each other out of our systems. The sex was good, and on the one fairweather day we got a walk up Schiehallion. Not bad up there. But by the end of it we were both ready to move on. And on each of those three nights she did some number puzzle. Not Sudoku, something else Japanese.

She said it was absorbing, left her just tired enough at some point to turn out the light, and she'd be asleep within a minute every time.

I was left lying there, those three nights, listening to her breathing. We hadn't even had sex on the third night. We did again on the final morning, but it was, I don't know what you'd call it, goodbye sex. Afterthought sex. What the hell, and might as well, sex. She came twice, (unless she was pretending, and I didn't even care by then), I came once, we showered, we packed up, and off we went. We chatted all right in the car on the way down the road, like strangers stuck on a train, and then I dropped her off at her place, and I drove home, and all I took out of that weekend was doing number puzzles to try to get to sleep.

So I bought a book of number puzzles, struggled to do one of the easy ones at the start, then never looked at it again. Finally tossed it in the bin a few weeks ago.

The lesson we learn from this, sports fans, is that you have to find your own thing. Ashley had her number puzzles, and I've got my masturbation.

Didn't help that I came to bed with feelings of such self-contempt. Came home, made myself a cup of tea, stood at the window looking down on an empty street. The tea tasted weak as shit, and it was nothing to do with taking the bag out too soon. Nothing to do with anything, except a young officer had fake invited me to a bar, and the greater the distance it got from the invite, the less fake I persuaded myself it had been, and so I stood there talking myself into going. Tasting the alcohol, seeing the effects of the drink in their eyes, spinning my bullshit stories, reeling them in. Thinking about Ablett, thinking there might be possibilities.

Got that feeling in the back of my throat.

Got my shoes on, got to the door, checked the time as an afterthought.

It was more than two hours since Ritter had extended the fake invitation. Two hours. Ritter and Ablett? You know, I'm sure they can have a far better time in a bar than I can, but on a Thursday evening, at the start of a major murder investigation, in the middle of a pandemic, there's no way they were still going to be there.

Now all I had was me turning up late at a bar, it having shut early, or it being not kicking the arse off closing time, in order to slam back a couple of vodkas before I got booted out, and then I'd be stopping at an off licence on the way home, drinking on my own until five a.m. and then going in to work, feeling as goddam awful as I looked.

I boldly, and bravely, turned my back on the night, took my shoes off, tossed my jacket on the floor, and came to bed. And though no one else had witnessed my own trial and ultimate triumph – boo-fucking-yah – I felt utterly pathetic for even having started down the road in the first place.

Since then I've been lying here naked, staring at the night, lost in a fug of depression. Or, you know, that poetic melancholy Kallas mistakenly thinks I possess.

Don't think about Kallas.

21

A morning of phone calls. Hello, this is the police about your dead mum, just checking whether or not you yourself might harbour a grudge against a man named Lord, to the extent that you would slice the shit out of the guy, slice 'im 'til he's dead?

No?

Sorry to trouble you. And sorry for your loss.

Next!

This morning, there's one woman who just straight out tells me to fuck off, then hangs up. Nice move. Trouble is, you have to call back. Have to. Even though you know – because of that honed gut instinct of yours that everyone talks about – that this is the most genuine call you've had all morning, and that this person really, really doesn't want to talk about her dead mum to anyone, least of all you, you insensitive police prick, you just can't know *for sure*. Because, of course, if you killed Harry Lord, and then out of nowhere you got a phone call from the police, wouldn't the cleverest thing be to act like the very idea of it really upsets you?

I mean, we know the killer telegraphed the connection between Harry Lord and the care home, so the bastard wants us to call him. He wants the challenge. He started the game, the last thing he's going to do is throw us off when we come calling. He's going to play until he's caught, that's who he is.

Nevertheless, when someone tells you to fuck off, you have to dial straight back, even though you may want to fuck off just as much as the person on the other end of the phone wants you to. I finally got to say that at the third attempt, after pointing out that if she didn't speak to me, I was going to have to go round there. And no one wanted that.

Ritter's out on a call, not sure where, or whether it's related to this – after all, we're still living in a shitshow of crime, it's not like the merry-go-round stops for the murder investigation – and now Detective Inspector Kallas takes Ritter's seat at the desk opposite.

'How are things this morning?' she asks, as ever, straight to business.

'If we're trying to be positive, I'm happily knocking the names of potential suspects off the list.'

'Have you placed anyone *on* the list?'

'Everyone's on the list until they're taken off.'

'Yes, very good,' she says. 'Have you investigated anyone who you subsequently left on the list?'

'No.'

'Very well. I have a list of Harry Lord's most recent lovers, as well as more significant lovers from the past. It is not comprehensive, and of course, if it was one of his former lovers who killed him, why place the mask on the door of the home, other, obviously, than as a distraction? Nevertheless, we are sadly still at a stage where we do not have any idea why or by whom Harry Lord might have been killed. So this we do, because we can.

'I prefer that we take these interviews together, as it is always good to get both a male and female perspective. However, given the current urgency of the situation, I think it might be better if –'

There's a phone ringing across the office somewhere, and Kallas obviously has the spider sense to know that it's coming from her desk, even though all the phones sound the same.

'Excuse me.'

She lifts Ritter's phone, presses a few numbers, says, 'Kallas,' in that way of hers that makes those two syllables sound the most efficient use of language anywhere in the world, and then she stares at me across the desk as she listens.

Uh-oh.

She's not the only one with spider sense.

'I will be right there. You will mobilise?' She nods, she's saying 'thank you,' as she's hanging up the phone.

'It would appear that this thing is not just limited to Harry Lord.'

'Another murder?'

'Yes. You will come with me.'

And up she gets, her eager and trusty manservant in her wake.

* * *

The old abandoned church up on Stewart Street. Here we are, out in force, the road blocked off, public allowed no nearer than a hundred yards. A few of them gathered at the tape, but people have got used to not going anywhere, not assembling anywhere, and so the crowd is much sparser than it would've been in the past.

The church was put into mothballs a few years back. I've no idea why the building wasn't sold, I expect we can get into that. It's an Episcopalian Church. The Church of Scotland sell their buildings off for biscuits, soon as they can get rid of them, they're so desperate for money. Give it a couple of years, and there'll be none left. I know nothing about the Episcopalians and why they wouldn't have sold a building. More than likely, there'll be some dispute over ownership, someone, somewhere arguing bloody-mindedly with someone else, because that's what happens. The old People Are Assholes rule.

The church has decent security. Solid fencing, topped with barbed wire around the perimeter, security cameras, good lighting, but not so good the neighbours would get upset. Consequently, the church hasn't been trashed the way many others would have been. They must have plans.

It does raise the question, of course, of how the killer got his victim inside the church unseen. More than likely, it'll transpire the cameras were disconnected as a cost-saving measure some time in the last couple of years. Or even if the footage is being recorded, no one will be looking at it live. Best-case scenario is that we get to watch film of the hooded killer lugging his victim onto the premises. We'll at least know what time it all started.

The church was largely cleared out of stuff, so that the nave is empty, not an old wooden pew in sight. The windows are still in place, but they're all plain glass, bar one long, thin stained glass window behind the altar. I don't know if the others used to be stained glass, and were removed for use elsewhere, if that was possible, or maybe they were placed in storage to await judgement day.

God knows if Episcopalians believe in judgement day. Do any of these people really believe any of the shit they bang on about?

Aye, all right…

The old wooden cross was left behind the altar, alongside an old stone table, which is physically attached to the floor. Would have been tough to move. As for the cross, someone could have had away with it at some point, I guess, but maybe

---

89

no one ever got in through the front door before.

There are fourteen of us inside the church. The body of David Cowal remains on the cross, though the blood has long since stopped dripping.

Cowal was widowed – his wife died of the virus this summer – and he was living with his adult children. Two daughters. One of them is an asthmatic student, living the student dream of never having to get out of bed in the morning, and if we'd been counting on her for the discovery of the corpse, the dad would likely still be alone on the cross, his body left to ferment in the chill of a long October.

The other daughter is a civil servant, works from home using a Samsung Galaxy she's had since April. Her dad had texted in the evening saying he wouldn't be home until late. Took the girl a while to realise he wasn't there this morning. Tried calling, obviously didn't get anywhere. Called his office in Baillieston, they said he wasn't in. Alarm bells were ringing, but she didn't want to call the police yet. I mean, can't really blame her, right? Who the fuck ever actually wants to call the police, particularly when it might just be your dad got a shag the night before, and he didn't want to tell his girls in case they were upset for the dead mum?

Then at some point she remembered that since the height of the great death in the summer, they've had family tracking on their phones, and by that means, she found her dad here, in this church, because his killer had kindly left his Samsung in the nave, perhaps for that very reason.

Cowal's body hangs limp on the cross, bound at the hands and feet. Not nailed, interestingly. Seems like a wasted opportunity to me. Perhaps tying him up there was just easier.

His corpse is covered in blood, head to foot. His toes, in fact, are only a few inches off the floor. Blood has pooled beneath him, bright red in the glare of the lighting which our team have set up inside, to the low hum of the small, mobile generator just outside the door.

Kallas and I are standing a few feet from the corpse, observing Fforbes make her initial assessment.

'A small man,' says Kallas. 'It would have been a tougher task to place the victim from Monday evening up there.'

'Yes.'

'Do you think you could do it?'

I glance at her, she's staring at Fforbes, though the question

---

was directed at me.

'Hold that little guy up so I could tie his hands to the cross?'

'Yes. You are of average build.'

Totally average, in every respect.

'Yes,' I say, 'I think so. I mean, like everyone bar the most emaciated old granny, he's still going to be a dead weight to lift, but I suppose I could do it with a bit of effort. You're wondering if it's a two-man job?'

'I do not think it is a two-man job. I think one person hauled this man up here. Hard, perhaps, but I do not think it would have taken exceptional strength.'

'If I could do it, so could pretty much anyone?' I say, unable to stop myself smiling grimly.

She looks at me now, unsure if I'm being facetious, then says, 'Yes, that is what I meant.'

Of course.

'You think you could do it?' I ask.

'I have been wondering. I am not sure. My upper body strength is not so great. I have never done the exercises.'

We share a look. Now I'm thinking about watching her walk naked into the Clyde, which may not be entirely appropriate for the setting but she was the one who started talking about her upper body. But, she's right. She didn't look muscular and strong. Just slim and soft and gorgeous.

For fuck's sake.

'What?'

Ah. She can't read my mind. That's good. It's probably because she's got all that logical shit going on in her head, and logically a senior detective sergeant wouldn't be thinking about his boss naked while standing beside a bloody corpse.

'It could still have been done by a woman, though,' I say.

'Yes.'

'Little guy,' says Fforbes from beside the corpse, then she takes a step back, so that she's standing beside Kallas and me. 'Not a huge amount of muscular development going on there either, so I don't think our victim did much in the way of working out. I reckon you might have been able to lift him up there, Kadri, but it would've been an effort, and we might wonder why you did it. So, I'd say your killer was either male, or a strong woman, who could do this without too much trouble, and I mean...' I get the glance. 'No offence, Sergeant, but probably stronger than you, unless he or she had a specific reason for putting him up here, in which case they might have been willing to make the effort. We know anything about him?'

'Not yet,' I say. 'The daughter's back down at the station.'

'She knew to find her dad here?'

'Used a phone tracking app. Didn't want to break into the church, called the cops, we turned up surprisingly quickly, then the kid entered with one of our constables.'

'That's the kid's vomit everyone's having to step over just outside the front door?'

'Yep. And when I say kid, she's in her late twenties or something.'

Fforbes gives me a glance, let's out a long sigh, turns back to the corpse.

'I've got all I need here for the moment,' she says. 'When the lads have done their work, they can get the body back to my office. I suspect, as you can plainly see, the discussion we have over the corpse will not be too dissimilar to the one we had three days ago.'

She indicates his groin, which is, naturally, completely covered by blood.

'Interesting to note that the penis has been flayed.'

Fuck me.

There's the involuntary squirming that comes with any kind of mention of the genitals being manhandled in an unacceptable manner.

'Is that the only area of flaying?' asks Kallas, while I'm still shuddering.

'There are four separate areas, so one more than the last time. The killer appears, however, for the most part to have followed the same process. Again, there would have been a lot of pain. Mr Cowal would have suffered.'

We look at his face, although, of course, we cannot see his face. Again, it has been covered by the same plain, white mask, the mask now, inevitably streaked with blood.

'How is the mask attached?' asks Kallas.

'Not sure yet. There's nothing obvious. It might just be the killer held the mask on the bloody face, and it wouldn't have taken long for it to adhere to the skin. No more than a few seconds. I'll be surprised if there's anything else.'

She stops, she turns, she looks at what Kallas and I are looking at. For a moment, what will be no more than a fleeting

---

second, the sun must have appeared in between the clouds, and the sunbeam perfectly catches the stained glass window, and falls directly onto the figure on the cross, casting the bloody corpse in an array of colours.

The others going about their business in the nave seem to notice it too, and for a second the activity stops as we look upon God's light shining on the crucified corpse.

Then the sun vanishes, the magical coloured light disappears, the moment is lost.

With a footstep, a cough, the scrape of a piece of equipment, the noise resumes, and we're back.

'OK, thank you, Doctor Fforbes,' says Kallas, with her familiar formality. Fforbes and I exchange our naughty glance, and then I turn away with Kallas and start walking back through the church, until we're out into the dull November morning, rain in the air, due to kick off at any minute. It will, at least, help wash away the girl's vomit.

'Rain,' says Kallas, stopping for a moment to look at the sky.

How British of her. She must have been assimilated to some extent these fifteen years.

'We'll need to come up with a plan for the mask,' I say.

We haven't revealed the existence of the mask to the public, so again there's the possibility of someone, somewhere finding another mask, the mask that provides a link, and not making any connection, because why should they?

'I know,' she says, as we pick our way through our people, back to the road, for the ten-minute walk down to the station. 'Let us see, first, if the mask presents itself in the course of events.'

And with that, as we begin our walk, the rain starts falling.

—

22

Here sit the sisters, grim, Anne and Samantha Cowal. Anne and Samantha, the parents were David and Mary, all very conventional and Scottish and middle class, living in their middle class home in Cambuslang, just off the Public Park, not so far from where Harry Lord lived.

Anne, the elder sister, the civil servant, turns out to be twenty-nine, and not, as you might suppose, living at home because of some Covid-related necessity. She just hasn't moved out yet. Won't need to now. She's doing the talking. Samantha, twenty-six, was summoned from her bed to the police station by her sister to be told the news. She doesn't appear to have spoken since.

'Can you tell us about your mum?' asks Kallas.

Anne looks at me, as she has done a few times, in that *would it be possible to speak to someone Scottish* way that people have, but really, anyone who thinks like that can calm the fuck down. Kallas is sharp as fuck, and it's not as though a little bit of an accent takes anything away from her. So I blank her, and she turns back to Kallas.

'She died in May,' says Anne, as though that might do it.

'Coronavirus?'

'Yes.'

'How did it happen?'

A beat, and then she lowers her eyes, her head shakes. 'I don't really want to talk about it.'

'If you want to help us find your father's killer, you are going to have to.'

'What does it have to do with mum?'

'We do not yet know. But there was a similar murder on Monday evening, and we believe it was related to coronavirus, so we have to give consideration to the possibility that your father's may be too.'

'He didn't kill mum,' she says, defensively.

Boy, that tone. Sounds like she thinks her dad killed her mum.

'How did your mother contract the virus?'

Her lips purse, she stares at the table, her head moves a little from side to side.

'Dad had mild symptoms,' says the other one. Samantha. The twenty-six year-old student.

Anne doesn't give Samantha the side-eye. Obviously accepts that it needed to be said, she just didn't want to be the one saying it.

'Continue,' says Kallas, sounding robotic, as she can sometimes.

Samantha glances at her sister, either looking for the all clear, or just to establish how much trouble she's going to be in later, but gets nothing in return.

'He likely picked it up at the supermarket. We all said he should start shopping once every ten days or so, maybe once a week at most, and he argued some bullshit or other, that he didn't want to be seen buying that much food with four adults in the house. But he was just going to the supermarket, that was all. It was what he did. Shopped on a daily basis. So he kept going. There was only one other person at his office, so it's possible he got it off them, but he said they were staying well apart.'

'Who was that?'

'Gill Something. I don't know, he just always called her Gill. She was kind of his work partn –'

'Blair,' says Anne, pitching in. 'Like the asshole Prime Minister.'

Like the asshole Prime Minister... Ha! He may have been an asshole, yet he only scrapes into the Top 5 asshole British Prime Ministers of the twenty-first century because there haven't been six of them. Not yet, anyway.

'Did he self-isolate when he had the symptoms?' asks Kallas, by the book as ever. I think we all know the answer that's coming.

'Said he'd be fine,' says Samantha, 'like he was a doctor or something. He didn't go to work for a fortnight, protecting Gill obviously. And he stopped going to the supermarket, bully for him. But you know, he still sat and had dinner at the table. If we said anything, he'd grab us and jokingly give us a hug. Started kissing mum in front of us, just to wind us up. Thought it was funny... That changed, at least.'

'You have asthma?' I chip in from the sidelines.

'Dad didn't give a fuck,' says Samantha.

'Sam,' says the sister, the elder, censorious voice from her left.

'If he had given a fuck, he would have stayed in his room. The house is big enough, he had an en suite, he had a desk in there, mum could've slept in the spare room, and she'd still be alive.'

'You don't know that.'

The bloody-minded certainty of youth.

Samantha has her tail up. She's talking now. We don't need to ask anything else, and I just indicate with a small movement of my hand for her to continue.

'I have asthma. When I realised how it was going to be with him, I stayed out of his way. I didn't eat with him, I didn't sit in the room with him watching TV. I basically sat in my room, which was fine, because, before my sister points it out, I spend most of my time in there anyway. Dad was pissed I refused to sit at the dinner table, but you know what, I didn't care. Mum, on the other hand, didn't have any option. Mum asked him to self-isolate, he refused, and there was nothing she could do, nowhere she could go. She was stuck, eating at the same table, sleeping in the same bed, breathing in his poisoned, virus-laden air. And dad, as previously mentioned, thought it was all a load of shit, and he could do what he liked.'

A beat. She holds my gaze across the table.

'Mum died.'

'Did your father take any responsibility?'

She laughs, bitterly, a snark of a sound. Anne stares at the table.

I ask the question, again, without speaking.

'He said he felt responsible,' Samantha begins, and her words have slowed, weighed down by sarcasm and resentment, 'because if he hadn't got the virus, then mum wouldn't have had to go to the supermarket, which was where she obviously picked it up. Can you *fucking* believe it? He genuinely said that. He genuinely appeared to think it. He genuinely wrote to Tesco to complain about one member of staff that mum had said had been coughing, and he spoke to a lawyer friend of his about suing them. The lawyer friend, btw, told him he could fuck off and not be so stupid.'

'That wasn't what the lawyer said,' says the sister from the cheap seats. Samantha, however, has taken the stage. Floodgates opened.

'Did your dad get tested?' I ask.

'No,' says Samantha. 'Didn't need to. He self-diagnosed. And you know, I admit it, I was kind of sceptical at first. I mean, he could be seriously full of shit…'

'Sam!'

'He could be full of shit. But I thought, well just in case you *do* have it, I'm staying the fuck out of your way. Anyway, then his temperature got bad for a day or two, and he never, like, got anywhere near needing hospitalised, but he had literally *all* the symptoms.'

'Yes, he did,' says Anne, sullenly from the sidelines, as though her sister needs verifying. Which she sounds like maybe she does.

'Did anyone else blame your dad for your mum's death?'

'No one blamed him for mum's death!' says Anne, looking angrily at the sister.

Well, we all know *that's* not true.

'Some of us did,' says Samantha to me.

'Who else?'

She pauses now. The break. She glances at Kallas, and then back to me.

Well, look at that, I didn't even notice the shift. At some point, Kallas interviewing Anne, has become me interviewing Samantha.

'Yes, sis,' says Anne, 'who else?'

So now, there either is someone else, and she's suddenly thinking, uh-oh, if I say so-and-so was pissed off at dad, it might be a motive for them to have committed murder. Or maybe she's thinking that there really is no one else, so it's only her with the motive for murder. Whichever it is, she's thinking all right.

'Who else?' says Kallas, the third to ask the question, her voice much colder than either the sister or me.

That, at last, seems to put Samantha's gas at a peep, and she lowers her eyes now, staring at the desk.

'No one,' she says. 'It's just me.'

Kallas has a steady gaze trained on her, such that Samantha has to finally lift her eyes to look back at the investigating officer.

'Look,' she says, 'I was pissed off at dad. I've been pissed off at him all summer.'

She breaks off before she gets to the bit about being upset that she's spent the last few months angry with him, and now he's dead.

———

Kallas leaves the silence there for a while, allowing it to mature. A few seconds, a few seconds more. Samantha stares at the table, Anne stares at Kallas. The few seconds become an eternity, that may be less than a minute, but who knows? Time disappears in it.

I love it. The poise, the patience. I wonder if this is Kallas's way of recapturing the initiative of the interview, with me having unintentionally snatched it away from her.

'Do you know if there was any connection between your father and a man named Harry Lord?'

Samantha doesn't lift her eyes, though there's the tiniest movement in the muscles in her face to indicate that the interview has shifted back. Kallas asked the question, Anne can answer.

'That's the man who was murdered earlier this week?' asks Anne.

'Yes.'

It's the talk of the town, she was bound to know the name.

'What does that have to do with dad?'

'They lived in the same town, they have been murdered within a few days of one another.'

'Was he, this Harry Lord, was he also crucified?'

'No.'

A beat. Anne looks a little lost, unsure what to say, which probably means she doesn't actually have anything to say.

'There are sufficient similarities in the method of murder,' says Kallas, 'for us to at least presume that the murders are linked. Do you know if there was a connection between your father and this man?'

'No,' says Anne. That's it.

Samantha lifts her head, guessing it might be time for her to contribute again.

'I'd never heard the name until I heard he was dead.'

'Did your father go to church?' asks Kallas.

Anne is about to say no, when Samantha cuts her off with that now familiar bitter laugh.

'Right,' she says.

'Did he play golf?'

'Doesn't every boring middle aged man?' she says, and Anne, once again, gives her the aggrieved sister look.

'Do you have to?' she says, and now her voice is breaking. 'His body's still warm!' escapes her lips, somewhere between a wail and an ejaculation, and the tone cuts her sister in half, and I think that'll do it.

And they both retreat now, staring at the desk, united at last in their sorrow and hurt.

23

Taking a short drive to Cowal's house, where we're going to set the team off in a thorough search of all the man's things, and then Kallas and I are heading into the mortuary, to get the initial results from Fforbes's scalpel. Totally unnecessary journey, as it could be done over the phone, or by video, or indeed, by e-mail, but it's part of the process. Spending time with the dead.

'Sorry about earlier,' I say.

The drive from the station up to the top of the town is five minutes, so the conversation won't get very far, and we've already spent the first three minutes in uncomfortable silence.

I mean, I say uncomfortable, but I think for a silence to be truly uncomfortable, both parties need to feel it as that, and I can't imagine Kallas ever thinking a silence uncomfortable. Me, on the other hand, have been uncomfortable around her since I fell in love with her.

Yep, there, I said it.

'What do you mean?'

'I didn't mean to take over the interview. When we were speaking to Anne and Samantha.'

'You did not.'

A beat. I glance at her, but she, naturally, is not looking at me.

'I thought I had. And I didn't mean to. So, I'm so –'

'I allowed it because I was quite happy for it to happen,' she says. 'You are a good officer, who asks good questions. You think, and you understand what motivates people.'

I give her another glance, but she still ain't looking.

'There is a reason, obviously, that you are still a detective sergeant at your age, but I've yet to see it.'

At your age. I'm going to give you a compliment, and then I'm going to ram it as hard as I can up your arse.

'It is interesting,' she says, then pauses.

I'm not sure that what she's about to say will be interesting. Not if it involves me.

'Your case file suggests that at some point you will go off the rails during this investigation, and I think it might have been better for you not to have been put on it in the first place.' She pauses again, as I turn on to the road, another couple of hundred yards to go. I think maybe we'll be getting there just in time. 'I wonder if perhaps the chief inspector gave you this assignment on the presumption you would mess up, intending to use that as a pretext to get rid of you? What do you think?'

Weird, isn't it? If Taylor had said something like that, I would quite literally have told him to go and take a gigantic fuck to himself. There are a variety of other people who could've said it, and I would've been a bit pissed off, or I would have laughed, or I would have rolled my eyes, or fuck it, I don't know. It would not have been a conversation.

But here I go, seriously answering the question.

'I don't know. Maybe she did,' I say, bringing the car to a halt behind the small police van. 'I don't know her well enough to know if that's the kind of thing she'd do.'

'You will endeavour not to screw up,' says Kallas.

I stare straight ahead. Hmm...

I already fell in love with the chief investigating officer. I've been fantasising about fucking the chief inspector on her desk. I damn near made an arse of myself over Constable Ablett last night, and although I never actually got anywhere near the bar, it was a much closer thing than it looked. And you know, there was something back in that room there, something uncomfortable going on, when the interview came to be between Samantha and me. Didn't matter that she was young, didn't matter that I was an old soak. She's the rebellious one. She's the one who doesn't give a shit, she's the one who will say what she thinks and do what she likes, smoke what she wants and bang who she wants to bang.

All of which describes me too. At least she's only twenty-six. She has an excuse. Fucking granddad here...

And all of that is dwarfed, monstrously dwarfed, by the plague of alcohol, which sits in the middle of my head, growing day by day, screaming, *buy me, you cunt, buy me and drink me. Only way to get through this. And one day when your liver gives out, won't that be fine? Won't that suit you, and everyone else, down to the ground?*

Life insurance still in place, Penny and the kids would benefit. Chief Inspector Hawkins wouldn't need to worry about her rogue, drunk, borderline useless detective sergeant. It might be a miserable death, sordid and sad and lonely and bad, but

101

what the fuck will I know about it? I'll be drunk. I'll be filling my boots. I'll be tasting the glory.

Am I not a romantic drunk? Hey, Kallas said it, didn't she? The melancholic drunk. Ha! Maybe I can go back to Switzerland, and sit at the side of a lake, and write rank awful poetry, then I can drop dead, and some eejit somewhere can find my rank awful poetry and declare me a genius, and I'll be a posthumous literary hero.

Met a girl,
Had some sex.
Soon enough,
She was my ex...

Or maybe I can just head off this afternoon, early this evening, late this evening, whenever, whatever, stop at the off licence along the way, fill up, go home and drown myself in it. Maybe that's all.

I'm jerked sharply from my plunge into the abyss by Kallas placing a cool hand on the back of my hand, which is still gripping the steering wheel.

'It is OK, Sergeant,' she says, 'you do not have to answer the question. Everything will be fine.'

She squeezes my fingers, I'm frozen by the touch and thank God do not respond, and then she's out of the car and walking briskly into the house.

Taylor never squeezed my fingers.

The feel of her touch stays on my hand, comforting yet mindfucking in its way after the quick descent into madness – suicide by vodka – and then I'm following her, staring at the ground, trying not to look at her, even though she's ahead of me and wouldn't notice me staring, and into the home of the latest victim, mind on autopilot.

* * *

It doesn't take long to find it. Five minutes maybe. Certainly no more than ten. The search begins in the victim's bedroom and home office. While a lot of people developed the home office during the lockdown, if they'd had the space, it's apparent that Mr Cowal, the independent filmmaker, had an office set up at home long before that.

He made films, in the way that guys in suits in offices make films. They move money around, they hire talent, but they don't actually have any talent themselves. So, the independent filmmaker, David Cowal, facilitated people with talent, and appears to have been pretty decent at it. Knew how to play the system, at any rate, even if he'd never had a really successful movie. Certainly not successful enough to get hired by one of the studios, or larger independents, but he did his thing, and made a decent living out of it. Knew where to get funding. Knew how to put a movie together, and to make sure it was finished, packaged and released. The keepers of the cash could trust him. A safe bet to look good on the annual report of Screen Scotland or Creative Scotland or whoever the fuck he approached for funding. They wouldn't have to worry about allocating fifty grand to some project that then faltered and died. Cowal would take that fifty grand, and add it to all the other funding he'd hoovered up, and that film would be made, and he'd make sure he got a decent producer fee along the way.

So, he had his home office, as well as his small office with Mrs Blair in Baillieston. Here first, there next, on and on we go.

I'm in the office, going drawer to drawer in his desk, trying to squeeze my brain into the autopilot box, when the call goes up from the next room but one, along the elegant upstairs landing, wooden floor, long, thin Moroccan runner in dark blue and orange.

I stay where I am. Whatever the news is, it will find me quickly enough. I continue to carefully rummage, each item taken out of a drawer and considered. Either put to the side to be placed back in the drawer, or put to the side to be taken into the station for further review.

Here, for example, in the large lever file drawer on the right of the desk, folders containing paperwork for seven different films, all seven projects still active, which is why they will be here. Given our digital age, the files are all slender, but there's still a lot to look through. It's easier than spending the however long it takes for our tech guys to crack his computer, and here is the bare essence of police work.

This is the victim's day job. The reason for his murder may well be nothing to do with his day job. The time spent trawling through this could well be time wasted. And yet, there could, in the tiniest footnote of the most insignificant looking page, be a thing. *The* thing. And so the time will be spent.

'Sergeant.'

I turn at the sound of Kallas's voice. Was relieved to not be in the same room as her, but now she stands in the office doorway, holding a white mask in her gloved fingers.

'He had yet to get rid of his wife's clothes. There was a walk-in wardrobe. This had been placed in her underwear drawer.'

'Buried, or at the top, easy to find?'

'The latter.'

'That's where we are, then,' I say.

'Yes. Emma is here now, we will leave her in charge. You and I will go and speak to Dr Fforbes, then we will visit Mr Cowal's office in Baillieston, and then we will consider the next step.'

A pause. For some reason I stay there like a lemon, kneeling down beside a desk drawer, the folder for a film entitled *Ballad In Blue* in my hand, until she lifts her eyebrows at me and says, 'We will go now,' and then turns and walks away.

24

'I have a theory,' says Fforbes.

We've retreated to the hospital café, drinking coffee. 'The coffee's terrific,' she said, by way of explanation, and she's right.

Fforbes is sitting across the table from us, eating a Danish. It's almost as though we're in interview formation. I, too, have a Danish. Kallas, the slimmest most gorgeously-bodied woman on earth, as I now know, is not eating a Danish. I suspect she eats a carrot once every three or four weeks.

Having taken a moment to chew her penultimate bite of maple pecan plait, and just as she's about to launch into her theory, Fforbes sticks the last piece of Danish in her mouth anyway and talks through it.

'Little Mr Cowal had much higher levels of GHB in his body. He also had more interesting bruising to his testicles. Earlier bruising. The flaying of the penis,' involuntary groin squirmage, 'was also early and fascinating. So, my theory is that his killer sees this little guy, thinks, this'll be fairly straightforward, shouldn't take too much intoxicant to incapacitate him, gives him the thing, but then it turns out the little guy has something going for him. I mean, the human body is the most extraordinary machine, after all.' She dabs her lips with a napkin, takes a drink of latte, and really, if the coffee's so great, which it is, why would you waste it by having *that* much milk, then continues, 'You just never can tell how it will react. So, I think perhaps the killer, wherever this took place, got a little more fight from Mr Cowal than they were anticipating. So, they went for his most vulnerable spot. There's a lot of testicular bruising. There was a violent, pre-thousand cuts attack on his testicles.' More squirming. 'Then, when the killer had regained the upper hand, if that's what happened, they injected way more than the required amount of GHB. Way more. Mr Cowal is out for the count. His body is moved, he's strung up on the cross, now the killer wants to wake him up, so they can enjoy the bloodletting together. Except, Mr Cowal doesn't want to wake up, because he's been so heavily sedated. The killer tries a variety of strategies. None of them work. So, in the end, they go for the strategy of pain.' She pauses. She looks across the table from me to Kallas and back, and then can't stop herself saying it. 'He flays the penis.'

'And that would wake him up?' asks Kallas.

Personally, I can't speak at the moment. That uncomfortable feeling in the groin has worked its way up my body.

Fforbes shrugs.

'Not sure. But it would've been sore. Am I right, Sergeant?'

She smiles wickedly, and I give her the appropriate look.

'So, who's your guy?' asks Fforbes, glancing at the café counter, contemplating another Danish, I dare say.

'He is a film producer,' says Kallas, having left a small space for me to answer, and realising that I might have wandered off mentally.

'Made anything I've seen?' asks Fforbes, in the way that people do.

'I do not know what you have seen,' answers Kallas, the literalist, and Fforbes looks at me for the kind of answer one might expect to that question.

'A lot of small Scottish movies, some TV,' I say. 'So, it depends. Look him up on IMDb. He appears to have been successful at getting films made, not necessarily at getting people to watch those films. Perhaps that's not what it's about at that level.'

'It's art, love?'

'Something like that.'

'So, what's your connection between the two?'

'Still looking.'

'You have further intelligence about the corpse?' asks Kallas, not ready yet to be distracted.

'Yes, of course,' says Fforbes. 'The first dose of the drug, what I surmise to be the smaller dose, was administered around eleven p.m. The penis was flayed around one p.m. The man was dead by two. More than half the cuts were administered post mortem. The killer very clearly keeps count, and on this occasion made sure they got to the required number, even though the victim wasn't alive to feel it. It does make one wonder if there's significance in the thousand cuts, and for whose benefit it is.'

106

'That is interesting,' says Kallas. 'The death was carried out with the same implement as before?'

'The very same,' says Fforbes. 'There's a small nick somewhere in the blade, an uneven serration. Almost as though the killer wanted to make sure it was apparent the murders were done by the same person, in case you might think there's more than one lingchi-ist on the loose. Just something else to tie it all together.'

'We have a showboater,' I say.

'That you most certainly do,' says Fforbes. 'And I think, sadly, that his work is not yet done.'

We nod together, we accept our fate, we drink coffee, while around us the tired work of a hospital, enduring the longest of years, continues.

* * *

'No, it wasn't just about that, it really wasn't.'

Kallas, having been filled in on my assessment of David Cowal's filmmaking abilities, has just put that assessment to Gill Blair, his former assistant.

'We had some success,' she says, 'and it was far more, *far more*, than a form-filling, financial exercise. Dave was passionate about film, he loved film. He dearly believed in every single venture he got involved in.' She's staring intently at Kallas, brow furrowed, eyes piercing, some sort of derangement about her, I'd say. Of course, her business partner, and quite possibly boyfriend, has just been horribly murdered, so there's probably all sorts of shit going on in her head. I mean, we've all been there, right? 'We had great viewing figures for our feature with David Hayman that was shown on the BBC. Very good feedback, *and* a Scottish BAFTA nomination.'

She's a little bit defensive there. Of course, she was defensive from the moment we walked in.

Decent-sized office. Bright. First floor, looking out on the main street. Venetian blinds on the large windows, which can be drawn when you're having sex on the comfy sofa. And there is, sure enough, as well as the two desks and the small coffee table, a large, comfy sofa. Easy to clean leather at that. I think we know why Mr Cowal continued to come to the office when the lockdown started.

'This can often seem like a very blunt question,' begins

Kallas, completely undaunted by Blair's nervy bullshit, and in those words are the acknowledgement, to me at least, that she's charged in bluntly without the preamble many times in the past, 'was there anyone in the business who held a grudge against Mr Cowal? Anyone who might have wanted him dead?'

'What? Really? Dave? What? That's… what?'

Kallas lifts a hand to cut her off, which is good, because for a moment I thought we were going to have to listen to Blair ejaculate in single syllables for several more minutes.

All right, *really* has two syllables. Fuck off.

'Do not sound so surprised,' says Kallas. 'Mr Cowal was brutally murdered. Someone, somewhere, wanted him dead. Otherwise, he would not be dead.'

'It must have been random,' she says quickly, the same strained tone in her voice. 'He must have been chosen at random. One of those, it must have been one of those.'

Kallas answers that with a vicious stare across the desk. I mean, the stare is blank really, but it's the most vicious blank stare you've ever seen in your life.

'Random murders happen,' blurts Blair.

'The killer took another victim earlier in the week. Both that attack, and the attack on Mr Cowal, were malicious and well-planned. Designed to inflict pain.' The hand to the mouth. *Oh, poor Dave, how he suffered…* 'We do not yet know for sure, but everything about the attacks suggests these men were picked for a reason. There was nothing random about either one.'

Blair has gone a little pale now, as she sits there, in her defensive bubble, behind a packed midfield, thinking about poor Dave.

'Do you know if Mr Cowal had any dealings with Mr Harry Lord? He was the –'

'Yes, of course,' says Blair quickly.

A beat. Kallas looks across the desk, just that hint of inquisitiveness about her, waiting for further explanation. It ain't coming.

'They had business dealings?' I chip in from the sidelines.

Good move, as Blair looks a little thrown, as though she'd forgotten I was there.

'Yes. Yes, of course.'

'Maybe you could give us the details?'

'Mr Lord had an interest in the arts. There were a few wealthy, private individuals who Dave felt comfortable approaching, if the project seemed appropriate.'

'So, you know that Mr Lord was murdered a few days ago,' says Kallas, a statement rather than a question, and I know where this is going, even if Mrs Blair doesn't.

'Yes,' says Blair. 'Everyone knows.'

'And now Mr Cowal has been murdered,' says Kallas.

The face across the desk goes through the logical progression of what Kallas is going to say next, her shoulders straighten at the realisation, someone somewhere having inserted something up her arse, then she says, 'No, no, I don't believe it. I just... I don't believe it.'

'You think these might have been two completely random, brutal murders in Cambuslang?'

'Yes, yes. That there might be a connection didn't even cross my mind. Dave, for the most part, made small arthouse films. He perhaps was not the artist himself, but he was an auteur.'

Kallas employs that stare again, says, 'You do not understand the meaning of the word auteur,' and Blair straightens even further. She might possibly be about to point out that of course she knows what an auteur is, she's in the movie business after all, it's just that she was assuming Kallas wouldn't. Instead, she stays quiet, and sits there in bolt upright stony silence, her lips pinched like a contracted sphincter.

'We need to know details of every deal that was done between Mr Cowal and Mr Lord. In particular, we need to know other people that might have been involved in those deals. We also need to know if there were any potential deals between them which fell through.'

Blair swallows, loudly and obviously. She doesn't like this, but there's no escape.

'Were you involved with Mr Cowal?' asks Kallas.

Much more delicately put than I would've managed. *Involved...*

'I don't know what you mean,' says Blair, but the tone says, *Oh yes!* 'We worked together, of course we were involved,' she adds, weakly.

Kallas holds her gaze for a moment, and then delicately, slowly, beautifully, casts a short glance in the direction of the sofa. Oh my fucking God, I love that!

Blair looks at the sofa, Blair, in fact, cannot take her eyes off the sofa, and then finally she turns back to Kallas, holds her gaze for a moment, then drops her eyes.

Guilty as charged.

'What about Mr Lord?' asks Kallas.

Jeez, she's good, hadn't even thought of that. But she's right. Harry was a bit of a lad.

Blair's head snaps up so fast she's probably going to need to wear an orthopaedic collar for the next month.

'What about him?'

'Did you sleep with Mr Lord?'

Nice. No surreptitious glances at the sofa this time. No need. She may have slept with Harry, but she's not upset about it.

Again she answers in silence, but the answer's there all the same. In time we'll get the details, but for now, really, we already know. Harry loved and left, Harry never hung around. Whatever they had sexually, it would have been brief.

'Did it suit Mr Cowal for you to have sex with Mr Lord?'

Oh, she doesn't want to answer that either. She's been trampled flat now, the stuffing knocked out of her. Defeated, the shoulders start to go.

'And what about Mr Blair?' asks Kallas.

'What about him?'

Words back out like a whippet.

'Does he know of your infidelity?'

'No.'

'Are you sure?'

'He doesn't know.'

Kallas allows the silence for a while, and then says, 'Perhaps he is a suspect, as you have cuckolded him with both murder victims.'

'No!'

Eyes wide. She stares at Kallas, she stares at me.

'You can't... you really can't say that. Will you just leave Tony out of it?'

Well, that just sits there, the words occupying a large space in the middle of the room, for a while.

'Your husband's called Tony Blair?' says Kallas, just before I ask the same question. Actually, I'd been going to preface mine with, 'no fucking way'. Then Kallas, sensible as ever, follows with, 'That is a nickname he was given after Blair became Prime Minister?'

'Yes. He was, I don't know, eighteen at the time. At

———

university. A bad time to get a nickname, as he says. It stuck.'

'What is his real name?'

'Finlay.' A beat. 'Everyone calls him Tony.'

'We'll need to speak to your husband,' says Kallas bluntly.

A deep breath from Gill Blair, and she dies a little more before our eyes.

25

Back at the ranch for the round table. The familiar faces in this investigation, everyone with their job to do, everyone compartmentalised into one stream or the other. Kallas and Harrison and Ablett and Ritter and Milburn and me, and I've been here before, so many times, and the crimes never seem to change, just the faces across the desk.

I can barely look at Kallas, I can still feel the touch of her fingers on the back of my hand. Soft and cool, something flowing through it, like some sort of weird Reiki shit. Yeah, I'm probably just imagining that.

Focus, you moron!

Connections between the two victims. The low-budget movie business. Golf. How their lives were impacted by the virus. Or, as it seems, how they impacted other people with the way they dealt with the virus. Could there have been a connection between the home at Garrion, and David Cowal's wife? Could there be someone who was upset by the deaths at the home, who might also have been upset by Mrs Cowal's death? And money, of course, there's always money. And Lord's lovers, with now at least one that he shared with Cowal. And don't forget the church, because even though everyone's saying Cowal wasn't interested in it, someone thought to crucify him in one, and that's coupled to Lord's church association.

So many routes, so many ways to go, so many things to break down. The coronavirus thing seems compelling, but then so is the business link, and so is the shared lover thing. Suddenly we have a multitude of possibilities. Think of a reason why some bastard might murder some other bastard, and if it's not already on the list, it's on the periphery, waiting to be added.

Naturally, when it comes to divvying up the spoils, I get Jesus. It was inevitable, right?

There's been a murder. What role did Jesus play?

Then it's wrapped, and we've all been packed off, and I'm heading out the station, on my way to walk the hundred yards or so to the church to speak to our minister again. Out onto the upper balcony of the woebegone shopping precinct, on a bleak, miserable day in October, darkness descending like a plague of demons.

* * *

The front door of St. Stephen's is open, and I enter the small hall outside the nave. There's a single light on in the hallway, and then I walk through to the nave, which is more or less in darkness.

Stop for a second as the door closes behind me, and then I stand at the top of the aisle, looking at the dark colours and shapes of the stained glass of the windows behind the altar, lit from behind by streetlights.

Silence.

I'd imagined the Rev Goodbody sitting in the same place as last time, second pew from the front, looking up at Jesus, searching for something. The pews are empty, there's no sign of life, the place so quiet, so dead, it feels as though no one's been in here for months. The kind of dark silence that takes you in its hand, and you feel it at first as almost a comfort, quiet, and full of ancient sadness; then slowly, so slowly that you barely notice at first, but slowly it starts to envelope you, the fingers of the hand close in around you, and soon enough it's smothering you, crushing you, and you don't know if you're ever going to be able to escape. That kind of dark silence. And at the far end of the nave, there's the cross, and there's the stained glass Jesus up there behind it.

But I don't feel any threat. This isn't a dark nightmare, when suddenly there'll be a jump scare, the phantom from the shadows, leaping out with his knife or his cudgel or his bared teeth or whatever it is the phantom would leap out with. Just me and the dark and the sadness and the decline of this church community, something that started a long time before Covid pitched up and decimated the demographic.

My phone pings, the sound muted in my pocket, seeming to come from light years away, a lifetime away, another world. Because this world here is not one of phones and instant communication, it's a world of faith and hope, of fealty to the unseen and unknown.

Take out my phone, look at the small pocket of light in the dark.

In the vestry. Door on the right at the rear of the nave.

113

Phone back in my pocket, time to get on with it. Head, as ever, seems to be in a hundred different places all at once, though of course, all of those places are familiar. Alcohol and sadness, women and melancholy, the feeling of being sucked into the void.

On and on and on, get on with it, down the aisle, through the door, another short corridor, only two doors down here, one of them with a light coming from beneath it, and I knock, wait a moment, she calls out, her voice soft, and I, with the thought in my head to get this over with as quickly as possible, to get back to the office to eat dinner at my desk, with all these good intentions, walk in, and there's the minister, Rev Goodbody, sitting at her desk, and I know I'm pretty much fucked.

I can try not to be, though, I really can.

'Come in,' she says. 'Take a seat.'

She's leaning forward, weight on her elbows. On the table beside her is a bottle of vodka, a litre, which she's only just begun. She has a shot glass in front of her, drinking the vodka neat. No ice. Needs must, obviously. There's another glass beside the bottle.

To the left of the bottle, pushed back towards the edge of the desk, is her dog collar. Her black top now just looks like a black blouse, top three buttons undone. She has the look of someone at the end of a shitty day at work.

Don't think about it.

'Sit down,' she says, indicating the seat opposite, and as I do so, she pushes the empty shot glass towards me. 'Fill your boots. You look as though you need it as much as I do.'

'Tough day?' I say.

I don't touch the glass.

I'm desperate to touch the glass. In my head I'm reaching out, lifting the bottle, and filling the glass and tipping the shot back in one, feeling that wonderful, warm, sharp kick in the throat.

I swallow.

'Tough day?' I repeat, after she's answered the first attempt with a hooded, hounded stare at the desk.

'Sure,' she says. 'If you call two funerals tough.' She looks at me now, eyebrows raised, as if seriously asking the question. 'What d'you think? Burying two people, comforting two groups of bereaved relatives, does that sound tough? After the spring and summer we've had.'

I have no answer, not that she's looking for one.

'I thought there'd be an end. We all thought there'd be an end. But it's been relentless since April. Death upon death. Five a week, six a week, seven, eight sometimes. Barely a day has gone by. They're not putting them all down to Covid, so sure, that's great. But people are still dying, and up it goes again. All that treatment that wasn't given, all those souls that just gave up...'

'I didn't think you had that many church members.'

'Most of them aren't. Not that we haven't been devastated, not that the heart hasn't been ripped out of the congregation... God, we talked about that before, nothing else to say. But most of these... I'm the parish minister, and that means I'm on call for funeral duty for anyone in all Cambuslang who wants a minister for their father or their mother or their whoever. Did they go to church? Did they Hell. Did they support the church community in any way whatsoever? Of course not. Did they give... did they give the slightest shit about God during the entirety of their life? Lip service at Christmas, but otherwise, no, they did not. You're not drinking,' she tosses into the middle of the conversation, then she continues, 'But refusal isn't in the minister's handbook. We don't get to ask those questions, we don't get to say, nah, my friend, your dad doesn't deserve God's blessing. That's not who we are. We allow all-comers to throw themselves on the death pile of sinners, repentant in the face of everlasting damnation.'

A head shake, a lifting of the eyes, and then she says, 'Jesus, you'd think they were all Catholics,' and she can't stop herself laughing at her own joke, and I can't really find it within me to fake laugh along with her.

'You're not drinking,' she repeats, and then when she sees the look on my face, she shakes her head. 'Sorry, none of my business. How can I help you? You find out some other interesting titbit about me and Harry you think I kept from you the other day? Wait, Harry didn't have erotic pictures of me on his phone, or something, did he? That'd be embarrassing.'

'Did he take erotic pictures?' I ask, somehow investing that curiously fascinating question with no drama and no interest whatsoever.

'Don't think so, but he was hardly above being surreptitious. He could be a bit of a cunt when he chose.'

No one swears like a vicar.

God, I'm thirsty. I shouldn't be thirsty, I'm not *thirsty*, but now my throat is dry and crying out for that vodka.

'There was another body discovered this morning,' I say, the words quick out of mouth, as I force the change in focus.

'I heard,' she says, her eyes dropping again. More tragedy. Perhaps she's thinking that that'll be another funeral she'll be required to take.

'Did you know David Cowal?'

Her head shakes, doesn't look up.

'Just another name. Seems like a small town sometimes, and then you hear name after name you never heard before, and you realise it's not so small, you realise just how many people are outside your orbit.'

'They found him in St Mark's.'

Now she raises her head, the look that's been on her face since I arrived, getting darker and darker.

'I heard that. I wondered what the story was. Was he just in there shooting up or something?'

'He'd been crucified.'

A beat. Another. Her lips are parted, genuine horror in her eyes.

'Jesus,' she says eventually, and then she lifts the shot glass, tosses the drink down her throat, and pours herself another, all in one continuous movement. Now she holds that small glass at the end of both sets of fingers, and stares into it.

'Why would someone do that?'

I don't answer, and then she looks up, and she starts nodding.

'That's why you're here.'

She rubs her hands across her face, pressing her fingers against her eyes, finally opening them wide, shaking her head, going through a routine of straightening out her thoughts, putting herself back in the right head space. If there is such a thing as right head space for hearing about someone being crucified.

'Was it a traditional crucifixion? I mean, nails in his hands and feet? The old cross they left in there was wooden, right? Was it even big enough?'

'It's not a large cross, you're right, but he was a slight man. And no, he was tied to the cross, and then... then killed in a particular way.'

'Definitely the same killer?'

As I start to nod, my eyes drifting with sad, crushing

---

inevitability to the vodka bottle, she says, 'We should hope so, after all. One psychopath would be bad enough.'

'What makes you think the killer's a psychopath?' I ask, and she gives me a look that implies the question might be loaded in some way, before tossing it disinterestedly aside, and drinking half the next shot glass.

I take a picture of Cowal from my pocket and pass it across the desk.

'I saw the picture online earlier,' she says. 'I didn't know him.'

'He never came to the church?'

'No. You know, in the old days, a minister might have struggled to answer that question, but not now. Now the incomers and the newbies, the fresh meat, stand out like beacons of the Lord.'

Fresh meat. God, this woman's terrific. Wonderful edge to her, she uses words like cudgels, and talks like she doesn't give a fuck.

'How well d'you know the congregations of the other churches in town?'

'Don't his family know if he went to church?'

'He has two adult daughters. They say he didn't. From them, there's nothing to suggest he might have had the slightest interest or connection to the church. Maybe he didn't. Maybe his killer just thought it would be a cool place to kill someone. There's something… that setting… an old abandoned church, the body on the cross, pool of blood on the floor, sun shining through a lone stained glass window, it feels incredibly cinematic. I know the stained glass would've been placed where it was in order that the sun caught the cross with the colours of the window, but it looks as though the death scene was staged.'

'So your killer knew about the church.'

'Must have done. It's been closed for several years?'

'Long time. Way before I arrived here. But I know they looked after it. God knows what they thought was going to happen. That people would return to the fold, congregations would grow, and they would have to reopen? Folly.'

She finishes the glass, pours herself another. She looks at the other glass, I can see her thinking about it, battling the demon that wants to give the alcoholic a drink, just as I'm battling the demon that wants to take it.

'How well d'you know the other congregations in town?' I

ask again.

She puffs out her cheeks, leans back in her chair, fingers never leaving the glass.

'Hardly. You'd have to speak to them. And you know the other Church of Scotland buildings in town closed a few years ago, right?'

'Yes.'

'Just not enough people anymore. Anyway, they say that was a shitshow.'

'It was.'

'Ah, a veteran. Nice. You worked with DCI Taylor on the murders that happened around the church mergers?'

'Yes. You know him?'

'Heard about him, heard the story.'

'Yeah, they… yeah, they fucked him, same as they fuck everyone.' I pause, I stare at the table. 'I speak to him every now and again. I guess, like all things, that too will pass. We'll just be people who used to work together, people who used to know each other.'

She looks at me curiously, and then settles back. A sigh, then her lips are pressed together, she makes herself comfortable, and then the noise of the movement goes, and she's stopped talking, and I've stopped talking, and now we're just two people sitting together in a small office at the back of a church. On the wall are aerial photographs of the other closed down churches in town, and a couple of the minister's certificates, and there's a print of what looks to the untrained eye like a Brueghel of some sort, and there's complete and all-consuming silence, like the silence is a thing, like if we sat here long enough, allowing our ears to become accustomed to it, we could hear each other's hearts beating, we could hear the blood in our veins and the white blood cells in the lymphatic system.

I close my eyes. In silence, faced with my own destruction. I could glug straight from that bottle of vodka. I can taste the alcohol, and it's right there, there for the taking, and I absolutely fucking hate myself.

'Have you thought of anything else you could tell me about Mr Lord?' I ask, opening my eyes, forcing words out of my mouth, to ask a question like I'm supposed to be doing, because it's my job, goddammit, clinging to the idea that I can get through this without fucking up, without drinking and missing work tomorrow, or turning up reeking of stale booze, hoping the chief will send me home with a bitter little blue pill to pop with a glass of liver salts.

And it's not just the alcohol that thrills you and tempts you, is it, you abject piece of shit?

'I said it all,' she says, then she casts a sober hand across the desk. 'Harry Lord took me with far greater alacrity across here than you're doing.' A beat, the acid mutual stare of revulsion. 'Perhaps you've just got more taste.'

There we go.

Fuck!

I have to get out of here. Hurriedly push the chair back, head shaking, almost drunkenly stumbling at the very idea of there being alcohol in the room, and I don't even look at her as I go, and I'm out the door, more or less bouncing off walls, and I already know I'm not going back to the station, and the evening stretches before me, and I'm thinking, vodka, vodka, vodka, and maybe I can be calculating about it, buy it now on the way home, drink it now, what's the time, not yet seven, stop yourself getting the big one, the litre, or the two litre, get the half litre, that'll do, get home, there's ice in the freezer, vodka on the rocks, don't need a mixer, drink, drink, hate yourself, maybe, fuck whatever, maybe watch porn, maybe fantasise about the sex you just ran away from, maybe about the chief, maybe about Kallas, except I know I won't be able to think about her, because when I do, I'll see how disappointed in me she is, and I'll hate myself even more for doing that, as though it's about her and not just about me, but it's not going to stop me, and I don't give a fuck that I haven't had a drink in six days, I'm not counting, I'm not ticking off boxes and making marks on the wall, it's a meaningless number, because I'm getting in the car, and I'm stopping at Oddbins on the way back to the house, and my next three hours stare gloriously and wonderfully and peacefully back at me.

26

'Sergeant?'

I stop. Don't immediately turn. I'd been fumbling with the keys in the dark, not that it's so dark beneath the streetlights, that's not why I'm fumbling. And I could've been surprised or jumped out of my skin at the voice, I could have whirled round, but I didn't because I knew it was coming. I knew I was being followed. I may be a fucked up mess, but the police gut is still there. And I saw her without seeing her when I entered the off licence, and she was still there when I came out three minutes later, and I didn't look at her, and I didn't care, but there was a small voice at the back of my head that I chose to ignore, but it means that when she speaks to me suddenly in the night, I'm not surprised, and there's no jump and there's no fright.

There isn't a voice I want to hear now. No one. Not Harrison, not the chief, certainly not Kallas. None of them would be welcome. But this one, even more than the minister, is the worst possible. And she's come to my house, and so I cannot leave. It will take me to stand here and tell her not to come in. It will take me to have morals and common sense and strength and an ability to say no.

'Sergeant?' she repeats, and only then do I realise that I'm resting my forehead on the door, eyes closed, trying to think the situation into oblivion.

Samantha Cowal.

I don't want you here. I don't want to talk to you. I don't need the victim's daughter on my doorstep. Victim's daughter? How about potential suspect? Victims are invariably killed by someone they know, someone with something to gain, something to avenge. We don't know of anything that connects the daughters to Harry Lord, but really? Is it at all a stretch to think Harry Lord might have met them at the house, and then slept with them? That's the first thought that comes to mind, but the options are infinite.

I swallow, try to form words, finally manage, 'Come and see me at the station tomorrow.'

She touches my arm with an uncertain hand.

Maybe I'll turn, yes I'll turn, and she'll have a knife, or a gun, and this tentativeness will be feigned, and soon I'll be getting drugged and slashed and…

'Sergeant, please.'

I turn.

She looks small and pale and beautiful and lost, and there it goes, my resistance, as if there was the slightest chance I'd have any at all.

* * *

Sitting at the table, my small table for two that sees so little use. Currently being used to do a jigsaw of the planets and the Milky Way that Rebecca bought me during the lockdown, before I came back to the force. I mean, like I needed a jigsaw, but your daughter buys you something, and you're aware that you're the shittest dad in all shitdom, you think, I'll do it, I'll do the jigsaw, and I did the most colourful bits, the easiest bits, the edges, the planets, leaving the trickier muddled middle of stars for whenever, a little bit every now and again, I think, though it has sat there for three months now untouched. And yet I don't break it up.

Samantha Cowal gave it little more than a glance, then I put a large placemat over it so it didn't get disturbed, and here now we have no food, no snacks, two large glasses, lots of ice, neat vodka poured over.

The first sip, the first taste, oh my fucking God. Like drinking an orgasm. Like drinking heaven. A feeling so good it's impossible to believe it could be bad for you. How can something that makes you feel this fucking amazing, this alive and kicking, this ready to grab the world by the balls, kill you? How can it turn bad so quickly?

If only one could take that first sip, that first taste, that first glass, and stop. If only one could capture that feeling and leave it there.

She's wearing a cotton top, top couple of buttons undone. Not unlike the minister I just left. Samantha Cowal, unlike the minister, is clearly not wearing a bra. Samantha Cowal has come to do business, and she can read me like a kipper. The no bra thing is my Kryptonite.

Ha! I'm such a dick. God, aren't we all in the private dungeons of our own heads?

'Why?' I say, as we sit over our first glass, the drink barely yet touched.

'My father was murdered last night.'

'That's not good enough.'

Having no trouble keeping my voice cold. I have vodka, I have a beautiful young woman, I'm giving in like the sad, wasted addict that I am, but I can still be pissed off about it.

'What d'you want?' she says.

'I want to know why you're here. I want to know why you came to see me, rather than Inspector Kallas. I want to know why you're not spending the evening with your sister, or with friends. I want to know why this couldn't wait until the morning. I'm a police officer, just doing my job. Investigating a murder. I'm not family relations. I'm not on bereavement duty. I'm not here to comfort you, or anyone else.' A short pause, but I've got the words flowing, and maybe I can get her to leave without actually telling her to, because I can't actually tell her to leave, as the part of my brain that wants her here won't let me. 'I can give you the number for victim support. Call them. Twenty-four hours.'

'I don't want that kind of support.'

She takes a drink, still at the stage where it makes her head snap a little. I manage to leave the glass in my hand, ice cold on my fingers.

'When was the last time you had sex?' I ask.

Yep, I go there. Straight there. Would Lewis have asked that question at this point? Or, I don't know, fucking Vera or one of those other bastards? Probably not. But the path of this evening is laid out, and we might as well get to it. Get it over with, or I can force her to leave with words and logic.

Yeah, sure, that's happening.

'That doesn't matter,' she says, although she doesn't look too upset about the question. No faux shock.

'When?'

She takes another drink, a shake of the head, then she says, 'About two weeks ago. Happy?'

'Go to that guy.'

'What makes you think it was a guy?'

Glib. Cheap. And why should she be anything else?

'You don't look any happier about you being here than I do,' I say.

'Nevertheless, here we are.'

I take another drink. Manage to make it just a sip. Manage to hold it in my mouth for a moment before swallowing, and manage to savour the taste. I shall sit here and glory in my few moments of restraint…

We stare across the table. Conversation isn't really necessary, but I force it anyway. Get her to say it out loud. Maybe if we talk long enough I'll say something genuinely hurtful or spiteful and she'll leave. I don't think, however, that I could hurt or spite her, regardless of how hard I try.

'Spell it out to me,' I say.

'We both know who we are.'

'I know myself,' I say, 'and that's as far as it goes.'

'You give off the vibe. You're not the team player, you're the, I don't know, you're the maverick. You're the copper who doesn't give a toss. You're the guy who does whatever he wants, surviving by the seat of his pants. Good enough to not have lost your job, but then, you're what, in your fifties somewhere… maybe you should've been an inspector by now. You're certainly older than the inspector on this case. So that's who you are… And you give off such an air of sadness. You're lost, Sergeant. And not little boy lost, but deeply and darkly lost, lost beneath a great welter of sorrow and horror, it's quite impossible to imagine.'

She pauses, eyes held on my mine, neither of us breaking the stare.

'And it's attractive to someone like me. That's it. Because I'm the same, but without this… this thing you have. I don't give a fuck, I do what I want. I've been a student for eight years. Drove dad nuts. But I like it. I drink, I fuck, sometimes I smoke pot, sometimes pop a pill, sometimes work behind a bar if money's getting low, and dad's refusing to cough up, but I don't give a fuck. That's who I am, and that's who you are. And that's why…'

And she indicates her and me and the table and the vodka, and she lifts her glass, and this time takes a longer drink, and now the world is unleashed, and I take my first long drink, and there's no savouring, and there's no hesitation, I swallow it, a long draft, and Jesus fucking Christ but it tastes good and feels good, and life pulses through me like a fucking firework.

Glass rested back on the mat, everything said that needs to be said.

'I won't tell anyone I was here.'

123

'Don't.'

'Don't what?'

'Don't say that. I don't know who you are, and the person you just described would tell anyone she felt like, if the mood took her.'

'I like you.'

'If you're as like me as you think, two hours from now, you'll hate yourself and anyone within a five-mile radius.'

She holds my gaze for a moment, and I see it in her eyes right there. She knows that feeling. She recognises herself.

'You know Dylan?' she says.

Jesus. Do I know Dylan?

I nod.

Suspicious. As ever. Paid to be, after all. Part of the job description. Is it entirely coincidental that she brings up the music I listen to more than any other?

Coincidences, as Poirot would observe, will fuck the detective up the arse if he lets them.

'He had a song earlier this year, *I Contain Multitudes*. You know that song? I mean, it's new, so...'

'I know the song.'

'Really?'

'Sure.'

Take another drink. Ice clinks against my teeth as I near the end of it. Plenty more where that came from, although now that I'm sharing it, not as much as there was going to have been.

'A lot people say they know Dylan, then it turns out they know the first line of *Blowin' In The Wind*, and that one Adele did, though they can't remember what it was called.'

I smile. Can't help it. Coincidence? Fuck it, sure it is. I've had my fill of people nefariously using my Dylan obsession against me. But she's got a nice smile, when she uses it, her hair is down over her shoulders, and over her face, resting on the top of her chest, the blouse is undone, her breasts are pressing against the material, the vodka glistens on her lips, and my gut – which incidentally does not waver upon the addition of vodka – is giving me the all-clear.

'I know all Bob's work,' I say, leaving it at that, and she toasts me and drains her glass, setting it down on the mat.

'When I heard that song... God, who knows? Maybe everyone thinks the same thing. Maybe everyone thinks, that's *me*, that's *me*! I *too* contain multitudes. I can be nice and I can be an asshole, I can be this and I can be that. Every-fucking-one of us contains multitudes. But, really, I don't know about anyone else. Tbh, don't really care either. There's just me, the only one I can really know. And Dylan nailed it. That line where he, you know, juxtaposed fussing with his hair, and fighting blood feuds… Oh my fucking God.'

I pour her another glass, manage to stay my hand and not add any to my own just yet. Look at me with my self-discipline.

She gives me a look to let me know she knows what I'm doing, but at the same time she immediately takes a drink. When your motto is don't-give-a-fuck, well, you're not really going to give a fuck, are you?

I take a drink, pause, drain the glass, set it down, don't immediately fill it back up. Still at a good stage. Early days, when it feels warm and fresh and harsh and delicious, and it just makes you want to throw off all the shackles.

Is there anything else to say? She's said her thing, and I've said my thing, and we are where we are, sitting across the table from each other on a Friday evening. The vodka works quickly, doesn't it? Five minutes ago I had two certainties. I didn't want her to be here, and I wanted to fuck her. The vodka has managed to straighten out the paradox.

'I need a shower,' I say.

Yep, that's how it is.

I mean, when I'm slaughtered, ugly drunk, staggering through town picking up anyone I can, even if I have to pay for it, I don't give a fuck. But in happier times – *here we see Tom in happier times!* – I need to wash before sex. I need her to wash before sex. Maybe I'm on a scale. Maybe I just have standards. I don't know. Tell you what though, I contain multitudes, that's for sure.

'Can I help you with that?' she says.

I stand, take her hand, she – true to herself – downs the second glass of vodka before she stands up – and oh, that's sexy, and there's a bit of me thinking, damn, I should've poured that second glass, but the vodka can wait, the vodka can wait, and when she stands she's immediately in my arms, and her lips are moist and cold and sharp with the drink, and the kiss is long and glorious, her arms around me, my hands on her back, holding her soft, cool skin, and I can't stop myself, and I run my hands over her body, around her sides, making her shiver, until I'm feeling her breasts, and she moans into my mouth at my touch

125

on her erect nipples.

* * *

I don't know if there's a niggle at the back of my head at the start. The *I shouldn't be doing this* niggle, the *I've been burned before, and more than once* niggle, the *maybe there's a camera or a microphone or a thing* niggle. But by the time we get to the bedroom, those niggles have long since been banished. And here we are, alone in my house, she walks naked into the room, no phone, no microphone, nothing about her person.

She lies on the bed, splays her arms above her head as she smiles, her breasts look amazing, her legs apart, so inviting, and I can't stop myself. I kneel between her thighs, lift her buttocks off the bed and slide my cock inside her. We both gasp loudly, what a fucking beautiful sound, and then I start slamming into her. I won't be able to last long like this, it's just to give myself the feeling, the sensational electric buzz of it for a few moments, and it's fast and riotous and frenetic and glorious, and when I feel it getting too much I stop suddenly, withdrawing, and not wanting to see any disappointment on her face at not following through with it until she came, I go straight down between her legs, her pussy so damned wet, like she's already been squirting cum, and I bury my face in her, licking along her lips, and then, as she gasps and judders, and presses her thighs against the side of my head, I settle into sucking and licking and biting her clitoris, and she's moaning and grabbing my hair and squirming and pushing back against me and soon, God, so quickly, she's coming and crying out and pushing even harder, and then pulling away, panting, her hand thrust down between her legs, pressed against her clit, the spasms still jerking through her thighs.

'Jesus,' she gasps, and I can't contain myself, can't wait for her to recover, and I lie on top of her and thrust my erection deep inside her again, and hold it there for a moment, our bodies hot and desperate, pressed close together, and that feeling, on the verge of frenetic thrusting, on the verge of glorious fucking, with still so much to come, is just the most extraordinary feeling you can imagine, and I kiss her, and she can taste herself on my lips, and she's gasping, and I'm breathless in the kiss, and then I start fucking her, my hands on her hips, my cock thrusting into her soaking pussy.

126

27

Three o'clock in the morning. A small flat, up one flight of stairs, on the north side of Main Street. A shop beneath, and a flat above, a flat on either side. The shop unit beneath has been empty since the spring. It will forever be marked down as a Covid casualty, and indeed it had been, closing at the start of the lockdown, the small café never with the slightest hope of being able to reopen. However, in the previous five years the unit had been vacant for around half the time, and in the other half had seen eight different businesses come and go. A charity shop, a clothes shop, a pound shop, a café, a clothes shop masquerading as a boutique, a community police office, Bob's Diner, another café, they'd come and gone, and then at the end, before the economy was sentenced to disappear without a trace, the third attempt at a café. Tea & A Scone, it had been chirpily called, the lettering in red against a white background. The S had fallen or had been removed and never replaced. No one knew why anyone would steal a capital S. People just do things.

The occupier of the small flat above the former café was Margaret Malone, fifty-seven year-old, three-time divorcee, as they'd say in the newspapers. Indeed, as they would say in the papers the day after next, when they got around to reporting her murder. Leader of an interesting life, although most of it sad. Depressing. The details of it would be polarising. A Marmite life. A living, about to be dying, misery memoir. Some people would breathe in the detail, absorb the horror and the desperation, the heaping of one act of sadness or madness upon another, while others would abhor the very mention of it, believing such a life either infectious, or simply too depressing to hear tell of.

Abuse and drugs and unwanted pregnancies and unwanted marriages, the occasional ray of light, quickly extinguished, one limping, hobbling, humbling experience to the next, a neverending cycle, but not a rollercoaster, because rollercoasters also go up, and the best she ever managed was to reach a level playing field for a few months, maybe just a few weeks, maybe some respite from the endless cruelty and awfulness of real life.

And now, living in a small flat on the main street of a small town, above an empty shop unit, people with not too dissimilar lives on either side, only just around the corner from the police station, but when it comes to it, it might as well be a thousand miles from the nearest police station because there's nothing the police can do when they don't know something needs doing.

Maybe her death will be a release. She's thought that often enough before, albeit the one time she slashed her wrists, she didn't make the cuts properly or deeply enough and the wound congealed before she bled out, and the first time she took pills and alcohol she didn't take enough of either, and she just felt fucking awful for two days, and the second time she took pills and alcohol it would've worked, except Bobby found her and called an ambulance, the stupid bastard, literally the only thing he ever did for her, and it was just about the one thing she hadn't wanted him to do.

Having said that, the following three weeks had been one of the times of a level playing field, and then, and then... what did it matter? There was always something.

Her eyes open. Small bedroom, a clutter, there's a spider that's been up in the corner for the last couple of weeks, large, a giant house spider, and she's been too scared to move it, and every time she opens her eyes, the first thing she does is look up there to see if it's still in position, and she feels a shudder of fear at seeing it if it is, and an even bigger shudder if it's not. If it's not, she sits straight up in bed, looking around, in case it's by her head.

So far, on the few occasions it has moved, it's always come back. It must like the spot in the corner.

She gets all the sounds of Main Street in this room. Cars and motorbikes, chucking out time, sometimes fights, more often arguments that go nowhere, crying children, the parade of life. Used to sleeping with the curtains open, the window open a little. Maybe, she thinks, if she leaves the window open the spider will leave.

The things she's faced, you'd think – she thinks to herself – you'd think she could laugh in the face of a spider, giant house spider or not. Big bastard for Scotland maybe, but nothing compared to the ones you see in Australian YouTube videos. One of the very many reasons she's never been to Australia. Now she will never go.

To be fair, she's about to never do anything again in her

life, bar lie on a mortician's slab, and rest in a coffin to rot.

She closes her eyes, does not wake up enough to wonder why it was she woke up in the first place. There are always noises, outside, to the left, to the right, above and below her. Noises don't mean anything. She wakes frequently during the night, and always enjoys the moment of looking at the clock, knowing she can go back to sleep.

Something in her arm. What was that? She doesn't open her eyes, rubs the mark at the top of her bicep, the nick, the bug bite. Mosquito? Midgie? In October? That'd be weird. Where are you now, Mr Spider? What's the point of you being in the room if you're not even going to take care of the damned bugs?

Her arm feels tired, heavy, she stops rubbing the mark. The thing, it's not bothering her anymore anyway. The midgie. Gone away. Maybe she squashed it. Her arm lies flat on the bed. She goes to move over onto her back, finds she can't.

What? That doesn't make sense. She should be able to lie on her back. Forces herself, all of her might, there's twenty-three and a half stones to move, that's what the scales at the doctor's said – Jesus, she could see how he looked at her, the cheeky, privileged bastard, he could get to fuck – and she flops onto her back at last, such a strange amount of energy to do that one small thing, and now she opens her eyes and there's someone in the room.

She goes to scream. The genesis of the thought is there, at least. Then a cloth is thrust in her mouth, and the scream doesn't happen. And she wants to sit up, she wants to jump out of bed. It's all there. All the thought processes. One after another in her head. Do this, do the next thing, meet the danger head on.

But she can't move. She can't scream. The figure stands over her, a knife in hand, clear in the lights of Main Street.

'I'll close the curtains.'

The prick in the arm. That must have been it. Just a small prick. A jab with a needle, a debilitating drug.

There's no terror, no fear, just anger. Doesn't know who it is. She got a good look at the face before the curtains closed, but didn't recognise it.

Fucking bastard coming into her bedroom. Well, go on then, steal something, you stupid fucker! The things she could say if she could talk. Mouth crammed with material, throat catching, loud breaths through her nose, and all she can do, her only fight, is the impotent look of rage and anger in her eyes.

129

'We need to talk,' says her visitor. A pause, a smile in the dark. 'Let's be honest, I'm going to talk, you're going to listen, because you have no choice. And then you're going to die.'

The killer pauses over her, then pulls back the sheets, tossing them to the side, then rips open the pink pyjama top, and pulls it sharply from beneath Margaret Malone's heavy body, before doing the same with the bottoms.

And then comes the knife, and with it, the beginning of the bloodletting.

28

She's gone when I wake up. I have instant recall of the night before, as I lie in bed at 6:14. Still dark outside, feeling vaguely shitty, though I've felt worse.

We finished the vodka. Lying here this morning I curse myself for finishing the vodka, grateful at the same time. I still reek of it. You don't drink half a bottle of vodka the night before and not stink of it the following morning.

Five minutes later I'm standing in the shower. Maybe I can wash it off. I hate myself, as usual in such circumstances. Slept with a victim's daughter, half my age. At this stage, the early stage, where everyone involved is a suspect, it follows that I also slept with a suspect. I have a history of sleeping with suspects. It never, and I mean, never, ever, ends well. You don't go sleeping with women involved in a murder inquiry, it's just monumentally stupid.

I stand in the shower for a long time. Wash repeatedly. Finally get out, dry off, clean my teeth, gargle with Listerine, walk naked through the apartment past the table with the empty bottle of vodka, the two glasses with melted ice cube water, damp circles around them on the mat, into the kitchen, just the right amount of self-loathing to perform.

Cold water and coffee. That'll do. Don't need any food. Check the time, still have nearly an hour before I need to head to work.

What can I do in an hour that would sweat the drink out of me?

Sweat by some means. Come on, you've had your moments of home exercise.

Drink water, make coffee, drink coffee, into the spare room where there's an old exercise bike, still hopefully plugged into the wall after all these years, and the bike and I look at each other with undisguised malice.

'Don't look at me like that.'

The bike, in its scorn, is too cool to reply.

I get on the bike, immediately do that man thing of going too fast from the start, having not turned my legs on a bicycle in

---

131

God knows how long. Set the timer at twenty minutes, put my head down, close my eyes, and get on with it.

Breathing heavily after five, feel pathetic for that, but keep going. Sweating after ten. Uncomfortable sitting naked on the seat, wishing I'd put on shorts. Dripping after twenty. Keep going for another few minutes, give it a final minute of exertion, the bike's resistance cranked up to full, and then get off, clutching for air, a few moments with hands resting on thighs, and then walking abjectly back into the kitchen. Grab a tea towel, wipe the sweat off, toss the towel on the floor by the washing machine, drink two glasses of water.

Wish there was an app for letting you know how much you still reek of booze.

Back into the shower. Time going by, always the chance to add being late to being drunk, but I'm sober and I can still get there in time, so just be like a little Fonzie, you prick.

More shower gel, more shampoo, I must stink of this shit, out the shower, more Listerine, into clothes, more water, more coffee, and finally I'm walking out the door, and in all that time I've hardly given Samantha Cowal a thought.

We drank vodka, we had sex, we drank more vodka, we had more sex, we fell asleep. Or, at least, I fell asleep. I have no idea what she did. Maybe she took photographic evidence. Maybe she'll turn out to be a plant from the chief inspector. Not a victim's daughter at all, just a test.

If that's the case, I failed. Or passed, depending on what they were testing me for.

Really, all the chief has to do to get rid of me is tell me she'd like me to fuck off, and I probably would.

Park the car behind the station, up the stairs outside, then just as I turn along the walkway on the first level, the door to the station opens and Kallas emerges at a rush, three officers behind her. Ablett's one, don't recall the names of the others.

We're beside each other in a second, then she's waving to the left, along the walkway, around the corner, on and on.

'Come on,' she says, as I fall in beside her, already at a jog.

'What's up?'

'You look fresh,' she says. 'Did you exercise this morning?'

I take a moment to adjust to this new reality, that not only did I take twenty minutes of exercise, but that it still shows on my face. That, and the inspector thinks it more worthy of conversation than the fact there are five of us heading out of the station at a jog.

'Yes,' I say brusquely. 'What's up?'

'There is a mask on a door around the corner, along main street. I do not have any other information. It could be nothing. We are going to check.'

Down the stairs, along past the boarded up shop fronts, the grill over the front of the off licence, the old charity shop, the key cutting/shoe repair/jack of all trades shop that everyone loved, and no one used, and so it had to close down, and the boards on the windows of what used to be a record shop, where once, a long time ago, in a galaxy far far away, I used to buy seven inch singles for forty-five pence.

'It was called in? No one knows a –'

'Constable Strong spotted it on his way into work. He reported it to me as soon as he arrived, and we're going there now. Given that, as you say, the public are unaware of the significance of the mask, this mask has worrying potential.'

Constable Strong, part of our five-person team. I knew that.

Across the road, past another boarded up shop, and then we're there, and sure enough, there it is, nailed to a dark blue front door, the mask of death with which we have become familiar.

'Fuck,' I say quietly, and Kallas, after a quick look up to the level above, and then across the road, rings the bell.

'You agree the mask is the same as the others?'

'Yes.'

She lifts her hands, already with gloves on, and runs her fingers over the mask, and then takes a step back.

'I assume this has stairs that lead to the next level.'

'Yep. I've been in these a couple of times.'

'The apartments are maisonettes?'

'No. The doors on this side lead to first floor flats, the equivalent doors on the other side of the building lead to the second floor flats.'

She rings the bell again. The other three stand behind us, and it registers that Ablett has a ram.

'Why do the British say flat instead of apartment?' asks Kallas, looking up at the first floor windows directly above.

'No one knows,' I say.

'It comes from flett, an old English word for dwelling,' says a voice from behind. A beat. 'Tolkien used it for the platforms the elves built in trees.'

Oh, do fuck off, Strong.

'English is an interesting language,' says Kallas. She leaves the perfect comic beat, then adds, 'Maybe that's why so few of you speak anything else.'

She carefully removes the mask from the door, and then looks round at Ablett and indicates for her to get to work with the chib. Ablett nods, steps forward, sets herself, then lets the ram hit the door with a whack near the lock, and the wood gives at the first crunch.

I go to head up the stairs, but Kallas touches my arm, and then walks quickly up at the front, the four of us behind.

She stops at the top of the stairs by the closed internal plywood door with no lock, knocks hurriedly, gives it no more than a couple of seconds, and then she opens the door, and walks quickly into the flat, saying, 'Hello?' as she goes.

She stops a few paces into the short corridor.

A door to an internal bathroom straight in front. Doors on either side at both ends of the corridor. Four rooms. Kitchen, sitting room with monster TV, and two bedrooms I dare say.

'Hello?'

Nothing still, just as we know there will not be anything, and then she throws, 'A room each,' over her head and walks to the end of the corridor on the Main Street side, and before anyone else has the chance to so much as open a door she says, 'Got it.'

She sticks her head back out from the room.

'Crime scene protocol. Looks like the same killer as before. I think we know the killer has already gone, but let's be careful. Can you call it in, Sergeant?'

And I'm already on the phone.

29

For now, just me and Fforbes in the bedroom with the corpse.

It's a small room, and there's a tonne of clutter. Not much room for anyone else, albeit Kallas has just walked out to take a call from the chief.

We're standing either side of the bed, the corpse in between us.

That, my friends, is a gruesome sight.

'Killer had a bit more surface area to play with this time,' I say, the words just appearing in my mouth without much aforethought.

Fforbes can't stop herself laughing.

'You're awful, Tom, you really are.'

'I do what I can.'

The smiles die away, and here we are again, me and her and a giant, bloody corpse, with the skin flayed from her face.

I mean, *her face*. That is some grotesque, fucked up shit. Her face, down over her chin, to about midway on her neck, is raw flesh.

'You think she was alive when that was done?'

'I'm afraid, I think I do.'

'Holy shit.'

'Hmm. Did you notice the spider up there in the corner?'

I look from the flayed face to the pathologist, who is herself still looking at the flayed face, and then I look around for the spider.

Jesus. Big bugger. No way could I sleep with something like that in my room. Would have to get rid of it. It'd be me or him. Or me or her. It's the ladies that are usually the bigger spiders, right?

'That's huge,' I say, turning back to the corpse.

The whole body is once again covered in blood, the white floral bed linen soaked with it. Impossible to tell how many cuts there are on the body, but it's not like we don't already know.

'Any other flayed areas you've spotted?'

'No, seems like the killer saved it for the face. That must have been…' and she finishes the sentence with an involuntary shiver. A moment, she nods to herself, then she says, 'She's pregnant, which explains the size, albeit she is naturally big anyway.'

I look at this great hulk of an overweight woman in her fifties, and think about the things we've already learned about her life, my brow furrowed, before finally a voice somewhere in the far recesses of my common sense gives me a nudge in the right direction.

'You're talking about the spider.'

'Yes, of course,' and then she looks up, a curious smile on her face. 'You're a piece of work.'

'I wasn't actually joking.'

'Not the most attractive spider, the giant house, but still useful to have around.'

'Have a lot of them in your house, then?'

'None. My cat kills spiders as soon as she sees them. Brutal little bastard.'

A moment. I don't really want to talk about Fforbes's cat. I don't want to talk to anyone about their cat. You want to own a cat, on you go, but I don't want to know about that cute thing it did, and I don't want to see a photograph. The minute you express the slightest interest in someone's cat, you might as well shoot yourself in the face.

'I'm going to be seeing that face in my dreams,' I say.

And it's not just a conversational filler, intended to get us off the subject of Fforbes's cat. Seriously, this bloody, eviscerated flesh-wound of a skull is the absolute stuff of nightmares. The face you see in the mirror looking over your shoulder when you straighten up from cleaning your teeth. The face you see standing at the end of the hallway. The face in the window when you pull back the curtains.

'Yes, we should probably cover it until the body is removed,' says Fforbes, although having said that she makes no effort to do anything about it, and we both stand there, enhancing our nightmares.

'If she'd been alive, she'd have been able to make some noise, wouldn't she? Something, when the skin was done like that, because there wouldn't have been a gag or tape around her mouth?'

'The gag could just have been thrust into her mouth,' says Fforbes, which is really quite obvious, and I nod along with her as she says it. 'Always effective. There would have been some noise escaped her throat, but nothing… nothing anyone would have heard. She lived alone?'

'Yes.'

'The downstairs unit is an empty shop, and next door and above…?'

'We've asked, so far no one heard anything.'

'People usually don't,' she says.

'The public have ears of convenience.'

'Nice.'

'In this instance, however, our killer has been pretty switched on. They know what they're doing. They're planning, they're thinking.'

'Which means each victim has been carefully selected.'

'Definitely.'

'Sergeant?'

I turn to Kallas at the door of the room.

'We should get on, though first I need coffee. You want to join me?'

'Sure.'

And we both nod at Fforbes, who says, 'I'll give you a shout when I'm ready for you,' and we're out the room and back along the busy corridor of the final home of the latest victim.

30

'You were drinking last night.'

The café in between the murder scene and the station. Quiet as ever. Two staff behind the counter, both wearing masks, three other customers. A couple of workmen, their credentials in their orange vests and the unwashed work trousers, and a young woman in a business suit, looking at a MacBook. Earbuds in, coffee in hand, this year's spectacles, hair pulled tight. Looks like she's about to go to the bank and fire everyone, before pocketing a bonus and flying to New York.

'Shit,' is all that escapes my lips in answer to that, and then I lift the coffee cup as though having that in front of my face might spare me the conversation.

'Thank you for trying to cover it. Most people won't notice.'

'How did you? I must smell of it.'

'It's your eyes. They had a certain clarity the last couple of days. I didn't notice at first, when we were rushing along to the crime scene, but the clarity has gone.'

Lower the cup, place it silently back on the table, lower my eyes with it.

Well, there's a feeling. Shame. Like my dad talking to me when I was fifteen. *I'm not annoyed, I'm just disappointed.*

Some shame. All it makes me want to do is head to the off licence, go home and start the process of forgetting. Jesus, why am I still here? Mortgage long since paid off, enough money kicking around I could meagrely survive until my pension arrives.

'You need to go to meetings,' she says.

'There's no point.'

'Why?'

'You need to want to go to meetings. You need to be driven to it. You need to have something to lose.'

'Your career.'

'Don't care.'

'Your life.'

I leave it a moment. The *don't care* is so mundanely

predictable that I don't even bother with it.

'Why are you still here if you don't care about your career?' she asks, as if reading the questions in my head. Of course, it's hardly a superpower, it's an obvious question. There's no judgement in it, however, rather Nordic-Baltic practicality.

Fuck do I know about Nordic-Baltic practicality? One just assumes they're practical, right? They have Ikea, and they say 'of course' a lot, and their houses are much warmer than ours in the winter even though they have wooden floors and the temperature's about fifteen degrees colder than Britain.

Of course, we're just shite at everything. Look at us. How in the name of all fuck did we ever rule anything, never mind the world?

Another quick drink, a small, calculated head shake to clear my mind, take the well-practiced punt of the self-pity to the sidelines. Jesus, when you feel sorry for yourself as often as I do, you get used its occasional practical ejection.

'It sounds glib to say I can't think of anything else to do, but that's the answer. Before I got called back this summer… what was I doing with myself? I read a couple of books. My daughter bought –'

'What books did you read?'

'Really?'

She stares at me. The look that says, *I am Estonian, why in the name of fuck would I ask you what books you read if I did not want to know the answer?*

'Fair enough. Hemingway. I thought, there was a heavy-drinking, cantankerous sod who killed himself, maybe I'll learn something. So, I read *The Old Man And The Sea*, and learned nothing. I mean, I could've looked it up and read what it was I was supposed to learn, and I could read about why he won the Nobel for it, because it said on the back of the book that he was given the Nobel after writing this, but I thought, what's the point, I'm not doing Higher English or anything? Then I read *A Farewell To Arms*, but that just contained endless pages of really terrible dialogue between him and the nurse, and I thought, this is awful, so I didn't learn anything from that either. But everyone says Hemingway's a thing, right, so I thought, it must be me, not him.'

'*For Whom The Bell Tolls* might have been a better choice, but you sound like you have had enough of Hemingway.'

'I have. I read something else that I forget the name of. It was too long, that's all I really remember. And my daughter gave me a jigsaw. Said it would be good for me. Absorbing. So, there was that. And before the lockdown started, I got out on the hills a couple of times, had a weekend away with Eileen.'

'You were in a relationship?'

'Just friends. Then the lockdown, and I just sat there like a lemon. Did my jigsaw, read Hemingway, went out for walks every day, made plans… Always making plans. Truth was, when the police called, I couldn't come back quickly enough.'

'If you like going out on hills, why not plan a long walking expedition? Give yourself some focus.'

'That's what I was doing. There I was, getting up in the morning with nothing to do and all day to do it in, and I thought, let's get out. Walk across Canada, or walk across the Silk Road, or walk the length of Africa or something. All plans, no action…'

'It probably would not take you very long to walk across the Silk Road.'

Her delivery is so perfectly dry that I stare at her for a moment, trying to recapture the words I just said, and then I realise, and I roll my eyes, say, 'You know what I meant,' and in very minor embarrassment lift the coffee cup for a drink.

'I like you, Tom,' she says, and she probably notices my eyes widening at the thought of where this is going. Unlikely to be good. 'But investigations cannot be about the officers. We are ciphers. We are facilitators. We are not the story, we unravel the story. Too often, your files suggest, you become part of the story. That cannot continue to happen if we are to work together.' She holds my gaze across the table, the words having been delivered in pretty much the same tone as she ordered the coffee, and in which she'll tell her kids to eat their dinner, or her husband to lie back so she can go on top.

'You need to start going to meetings, you need to stop drinking. Today you are OK, but we both know it will not last. If you do not want to go to meetings, you will have to leave the police service. I cannot mandate this, I should not even be saying it, but I am being practical. The combination of your drinking and your job is a bad one.'

I'm nodding along at the Estonian pragmatism of it all. Jesus, this woman holds me in the palm of her hand. Not that I'm about to rush off to a meeting. Maybe it's time I seriously planned to walk across the Silk Road. That would be the adventure of a minute. I could write a book about it.

'You had sex last night, too?'

'No.'

She holds my gaze, a couple of feet away across the small table, our hands on our coffee cups, and she knows I'm lying, and she knows I know she knows, and I'm thinking, Jesus fucking Christ, do I have last night's orgasms stamped on my forehead, but really it's just her, just Kallas, who reads everything about me, and who will know the order of the drinking and the sex, who will know about me waking up early, and about standing twice in the shower, and about getting on the bike purely as a means of expunging the alcohol fumes, and if she pushes me now I know I'll tell her everything, even though she likely already knows it, then she says, 'OK. It is not my business. Be careful, Tom, that is all. We should get back to work.'

She takes another drink of coffee, then sets the mug down. She pauses, thinking about something, I wonder what further devastation she will lay calmly at my doorstep, then she lays her hand on mine, I feel the shock of the unexpected touch, the touch as exhilarating and warm as it was previously, she squeezes my hand, has no words, and then stands.

'We should go.'

I dissolve in her presence.

What a fucking clown I am.

I need to look at flights to Samarkand when I get home.

31

Sometimes leads come quickly. Sometimes not at all. Anything in between. Some leads might not be leads, and you'll never know until you've followed it to its very end, like the source of the Nile.

Now, Kallas and I on a small film set on the Gallowgate, where they've closed down the road for a day's filming around Barrowlands.

We spent the morning on the life of Margaret Malone, with a focus on any potential Covid connection. That's the clear assumption we're working to here. The death masks placed on the door of the care home, and the one in the personal things of the dead wife of the second victim, seem to clearly indicate these are revenge killings, related to the spread of Covid. Of course, we don't know if that's a cover, the carefully laid red herring. That the killer would want to throw us off course, is just as possible as the killer leaving the message for others. Beware all you who perhaps unwittingly, but foolishly and unthinkingly spread the illness.

There are going to be an awful lot of people to kill.

From what we picked up so far, that was one hell of a depressing life Margaret Malone was leading. Well, it's not like we're not used to investigating the depressing life. For a kick-off, most lives have taken a depressing turn when we get involved, and these ones, the ones that begin in squalor, with abuse and drugs and alcohol and pain, they tend to continue in such a vein.

As the victims grow in number, you need to know the link, because if you can't find it, then you're scrabbling around, investigating every aspect of their life, and you never know which one is going to present the bullseye. Here, however, almost straight off the bat, we have a hit.

Not Covid, but the other Holy Grail of this particular investigation. A connection between this woman, who had nothing, and whose life was a complete mess, with the two previous victims, livers at the top of the town in the large, old Victorian houses where the money is.

Last autumn, in a lifetime before the virus, before the lockdown, David Cowal produced a small movie entitled *His Grey Return*. I mean, that's a shit name for a movie, but it is what it is, and it was *His Grey Return*. Filmed in Strathclyde Park, amongst other places around here, with some filming in the Trossachs. Lake of Menteith area. Funding for the movie came from a variety of sources, but one of the principals was Harry Lord. And that shittily-titled movie, about a prodigal son returning to Glasgow after having run away from home aged fifteen, featured a character he meets in a bar with the name on the cast list, Fat Whore.

Fat Whore. Someone might have objected to that somewhere, if anyone had ever actually seen the film.

The film has all the hallmarks of being, like, a proper film. One that got made, packaged, released. It has its IMDb page, it has its cast and crew list, and its release date. The release date was sometime in May. Well, the cinemas were closed in May, of course, not that this small piece of arthouse domestic grievance-cinema would have made it anywhere near a picture house in any other May, not when it had to compete with *Mission Impossible 11* and *The Avengers Tight End* and God knows what piece of Hollywood garbage, three seconds of which was filmed in George Square doubling for Philadelphia, so we can pretend it's actually got something to do with Scotland, and by showing it fifteen times a day at the multiplex they're somehow supporting the local film business more than if they showed a small budget Scottish movie with which people might connect.

Maybe it made it to Netflix or Amazon Prime? Definitely not. The BBC? Nowhere near it. So it's just there, existing in the ether, unwatched by anyone. Wasn't issued as a DVD, isn't available on any platform, from iTunes to YouTube.

But it has its IMDb page, so at least there's that. The actors and crew involved can put it on their CVs, and perhaps there's a clip or two circulating between them they can use in a highlight reel.

We've come to talk to the director of *His Grey Return*. Between cast and crew and producers, there are twenty-seven names listed. Could be any one of them we need to speak to. Or it could be none of them. The director seems like an important enough person with whom to start, so we'll speak to him, see where it takes us.

They're filming a scene with two guys having an argument

outside one of the Celtic pubs, across the road from Barrowlands. The scene is painted in tidy shades of green and blue, one guy in a Celtic strip, the other in Rangers.

Maybe it's a metaphor.

The director calls cut after they've been shouting *fuck* at each other for a while, and the Rangers lad has the Celtic lad by the neck up against a wall, and the actors fist bump as they pull apart, someone else from the crew clapping as the director says, 'We're good. Matt, can you get to work on twenty-six, please?' and indicates for a young woman wearing a multi-coloured face covering, a tablet in her hand and earphones on, to follow him to a small area set up in the building next to the Barrowlands, from which the film crew are operating.

They're just starting to talk when Kallas cuts them off, and the director, James Crawford, gives her a classic shit-on-my-shoes look.

'Mr Crawford?'

'God, we're trying to work here, where's security?' looking over her shoulder.

She produces her ID, his brow furrows, and he regards her contemptuously.

'Jesus, what? The police scenes aren't until, what… next week some time, is it, Jenny?'

He looks at Jenny, Jenny clearly understands the situation better than James Crawford, so she indicates the badge and says, 'I think this might be the actual police.'

'What? Seriously, what? We got the bloody permits three weeks ago. Where's Roger?'

* * *

He keeps his arms folded, no relaxing into the situation for this prick, even though when he writes his shitty autobiography, he can have a paragraph or a page or a fucking chapter, depending on how it works out, on the time his shitty movie got shut down for twenty minutes while he got interviewed by the police.

'We've got Martin for three days. Three days. So, you know, this is a nightmare. Can we just get this over with as quickly as possible?'

'Who's Martin?' asks Kallas.

'Compston,' he says, in that way that suggests she's supposed to know who he's talking about. Kallas, not being a watcher of television, has no idea.

That explains why I thought I recognised him. That was him in the Rangers jersey. Funny.

'He's a more famous copper than you'll ever be, darling,' says Crawford, as though *that's* supposed to be a thing. What a prick.

'This is a murder enquiry,' says Kallas. 'A real one. We'll take as long as it needs, while being sympathetic to your requirements. Perhaps, if this takes too long, you could get your AD to take over for a couple of takes.'

AD? No idea.

'Oh, could I? You know who my AD is on this movie?'

'Her name is Geraldine Colquhoun and this is the first film she's worked on. I presume this is a small production, and you have had to cut corners.'

'Well, you seem to know what you're talking about, at least, but then you should also know it's completely unrealistic to think that we have one of the most famous UK TV actors in our fucking midst, and you want me to put a twenty-one year old who doesn't know which way to point a fucking camera in charge.'

'We need to talk about a film you made last autumn, *His Grey Return*.'

There's a look. Interesting. The very mention of the movie casts a grim shadow across his face. You can see his shoulders relax, although the arms stay firmly folded across his chest.

'What about it?'

'You'll have seen on the news that one of the producers of the film, David Cowal, was found murdered yesterday.'

'Jesus.'

'You heard?'

'Yes. Look, he was an exec producer, don't go getting the two mixed up.'

Keep the eye roll to yourself.

I know fuck all about movies. Spent fifty years looking at lists of producers and executive producers without having a Scooby.

'Did you hear about the death of a man named Harry Lord on Monday?'

'Of course. You people are conflating the two.'

'Connecting, not conflating,' she says. 'We are entirely confident the murders were committed by the same person. Was

---

145

Mr Lord involved in the filming of that picture at all?'

'Mr Lord? Of course not. Neither was Mr Cowal *involved*, for that matter.'

'If a financier took the opportunity to visit the set of a production he had helped make happen, it would surely not be the strangest event in the world of film.'

'I never met Lord, never saw him, never talked to him.'

'A third body was found this morning in Cambuslang. The woman's name was Margaret Malone.'

'I don't know her.'

'She played a small part in *His Grey Return*.'

'Which part?'

'Fat Whore,' says Kallas, investing the character name with zero judgement.

I'll give him his blank stare. Don't think he's putting it on.

He takes a few moments, he starts nodding, he remembers the scene, he remembers the woman, he thinks on it some more before finally shaking his head.

'What?' he says.

'Three people involved in the making of that picture have now been murdered, Mr Crawford. Looking at the cast and crew list available online, it was not big. There were only twenty-seven names. Since Mr Lord wasn't one of them, that means that two of the twenty-seven, or seven-point-four-o-seven per cent, plus one other individual, have now been murdered.'

A beat. His eyes widen a little. Mine too, at the seven-point-four-o-seven thing. Maybe the inability to have normal conversations isn't just because she's Estonian. Maybe she's on the maths-genius-but-also-a-bit-weird spectrum.

Maybe it's just not that difficult to work out two as a percentage of twenty-seven. I have trouble working out two as a percentage of four.

'Wait, d'you think I could be in danger?'

Oh, here we go. The selflessness of the true leader.

'Yes,' says Kallas, and I almost laugh.

I mean, fucking nailed it. The guy's going to stop giving a fuck the minute she tells him he's got nothing to worry about. But let him think *his* neck might be on the line, and the clown is going to be all in.

Truth is, of course, we have no idea whether he's in danger. Maybe he is, maybe he's not, and that's all. The narcissist needs to believe, however.

'What happened to the movie?' ask Kallas.

'What d'you mean?'

'Internet Movie Database states that its release was five months ago, but there's no sign of it actually being available anywhere.'

'Oh, that. It was never happening.'

'Why?'

'It was a business film. People needed to use budgets, people needed do favours for people, people needed to meet targets. What does it matter if anyone actually ever sees it, right? I mean, seriously, what difference does it make? It's kind of scream in the forest territory. Wait, no, I'm getting crossed, a tree falling in the forest territory, right?'

Where we're standing, I get a waft of booze from across the road, as a guy comes out the door of one of the pubs. He's wearing an old, tight-fitting Celtic t-shirt, he's carrying a half-full pint glass, and he bares his gums and squints as he looks around at the film set, experiencing broad daylight for the first time in forever. He has a trickle of dried-in blood on his face, and three teeth.

But the smell of the booze. Stale and depressing, yet with the hint of sweetness that makes it a siren's call.

The three-toothed guy lights up a fag, holding the pint glass clumsily as he does so.

'You made a film that you didn't bother if anyone saw?'

'It's still a movie, and I still directed it. I have a copy I can show, should I think it worthwhile. I can use it, as can anyone who was involved. It's part of the process of getting from here,' and he waves a small hand across the put together set of a small-time movie, 'to the big leagues. That's all.'

'Is it possible someone was upset about the movie not getting any kind of release?'

'So upset they've started killing people?'

'Yes.'

'Really… it was just a movie, these things happen all the time, they really do. That's why, when you look down a jobbing actor's screen credit, you'll barely recognise anything. There's so much of that kind of thing, and it's all about taking the next step up the ladder,' and he gestures around, this production, with an actual actor people have heard of, presumably constituting that next step.

'Was there *anything* about the movie that might have

inspired murder?'

Finally, finally, the arms uncross. He must think we're justified in asking the question. That's big of him.

'Look, it all seemed pretty straightforward to me at the time. Just a job. Four-week shoot, pretty normal for this kind of thing, everyone doing what they had to do, film got made, we took it away, did some editing, got a couple of students at the Conservatoire to do us a score on the cheap, just piano and cello mostly, nice though, nice, the lad played the Bach, you know the Suite in G Major, I mean really, could've been Yo-Yo fucking Ma, no one could tell the difference.'

Sometimes it's worse when they start to talk.

'How was your relationship with Annabeth Blake?'

The producer. That's the person who runs the operation, unlike the executive producer, who organises a bit of funding, then has sex with someone he shouldn't, before playing a round of golf.

The guy's got no poker face, I'll give him that. Unless he's cunningly displaying no poker face in this regard to fool us, in order to give more credence to the other denials that spill from his lips.

'She's a cunt.'

Ha!

'What kind of a cunt?' asks Kallas.

Behind me there comes the sound of bitter coughing, a raking, rancid hack drawn from the back of the throat, and then as I turn, the guy in the Celtic t-shirt, in a paroxysm of spluttering, drops his pint glass and it shatters, and he manages a loud and throaty, 'Fuck's sake,' into the early afternoon air.

32

With another couple of interviews to be conducted on an afternoon that seems to be shrinking, we finally split up. I get Mr Blair, the cuckold, who's been known as Tony since the bright Friday morning in May 1997 that heralded the dawn of Cool Britannia, a period in our history which turned out to be pretty much just as shit as all the others.

'You're a gravedigger?'

He looks at me over the top of the shovel he's leaning on. Despite the shovel, he is not currently digging a grave. We are, however, in a graveyard. South side of town, on a bleak low hill behind a church, not much of a view beyond the surrounding streets.

'I work for the council,' he says, the tone of his voice fitting perfectly with the dismissive look. 'I'm employed as a Grounds Maintenance Operative.'

'What does that mean?'

'You taking the piss?'

'Just asking what you do.'

This guy is not happy being interviewed, but then, I guess he knows why I'm here.

'I'm a groundsman. A park keeper. One of a team of twelve for this... district. One of the jobs involves graves.'

'So you're a gravedigger,' I say, and can't help smiling.

'Fuck off, mate.'

In an attempt to reset the conversation, which, to be honest, I'm making a bit of an arse of, I turn away for a second, looking around at the grim day.

'The graveyard is attached to the church, or it's a separate council property?'

'Really?'

I turn back to him.

'Sure.'

'Whatever. Used to be part of the church, back in the old days. Then it went, I don't know, it was like dormant for a while, then the council needed it, they bought some land next door, they expanded,' and he indicates the newer section of the cemetery to the left, which is still bleak, 'and they took over the running of it. Don't ask me when that was. Well, you can if you like, but I don't fucking know. Mind if I smoke?'

Like he cares if I do, as he takes out the cigarette and lights up without waiting for a reply. I don't say anything, but I am quite happy to stand here and breathe in the second hand fumes. I'll take anything.

That's a great smell. Fresh nicotine on a dull, shitty afternoon in Glasgow.

'You knew your wife's boss?'

'Ha. Here was me thinking you'd come to do a feature on my work.'

'I never said I was a journalist, did I?'

Snarky is as snarky does. This isn't going well.

I need a drink.

'You knew your wife's boss?'

'No.'

'You'd never met him?'

'No.'

'Not even at, I don't know, like a film premiere or something?'

He takes a drag, looking moodily away across the graves, head shaking.

'Whatever. Might have met him a couple of times. But I hated those things, hadn't been to one in five years.'

'The two of you,' I say, not really thinking it through, 'you and your wife, you don't go together.' Unlikely to help on the snarkiness front.

'What does that mean?'

'Maybe… I don't know, you look like you come from this world, she looks like she comes from a world of movie premieres.'

'I'm too working class for that shit?'

'Yes,' I say bluntly. It's what Kallas would've said.

He takes another pull on the fag, nodding as he does so, then leans again on the shovel, does his manly staring across the graveyard thing. Hmm, not bad from me. The interviewee appears to have appreciated the blunt approach and extraordinary perspicacity of the investigating officer.

'Yeah, whatever. Gill and I. Met at uni, she was already, you know, I grew up in Garrowhill, she grew up in some posh bit of Cambuslang…'

———

'She's from Cambuslang?'

He shrugs.

'Suppose. I mean, they like sent her to Hutchie, then they moved at some point, when she was thirteen or something. Went to Bears-fucking-den. But look, we go to uni, and we're both studying film, so what difference does it make? We hit it off, got together, man that's all she wrote, as Springsteen would say.'

'No kids?'

'She never wanted them. I don't know anything about them. We don't talk about it. Why?'

'How come you didn't end up in film?'

Another long drag of the fag. Slowing it down. Can see he's slightly discombobulated by the razor-sharp, quick-fire questioning from a police officer at the top of his game.

'S'lottery, in it? Hardly any jobs going. We interviewed for the same one, way back, like ten year ago, something like that. She got it.' He shrugs. 'I needed the money. I got this. Here I am, all these years later.'

'And you don't like the movie world?'

'Fuck, man, who does, apart from all the narcissistic wankers who work in it? It's just avoiding real life while you can, right? Do it all your life, can you say you ever really lived?'

I hold his gaze for a moment, then look around the graveyard. By that measure, would you call *this* living?

'Do you and Gill get on OK?'

'The fuck does that mean?'

'Seems your lives have diverged. So, has th –'

'Fuck that, man. She's got her job, I've got mine. We do our shit, but we still end up back in the same fucking bed at night.'

The rapprochement didn't last very long. On the verge of spitting out a question about her affairs, I look away, give myself a second or two.

'So, tell me about David Cowal,' I say instead.

'What about him? I didn't know him. I said I didn't know him. What d'you want?'

'You think there was anything going on between him and Gill?'

I get the look then. The anti-police glare, like I'm supposed to be intimated by it. Would be nice if we could just arrest people for looking at us funny. I mean, they can do that in America, and that's almost a functional country.

151

'You mean, were they having an affair?'

'That's what I mean.'

'No.'

'You don't think so?'

'No.'

'Does she ever work late? Travel? Spend much time away from home?'

He doesn't answer that straight away, choosing instead to give me the spiteful look of the aggrieved interviewee. But we know where that look comes from. That's the staring-into-the-abyss-of-the-truth look. We've all done that. Hurts like fuck.

'Does she ever work late? Tra –'

'Aye, all right. She works late. She travels. She does all that kind of shit. What d'you want from me? Doesn't mean she was shagging the boss, does it?'

I give him the look that says, *we all know she was shagging the boss*, but strangely it doesn't break his look of defiance. I do believe he thinks I can go and take a fuck to myself. Very respectful of him to so far avoid actually saying it.

'Has she ever mentioned Harry Lord?'

'Ha!'

A beat.

'That it?'

'What d'you want from me? That's the guy who got murdered the other night?'

'Aye.'

'No, she never mentioned him. Why would she mention him?'

'She and David Cowal worked with him.' Leave the pause. Brace myself for the reaction to the next line that pops into my head. 'Maybe she shagged him too.'

He unthinkingly snaps, grabs my collar with both hands, drops the cigarette, teeth gritted, mouth in a snarl, a splash of spit on my face, his smoky breath in my nose – try not to breathe! – and I await the assault, deciding I'll take it from there if it actually comes.

It doesn't. He grunts, he pushes me back, turns away, kicks the gravestone that we'd been standing beside. I will not think about how easy a virus can be transmitted in such an altercation.

'Christ's sake,' he says.

'You ever had an affair, Mr Blair?' I now toss into the mix, and his head starts shaking before he turns to look at me.

'The fuck has that got to do with anything?'

'Could make you more tolerant of your wife having affairs with a couple of guys she worked with.'

'Fuck off.'

'Not necessarily, of course. Plenty of husbands have the *one rule for me, one rule for her* rule.'

'None of us were having an affair.'

'While, on the other hand, were you the spurned and hurt cuckold, that might make you more likely to seek revenge against the men who bedded your wife.'

That stops the ill-natured interview in its tracks. He's had his outburst, he's come close to throwing a punch, he managed to stop himself, and now he just wants out.

'You're asking me if I killed that Lord guy, and Gill's boss?'

'Yes.'

He's breathing heavily through his nose, the caged, raging bull.

'No,' he says finally, the word spitting out.

We hold the angry stare, the Mexican stand-off in the graveyard. The perfect time for the informed and instinctive officer to make a judgement on whether the accused might be hiding something.

Well, I fucked it. I've conducted the entire interview like a moron, and so I can't tell anything. Haven't even got anywhere near asking about Margaret Malone. He's pissed off, and it's impossible to tell what anyone's thinking when they're this angry. Easiest thing in the world to hide behind. You don't have to fake innocence, when all you've got is rage. And why shouldn't you have rage when some moron comes tripping up to you at work out of the blue and accuses your wife of sleeping around?

'We're done,' he says, which is not really his decision to make, but which I was thinking in any case. Time I got out before I did any more damage.

He gives me a final glare, a final dismissive shake of the head, and then he turns away, lifting the spade and carrying it in the centre of the handle, horizontal to the ground.

I watch him for a while, and then shake my head, at myself rather than anything else.

'Fucking useless,' I mutter to the quiet earth and the buried dead.

33

Late Saturday afternoon, me and Harrison and Kallas and Ablett in the situation room, going over what we have so far.

The first murder on Monday evening, and now here we are on Saturday afternoon, there's been a further two deaths, and really, what do we have? A link between the three, which promises a long investigation with God knows how many dead ends. A clue left by the killer that all the deaths might be Covid-related, but we've found nothing to indicate Margaret Malone doing anything of the nature of the other two, and even then, when a killer intentionally leaves you a clue, it's not usually something you can trust.

Impossible to tell if Kallas is feeling any strain, but one presumes she would be. First big murder investigation at her new station, buck effectively stops with her, even if the chief will pull some buck-stops-with-me crap, and in four and a half days we've made little progress.

Kallas under stress looks not unlike Kallas drinking coffee in a café and Kallas getting undressed and walking into the Clyde.

God, that seems a lifetime ago.

'You've got anything more on the film, Eileen?'

I've done my bit on Tony Blair. Stopped short of a full admission of my perceived view of my own incompetence, but did at least admit to not even coming away with any kind of feeling about him. Certainly not in a position to strike him from the list, which means nothing at this stage, as we've more or less not struck anyone from the list.

'I spoke to Annabeth Blake,' says Harrison. 'She's happy for us to go and see her. Tomorrow morning, she lives near Bridge of Allan.'

'Good.'

'She described the film in pretty much the same way as you said Crawford described it. It was a dead end, never likely to see a release. People are just doing jobs, no one's really caring what happens to the movie. Expectations are zero. If it gets released, and becomes a thing, and suddenly it really matters to their career that they were in this movie, then sure, they can get excited about it. But at this stage, everyone's just glad to get four weeks' work, four weeks with something to do and a small pay cheque.'

'Was there any dispute during filming?'

'She sounded a little cagier on that, I have to say. I think it'll be worthwhile having a word.'

'OK, thanks, Eileen.'

Kallas looks up at the board. She's sitting at the end of the desk, then there's Harrison, Ablett and me in a line. Ritter was off today, back in tomorrow. Milburn still out there in the wilds, chasing down leads.

The three victims in a row on the board. Lord, Cowal, Malone. The money guy, the movie guy, and the Fat Whore. Yeah, I know, that's terrible. I shouldn't be thinking of her as a whore, just because of some stupid movie, and I shouldn't even be thinking she was fat, even though… well, she was fat as fuck. Just was.

I may get drunk again, and I may be a twat, and I may have sex with someone inappropriate, yet I'll manage to never refer to the victim as the Fat Whore out loud, so there's that. Bully, the fuck, for me, I'm practically a fucking Millennial.

The door opens, Milburn pitches up, slightly flushed, out of breath.

'Katie,' says Kallas, 'you did not need to rush.'

Milburn makes some sort of gesture to imply she hadn't been, but then she obviously had, so in the end she just kind of lets it go, and then takes a seat at the far end of the table from Kallas, next to me. She doesn't give me so much as a first glance, never mind a second.

'You spoke to Margaret Malone's sister?'

'Yes, I did,' says Milburn, and she takes out a notebook and has a quick read over her notes. An old fashioned look about her when she does that. I like it. Her breath just about back to normal. 'She hadn't seen her sister in a couple of weeks. Said they were a bit up and down with regards communication. Margaret hadn't been working for a while. Her last job, in fact, was last year, working behind the bar at the Red Lion. Did it for about six months, then got let go after Christmas.'

'The sister knew about the film?'

'Yeah, she said Margaret got that from a guy she met in the pub. They all thought it was funny, apparently, having someone that heavy and unattractive playing a hooker. She said Margaret didn't care. Or,' glances at her notes, 'couldn't have given three

---

155

fucks, to quote her more precisely. She just liked the idea of a movie, got paid a little in cash, had a day on the set. Everyone wants a little bit of that movie magic,' she shrugs.

'Was there any follow-up to the movie, any takeaway, anything that might have come back to haunt her about it?'

'That was really the limit of her knowledge. Didn't think it played any further part in Margaret's life, and it certainly didn't lead to an acting career.'

'OK. Any possible Covid connection?'

'She said she hadn't been infected, as far as she knew. Really nothing hugely tangible, though she might have done some stuff online.'

'OK, we'll get into that. Anything else that's viable?'

'She had three ex-husbands, and didn't speak to any of them. They all hated her, and she hated them. The sister, in fact, unaware initially that there might be a connection to either of the previous murders in town, was assuming the killer must've been one of Margaret's exes. She said they were taking bets within the family which one it might be.'

We all smile except Kallas, who, being an automaton, doesn't understand that that's something to smile about.

'We need to speak to the ex-husbands,' says Kallas. 'Can you make some calls and fix it up for tomorrow? How recent was the most recent ex-husband?'

'Got divorced in July last year.'

'Do we know if they had any kind of on-going relationship?'

'The sister didn't think so. She didn't think they were capable of it, though she did think him capable of killing her.'

'OK, that is a start. We will have a busy day tomorrow.'

She looks back at the wall, eyes running over the mass of information and photographs and names, trying to make the connections that are not immediately obvious.

'We cannot allow ourselves to be completely side-tracked by this film, even though it does present the most obvious connection between the three.'

She looks like she's going to add to it, but perhaps she decides all she's doing is adding words that don't need to be spoken, and then she says, 'That will do for today, I think. Thank you all for your work. Back in tomorrow morning, I'm afraid, and we can split up the interviews.'

There are murmurings around the table, and we rise and

head to the door. I like the way she said *I'm afraid* there, like she didn't really understand why one would say those words at that particular point in a sentence, but she knew, nevertheless, that it was appropriate.

'I'm heading over to see Dr Fforbes now, if you care to join me,' she says as I'm heading out the room.

'Sure,' I say. 'Wasn't about to leave anyway.'

'You should. We will see Dr Fforbes, and then we will be finished for the day.'

I look at the clock, nod in agreement, even though it means that I'll likely be walking back into my house at seven-thirty on a Saturday evening. Kallas is obviously one of these new-fangled bosses who believes in a work/life balance. Tickety-boo when you've got a family at home. When your life consists of an unfinished jigsaw of space, however...

I really don't want to have that much time. Maybe I can be completely hammered by ten, then have more time to sleep it off before I need to come into work in the morning.

'You all right?' asks Harrison, appearing by my desk, as I'm getting my shit together.

I nod.

'You going to come back in here anyway?' she asks. Must have overheard.

We hold the gaze. She knows what I'm thinking.

'Would you like me to come over?'

'You've got plans for the evening,' I say.

'I can cancel them.'

'Don't you dare. You have plans for the evening that you've been looking forward to, so don't mess with them.'

She holds the look, her concerned Emma Thompson face that I find so attractive.

'I can cancel.'

'Don't. After all...' and I nod over in the direction of Kallas. 'Who knows what the DI has up her sleeve, eh?'

'Yeah, it was funny when I was taking the piss out of you for it, mate,' says Harrison, 'but it's not happening.'

'I'll be fine,' I say. 'Call me around ten or something, if you're worried, you can check up on me, then go back to your thing.'

'What will you do?'

'Really?'

'What will you do?'

A pause. It's Harrison. She can see through me just the same as Kallas, and Harrison will just get it all out there, opening me up like she's gutting a fish.

I swallow. Shove my hands in my pockets, aware of the slight tremble. Fuck's sake.

'I'm going to stop at Oddbins on the way home. I'll pick up a bottle of vodka. And some tonic, this time. I'm going to go home. I'll… fuck, I'll do Rebecca's jigsaw. I can sit at a table, on my own, drinking vodka and doing a jigsaw, and hopefully, since it's, I don't know, about fifteen years since I got a good night's sleep, I'll feel tired before the evening's too old, and I can go to bed.'

'And you won't go out anywhere?'

Fuck me.

She's right, of course. Bad things happen when I have a drink at home and then go out.

'Yes, mom.'

'Don't do that.'

'I'm not doing it.'

I can't get annoyed at Harrison when she's telling me off. She's right, and I love her. That's all.

'We're good, don't worry,' I say.

Clench my fists in my pockets. Smile. Do my best to smile.

She does the concerned friend thing, her hand resting on the desk.

Taylor used to stand there like that, his hand resting on the desk as he talked. Then he'd tap the desk before he walked away.

Don't think about that.

'You better go out and enjoy yourself,' I say. 'You've put up with my shit for too long. I want a full report tomorrow morning of a night of filthy sex.' A beat. She stares at me. Time for a regular, well-used joke. 'I'll want to see video as confirmation.'

'Take care of yourself, Tom,' she says.

'It's cool.'

A moment, she finally makes the resigned I've-done-what-I-can face, then turns to walk away. Before she goes, she taps the desk.

I wish she hadn't done that.

34

Check my phone for the whateverth time. Nothing from Samantha. I want her to text and say she's coming round again this evening, roughly the same amount as I don't want her to. A real conflict, not an ounce of indifference to be seen. I never want to see or hear of her again. I was an idiot for sleeping with her, and I hate myself today – just that tiny bit more than normal – for having done it in the first place. But, Jesus, it was sensational, and how can you not want to do something *that* good again?

'There is something we should not get away from while we are pursuing the film lead,' says Kallas, as she pulls the car into the hospital car park, as if recognising that I need to be brought back to the case. 'These three murders have all been in Cambuslang. That is not necessarily odd in itself, three murders in Cambuslang, but it is odd if it is related to this film. The film itself is not Cambuslang-based, the people were not, the company was not.'

'The exec producer was, that's the start,' I say. Look at me with my *exec producer* schtick. Got the lingo. 'Then some of the money. But then, you're right, in that Harry Lord was just one source of financing. It looks as though the money came from about ten different places, so why specifically Harry Lord…?'

'Unless the killer is Cambuslang-based.'

'Which would tie in with the murder of Margaret Malone.'

'Yes.'

'And Gill Blair, I forgot to mention that.'

'What about her?'

'Born in Cambuslang. Didn't go to school there, but lived there until she was, like, fourteen or something her husband said.'

'Hmm. Well, we will add her to the list. I will speak to her again tomorrow. She is an interesting character.'

Car parked, masks on, and we're out and walking into the hospital, past reception with a nod, quick squirt of hand sanitizer, then down the long white corridors, a few people around, the walls covered in Covid warning posters, innumerable pictures of people with face coverings, and hands beneath running water.

'I made some more calls,' says Kallas, as we pass a man in blue scrubs washing his hands in a corridor sink, while he stares straight ahead at the white wall, looking as though he's been standing there, in that position, hands endlessly going around and around each other, trapped, for several days. 'Another check to see if there have been similar murders elsewhere. There have been four murders in Scotland this week, eleven in England.' A beat. Down a flight of stairs, along another short corridor, blazing white beneath fluorescent lights. 'All were either domestic or alcohol related. Or both, naturally.'

'Good to confirm our lingchi killer is a little local difficulty.'

'Yes,' she says, and we're at the morgue, and Kallas taps her knuckles quickly and lightly against the door and in we walk.

All my confidence and that sort of laissez-faire, don't-give-a-fuckness, about turning up at the mortuary, particularly when it's like the fiftieth visit of the week, disappear when suddenly I'm standing there at the table beside an enormous dead body, there's a huge cut down the gullet, every inch of the skin is lacerated, and of course, there's that face. Like, fucking Red Skull out of *Captain America*. Not that Hugo Weaving looks much better when he's got skin, by the way. Fucking miserable elven *Lord Of The Rings* bastard that he was. *Men are weak…* Too fucking right we are, you ancient cunt.

'This is horrible.'

There, I said it.

Fforbes glances up at me, gives me a strange kind of a smile, then continues to work on the area of the lower left leg which she's cleaning up.

'I agree,' says Kallas, surprisingly. 'I find it extraordinary that you can do this with continued good humour, doctor. It must be very difficult.'

'Weird thing is,' says Fforbes, straightening up now, and laying down the surgical cloth with which she'd been wiping away the congealed blood on the leg, 'I rather enjoy it. The human body's fascinating. How it works, how it stops working. I always… when I was young I used to wonder, when you see people in TV shows, and they get shot in the stomach, and,' she snaps her fingers, 'they're dead, just like that, I always thought, why? Why are you dead because you get a bullet in the stomach? Right away, right then, why does your brain instantly stop working? Why can't you move your muscles for a while longer, why can't you think? Isn't it fascinating? When does life actually leave the body? Even if you get a bullet in the heart, why does the brain stop sending messages that very instant? Why can't it limp on a little longer, just because the heart has stopped working, and the blood has stopped flowing?'

She looks between the two of us.

'It's such an extraordinary machine, and it's all tied up with this,' and she taps the side of her head, which is fine wearing a bloody glove, because she's also wearing a surgical skull cap.

'Yes, I understand,' says Kallas.

'When I was a kid my dad told me the story of Frederik Ruysch.'

'Full back for the three-time European Cup winning Ajax team?' I venture.

The fool and his frippery are not easily parted.

'Seventeenth century Dutch anatomist,' says Kallas, nodding.

At least I got the nationality right. I can cling to that so as not to feel like the idiot in the room. Imagine being the only person not to have heard of Frederik Ruysch.

'He was fascinated with the human body, and how it worked. He developed a method, far exceeding that of anyone else at the time, of preserving body matter. He dissected bodies, he preserved them, he preserved animals... he built a collection. Ruysch's cabinet.'

'Sold it to Peter The Great for thirty thousand Gilder,' chips in Kallas.

'Thirty thousand Gilder,' repeats Fforbes, like she's yon woman repeating everything her husband says in that *When Harry Met Sally* clip. 'Then he built up another collection, starting when he was in his eighties, and that got sold to August the Strong.'

'King of Poland, Grand Duke of Lithuania,' chips in Kallas, as though we're on *University Challenge*.

'Your dad told you this story?' I say. 'I remember my dad telling me about Willie Woodburn getting sent off four times for Rangers, and getting banned for life as a result.'

'Dad's a mortician,' she says. 'He likes talking about his

work.'

She smiles. There's potential for this kind of conversation to make a chap feel a bit stupid, but not with these two. Fforbes is funny, very, very likeable. And Kallas…? She can say any old shit to me, I don't mind.

'Is there anything significantly different?' asks Kallas, getting the meeting over Giant Red Skull here back on track.

There's a natural efficiency about Estonians. When they say a meeting will start at ten, it starts at ten. Arrive a minute late, you miss the first minute. She says that in Tallinn when a cinema lists a movie start time as six-thirty, it starts at six-thirty. There'd be bedlam if they tried that in the UK.

Of course, soon enough there will be no more cinemas in the UK.

'The significance, once again, is in the similarity. Mrs Malone was injected with GHB. We can surmise, although obviously this is more your territory, that the killer attacked her as she lay in bed because…' and she indicates the prodigious body lying before us. 'Mrs Malone was not getting crucified.'

'Not without the use of a crane,' I throw in, and Fforbes can't help herself laughing.

'One thousand cuts?' asks Kallas, keeping the discussion focused, though there's no censure in her voice. Observing that you would need a crane to lift Mrs Malone up onto a cross would probably be entirely logical to her, rather than a joke.

'I haven't catalogued them all yet, but I'm at nine hundred and seventeen, and, as you can see, at the lower legs. I'll have the final number before close of play this evening.' This woman doesn't have a life. Lucky her. 'It would be interesting, and potentially significant, if the killer changed the number. Just a small change, however, and you have the quandary of whether they've done it intentionally, or whether they miscounted.'

'It does not seem that they miscount.'

'Nope.'

'You have been into the stomach?' asks Kallas, indicating the slit through the abdomen.

'Yes. I completed the study of the upper body lacerations, then did the internal. She ate and drank, well, copiously, it seems. She had two bottles of red wine, and two pizzas. One chicken, one meat feast I'd say…'

'It wasn't one giant pizza?' I venture, albeit, it's kind of a moot point. We do like detail, though. Always helps.

———

'These were two giant pizzas,' says Fforbes. 'Quite a lot of garlic bread, a lot of doughballs dipped in some kind of tomato sauce.'

'Pizza, doughballs *and* garlic bread?'

'Yep.'

We look down at Margaret Malone.

'How was her heart?' I find myself asking.

'Almost perfect. She had a long, long way to run yet, despite the morbid obesity. Obviously flourished on her white flour-based carbs.'

'Would she have been drunk?'

'Hard to say. I kind of doubt it, given her size. Slowed, maybe, but she ate well, she drank well, so she may well have slept well. If she was doing that, her killer might not have had too much difficulty breaking into her apartment and administering the drug. Once that was in her system, and again the killer took no chances and delivered an explosively large dose, once that was done, she wasn't going anywhere.'

Kallas stares along the body, foot to head, finishing up at the red skull.

'You think she was awake for the torture, despite the dosage.'

'Yes, but haven't nailed that down yet. Let me get the tests back on the brain.'

We stand in silence for a few moments, looking down on the corpulent, bloody mess of the now dead Mrs Malone.

'She really was remarkable,' says Fforbes. 'A fascinating case. I'll maybe... sometimes you'd like to be able to speak to the family.'

'How d'you mean?'

Fforbes holds my gaze for a moment, thinking about something, makes the decision, and then leans over the corpse and pulls apart the large cleave down the centre of the diaphragm, revealing the mass of organs beneath. Having done that she stands for a few moments to admire it, while I reel a little at the pungency. Kallas is a rock, as ever.

'Look at it,' says Fforbes.

'I've done that.'

'When you see someone like Mrs Malone, you make judgements. We all do. We may approach those judgements from a different perspective, but we judge and we can't help it. I see someone like this and I think, my God, what will her blood vessels be like? Her liver, her bowel, her pancreas... And, of course, her heart. I mean, how do all these pieces of human kit, evolved to carry someone of, what, ten stones, keep functioning with someone more than twice the size? And yet, look at this. It's gorgeous.'

Kallas and I stare into the visceral mire.

'No sign of a fatty liver, no degenerative joints. Heart in perfect working order, she had the bowel of an Olympic athlete, lungs just full of life and energy and bursting to keep working for decades to come. Wow...'

Fforbes really is looking at the corpse with the appropriate wonder on her face, eyes wide, head nodding.

'It is remarkable,' Kallas manages.

'That it is.'

'We should go now,' she then says, snapping the moment. Or rather, stamping efficiently on the moment.

'Yep, I'll crack on,' says Fforbes. 'Shouldn't take me too much longer. The report should be waiting for you in the morning.'

'Very good,' says Kallas. 'Thank you.'

She nods, she turns, she walks back to the door. Fforbes and I smile at each other, the familiar look, and I nod in the direction of the intestinal melange.

'Fill your boots,' I say.

'Bugger off, Sergeant,' says Fforbes.

* * *

We sit in the car in silence for a while, but the drive is not long.

'I will drop you at your apartment, and not back at work,' says Kallas, not giving me the option. 'If you like, I can pick you up in the morning, since you won't have your car.'

'I'll be fine,' I say.

I've walked in often enough. Though that does require getting out of bed in time.

We drive on in silence, now doing thirty behind a yellow Ford, now sitting at a red light. Kallas doesn't listen to music. It probably constitutes unnecessary enjoyment.

There's an elephant in the car.

Wait, is there an elephant in the car? And if there is an elephant, is it the elephant I think it is?

Who am I kidding? And she's got that say-it-first-never-

164

think-about-it approach to absolutely everything, so why should there be any elephant?

Time moves with the car. We get to my street, we park outside my door. Like a movie, a decent-sized parking space right there, where and when we need it.

She puts the car in neutral, and the engine cuts out.

Silence.

We don't look at each other.

I think about my trembling hands and realise they're not trembling any more. And they weren't trembling while being bludgeoned by the sight of the naked and dead and flayed Mrs Malone. God, I'm still getting that drink in when she's gone, but right now, the need for drink has been temporarily displaced.

Mind all over the place.

'Perhaps you could make me a cup of tea,' she says.

Hmm, inviting herself up. Did she make a deal with Harrison? I didn't see them talking. Did Kallas get Saturday evening duty? Make sure the sergeant isn't a dick?

That doesn't make sense. For Harrison, perhaps, we're friends, but not Kallas.

Wait. That means this isn't about me, it's about her.

Uh-oh.

'You don't have to get home?'

'The babysitter is at home. There is no rush, though I would like to see the girls before they go to bed.'

'Your husband's not home?'

A beat. The silence returns like a positive force, wrapping everything in its morbidly tight and strange embrace.

We're both looking straight ahead. I'm a little lost in the moment, to be honest. It's so long since I did actual emotion with a woman. For years now it's just been a rough calculation about sex. Maybe that's all it's ever been. Schrödinger's shag. Either it will happen, or it won't, and you won't know until you make the positive move.

This isn't that, though. This is fuck all to do with Schrödinger.

'He left on Thursday. Went back to Estonia.' A beat. 'He is gone.'

Oh, fuck.

There's a game changer.

I mean, here I was, thinking, you know, romantical thoughts, imagining the DI getting carried away, doing

---

165

something stupid that would lead to awkwardness, but at least would get me an outrageous and unexpected shag out of it. But not like this.

Anyway, no way she's sitting here looking for sympathy sex. A cup of tea, that's all. Maybe she won't even need to talk.

'Come on, I'll stick the kettle on.'

35

Nine-fifty. How an evening changes on a sixpence.

Two hours ago I was sitting here with Kallas having a stilted conversation about her marriage. She didn't really want to talk about it, and I ended up burbling on about all the times I fucked up my marriages, while we drank a cup of tea each.

When she left, she said it had helped. Who knows? For someone who can be so expressionless, got to say she looked incredibly sad. Jesus. Three kids, newly promoted, big-ass murder investigation, asshole husband buggers off. She even said she wasn't sure she would ever see him again, which sounds dramatic, and a step or two up from just leaving his wife. I asked if there was someone else, she said she didn't know. I asked, boldly, why she went swimming naked in front of me the other day, and if that was some sort of self-power play on her part, doing what the hell she liked, doing something she knew her husband wouldn't want her to do, because she knew they were in trouble, and knew his departure was imminent. She said, 'No, I felt like going for a swim and did not have a swimming costume.'

She left after thirty-five minutes. Not the easiest thirty-five minutes of the year, although there have been, and will be, worse. I kind of melted when she left. Relaxed, at least. It had just felt so intense. And yes, there was an elephant, big as a fucking house.

We got nowhere near talking about the elephant.

And I'm still in love. I'm, like, one fucking step from the bastard love child of Hugh Grant and Richard Curtis.

She left, I gave it a few minutes, looked out of the window to make sure she wasn't sitting in her car weeping – she was never going to be sitting in the car weeping – moved a sweet and sour chicken with egg fried rice from the freezer to the microwave, then nipped along the road to the off licence for a bottle of vodka and some tonic.

I'd been telling myself all day I'd just be buying a half-litre, maybe even something smaller. I could do that, no bother. I bought a litre, and only the thought of a series of women at the

167

station looking disappointed in me stopped me buying two. On the plus side, I got the tonic, so I could drink half and halves and spin it out. Then I thought, on the other hand, if I drink it far too quickly, and drink it all, that's more likely to make me vomit, which increases my chances of not being an obvious, drink-soaked moron in the morning. Though, in my favour, my first engagement is coffee with the film producer in Bridge of Allan at ten, so I've got until maybe midday to sober the fuck up.

Yeah, all right, wouldn't be great to conduct an interview while still drunk.

So, that settled it. Decision made. Don't eat, drink quickly, get it over with.

So, here we are, me and my bottle of vodka, nine-fifty in the evening. Still sitting at the table with my space jigsaw. Mercury: Distance from earth, average 149.95 million km, temperature 450°C, length of year, 88 earth days.

I'll have forgotten that by the time I get to the end of this sentence, but there it is, right there. Of course, since I haven't touched it before tonight in three months, the jigsaw exists to more or less just taunt me. This is who you are, Hutton, the jigsaw says. You start something you can't finish. Not even a jigsaw puzzle.

Well, fuck you Mr Jigsaw Man, just watch as I finish this bottle of vodka. Yeah, exactly, so fuck off.

The first vodka tonic was pretty sweet, as was the second. And the third. Was it the fourth or fifth when it started to go a little awry? Can't remember. Bubble bubble, boy's in trouble. Now, fuck, we're at the bitter stage. No one knows how many drinks in we are. The bitter stage, when the alcohol and tongue have fallen out of wedlock, and no longer want to be acquainted with one another, but when the brain refuses to back down.

Starting to feel a bit sick, but my hand keeps pouring vodka into the glass, and getting more ice from the freezer, and pouring out tonic, and my arm keeps lifting the glass to my lips, and my tongue and my throat just have to accept the situation.

I did three pieces of the puzzle in the first half hour, and then I spent another thirty to forty minutes looking with blank eyes, and then it got too tiring, and now I'm just sitting here, drink in one hand, head resting in the other, feeling tired, and wondering if I'll be able to fall asleep, and stay asleep, before I need to throw up.

Another drink drained, ice still extant, pour the vodka, pour

168

the tonic, swirl the glass around, listen to the pleasing clink of ice in glass, take a drink, do the loud satisfied sigh, even though it's no longer satisfying, not by a long fucking way, head snaps, forcibly allow myself a second twitch, and then a thought formulates in that slow, thick head of mine, and I get up, drink still in hand, stagger a little, bump my thigh against the table, the bottles wobble, the vodka manages to hold its nerve, the tonic topples, and of course, of course, you rat-arsed skunk, you fucking loser, full of washed out spunk, I hadn't tightened the lid properly, and it sploshes onto the carpet, just a little, as there's not much left, and I bend down to pick it up, and in doing so, spill a little of the drink from my glass, and I right the tonic, but leave it on the floor, and stand up, the sharp movements up and down making me feel even more like vomiting, and I stand there trying to think of what it was that made me get up in the first place, and I'm standing, and I'm standing, and I'm standing, and so I down the drink in one long pull, and feel absolutely fucking terrible for it as it goes down, then I lay the glass back on the table, keeping it away from the jigsaw, and I remember what made me stand up, and it wasn't to vomit, though that may be on the cards now, and I go to the window and look down onto the street, and there she is, sitting in her car, maybe fifty yards along the road.

Sergeant Harrison, spending her Saturday evening making sure I don't go out and do something stupid.

Sober, I'd love her for it. Drunk, feeling this shit and drunk, I don't care either way. Ruin your evening, for me, I think. Seems stupid, but if you want to crater your night at the altar of a craven fuckweasel like me, on you go. Standing here drunk and shallow and alone and exactly the kind of man Elrond was talking about, I'm so glad Eileen didn't invite herself in. I don't want to face loving her and not being able to have her tonight.

Wasn't it the DI you're in love with?

Ah, OK, in love with two women at the same time. I can do that, I contain multitudes.

Having been standing, staring down the road for several seconds, I lift my hand. No point in pretending we don't see each other. She lifts her hand back. I neither signal for her to go nor to come in, and then I turn away, turn my back on her, and look down on all the sorrow.

Tonic on the carpet, a jigsaw puzzle that defeats me, a

hollow Saturday night, the waste of a life.

I feel the vomit rising.

* * *

I dream of the war in Bosnia. My part in the abomination.
There's me and a group of women, and I have a gun, and I've
told them they all need to lie there, because I'm going to rape
them one by one. There's Eileen, and there's the chief, and
there's Kallas, and there's Samantha, and there's Fforbes, and
there's Margaret Malone, and Taylor's there too, standing off to
the side, his arms folded, watching me. He's not stopping me, he
seems disinterested, he doesn't move.

And I order Eileen to get undressed, and she does, and she
lies back on the forest floor, and there are bugs and spiders
starting to crawl over her body, and I kneel over her, and that's
when I realise how flaccid and useless my penis is, and I'm sure
I'm turned on, I'm sure I want to do this, and my penis is like,
don't be daft, son, and Taylor starts mocking me, and then the
women start mocking me, and I want to run away from them, but
I can't, I'm stuck here, on my knees, and now Harrison is fully
clothed again, they all are, and I'm the only naked one, and
they're all laughing, and there's nothing I can do about it, and
when I look down at my penis to try to talk some life into it,
there are bugs crawling all over it, and that spider from Margaret
Malone's bedroom, big and long-legged, starts to crawl up my
stomach, then suddenly it's racing up my chest, and I swat at it,
and miss, and I can't hit it, and it's getting higher and higher…

I wake feeling indescribably awful. I wake feeling like they
will know, that I will wear that dream on my face. At work, the
women will know I dreamt about them. They will know what I
intended doing to them. They will scorn me, and I will deserve
it.

On top of that, however much vomiting I did in the
evening, it wasn't enough.

Six thirty-nine a.m. Out of the bathroom, still drunk,
corrosively hungover, hands shaking. On my way to the kitchen
I see the vodka bottle on the table. Unfinished. Still with
something to say for itself.

How low are you prepared to go, Sergeant? That's exactly
what it's saying.

170

36

We have no idea, we really don't. About movies. We have no idea about movies. You watch a movie, you see, I don't know, George Clooney and Ewan McGregor, and all those other bastards. They're the face of it. They're the ones you think of. Some directors are famous, but the producers and moneymen? Unless you're descending to geek level, you don't know any of them. Why should you?

But however much your famous guy is getting for the movie, there's someone you never heard of before getting that little bit more.

Now, here we are, Sunday morning, and it's Bridge of Allan, not Beverley Hills. Nevertheless, this is the house of someone who's made a fuck tonne of money in the movies, and I've never heard of her, and I expect most other regular people haven't either. Don't even think you would've if you'd read Empire magazine.

I'm standing in the study, waiting for Annabeth Blake to return with the coffee. I walked to the station, didn't go in, picked up the car, headed out of town. Now I'm here. When I arrived Blake took one look at me, offered the coffee, then asked if I wanted something stronger. The dog, a big bugger, sussed me out, and obviously decided I was too wasted an individual to be any kind of a threat, and left.

So, I stand at the window, looking out on the lawn, with an interesting tree and plant selection around it. Interesting is pretty much all I've got. There are trees and there are plants. My ability to describe them would be on the level of that first year French you did in high school. There are trees. The trees are big. The leaves are yellow.

At the bottom of the garden there are two trees with a gap in between which perfectly frames the view of a mountain in the distance. I've been walking in those mountains. Ben Vorlich maybe, or Ben something else. From here, I've no idea which one I'm looking at.

The room, the study she introduced it as – 'this is The Study' – like she was introducing me to an actual living being of

---

171

some species or other, holds the memories and triumphs of her movie career. Awards and film posters, signed photographs, pictures of her and several well-known actors. Tom Hanks and Charlize Theron, Al Pacino, some guy who was in a thing, whose name I forget. Spielberg and David Lynch. Harvey Weinstein. Hmm, interesting. A talking point, I suppose, regardless of what you think of the bastard.

My one act of determination through the fug of hangover, is not to let her catch me looking at all her movie shit. So, I'm standing here staring at a view of the hills, which is something you can do from tens of thousands of homes in Scotland.

Damned movies. Such a bullshit world.

I can feel her behind me, a noiseless presence entering the room, and then she's laying the tray down on the coffee table, and I turn, just as she's bending over the table, and the airy, Asian type of top thing she's wearing, is floating around like a butterfly, the neckline hanging low, and I wonder if she was just going to stay there, bent over the table like that, until I turned, and she straightens up and smiles, and says, 'There's fresh pain au chocolat, I wasn't sure if you'd want something to eat.'

I swallow, nod, certainly don't say yes, and then we're sitting down, the coffee is poured, the fresh pain au chocolat remain where they were on the tray, the smell of them haunting the air.

She smiles, studies me with a filmmaker's curiosity. She can fuck off with that shit. Of course, I'm studying her. Early sixties, got that Hollywood look about her, which is, as it always is, slightly incongruous with her Scottish accent, although there's none of the Hollywood sixty year-old woman's clutching at former glory, skin stretched and lips done, the start of the descent into plastic, manufactured abomination. She's natural, the wealthy woman's healthy glow about her, her only nod in the direction of American dreams of perfection, the iridescent, snowy-white teeth.

'Did you sleep with Harvey Weinstein?' is out of my mouth before I remember I wasn't going to ask about any of that movie shit. Of course, I'm here to talk about her making movies, and it is curious why someone with all this paraphernalia, this homage to movie success, was making a shitty, low-budget Scottish film that was never going to get released.

She smiles.

'Harvey's a darling,' she says, then she smiles. 'Unless

he's a cunt. You take the Harvey you get, I'm afraid, but is that so different from any of us? Harvey's just a little larger than life than most, so the highs and the lows are so much higher and lower.'

Yeah, all right, that was a lousy first question. I don't give a fuck about Harvey Weinstein.

Take a moment to have a drink of coffee, composing the first proper question in my head, and she fills the gap.

'You're an interesting looking character,' she says.

'It's not about me,' I say, putting the cup back down.

That is good coffee. Holy shit. What the fuck *is* that? I don't want to ask. I don't want to give her the pleasure, nor, for that matter, find out just how much it cost.

'Why not? Your life is about you. Life is about people. There are stories all around us, and you must see that more than most. And now look at you.' Do I have to? 'Come to conduct an interview on a Sunday morning, terribly hungover. You probably shouldn't have driven.'

'I'm fine.'

'Maybe you are. Maybe you can conduct yourself like this, carry out your duties, because you're used to it. But a police officer on a big murder case, and you're getting horribly drunk on a Saturday evening. What are you, early-fifties? Interesting. I take it your divorced?'

I take another drink of coffee, staring at her over the top of my cup as I do so. Damn, that's good shit.

'How many divorces? Two, three? I've had five myself. Rather wonderful the way one allows oneself to believe, isn't it?'

'Three,' I say.

'Ah, yes. And…' and she cuts herself off, smiling, leaning forward to take a drink of coffee. I glance out of the window, just in case. 'You have such an air of melancholy, Sergeant. Such a man of sorrow. One can only imagine the things you've seen.'

'I'd rather not.'

'You'd make a fascinating subject for film.'

'I don't think so.'

'Oh, you would. Look at you. Damaged. Women love damaged. Men, too, depending on how they react to it. But women, they would really go for your character. And I bet they do. Damaged, with that hint of danger. The unexpected.

173

Knowing that you're always going to be let down. How thrilling.'

'You've got all this,' I say, moving the conversation along, or trying to, indicating the movie room, and the house, and the view, and the yellow leaves on the large trees, 'the trappings of a successful Hollywood career, and your movie page reads like a fucking Blockbuster Video encyclopaedia, so what were you doing making some shitty, low budget Scottish movie that was never going to be released?'

She does the thing, she actually does the thing, where she holds her hands up, making the camera frame, the ends of her thumbs and forefingers pressed together, viewing me through the lens.

'I'm thinking McAvoy. No, wait, he already did *Filth*. I feel your story might be a little too close to that one. Though you're... you're better than that. More complex, what d'you think? And you don't *need* to be Scottish, it's not the Scottishness that defines you. We don't need to think about Ewan or Gerard, though neither would be bad, of course. But we could put you in the States somewhere, or Canada maybe. Why not? Might as well think big. Ryan Reynolds, I mean he can do... Ryan can do everything. He's funny, tragic, bombastic, cripplingly melancholic. Ryan's tremendous. Might as well dream cast at this stage, am I right?'

Jesus fucking Christ.

'What are you doing? Seriously, are you trying to distract me with this movie bullshit? I don't care. I gigantically, explosively, on so many levels there isn't a Burj Kalifa tall enough to take them all, don't give a fuck. Ryan Reynolds... Why, when you've had this career, and you've got all this, and you've worked with all these people, did you end up making some tiny, shitty little Scottish movie?'

She takes another sip of coffee, and now puts one of the pain au chocolat on a plate, which she first offers to me, then takes for herself when I shake my head. Pushing back at my annoyance with her equally robust and determined insouciance.

Yes, insouciance.

'You're no fun, Sergeant.'

'It doesn't sound like fun,' I say, 'it sounds like you're avoiding answering the question. Keep at it and I'll be suspicious enough to suggest you come back to the station with me, and you can speak to the inspector.'

174

'And what's he like? Even more terrifyingly damaged? Wait, he could be played by Matthew McConaughey.'

I won't even bother with the gender thing.

'Tell me about the movie.'

She takes a small bite, an LA diet-sized bite, of the chocolate croissant, then lays down the plate, shaking her head as she does so.

'Very well, very well. All this, glorious and wonderful and exciting as it is, is rather old now. Wearing at the edges, wearing thin, wearing away. Little to say for itself. You may have just been betraying your age with your Blockbuster Video line, but it's not entirely inaccurate. The Blockbuster Video days were my heyday.'

'What happened?'

She shrugs, takes her time over the answer, lifts the plate, takes another bite of pastry, lays the plate back down.

'A bit of everything, really. I'd made it up the ladder, from Bargeddie to Hollywood, a long climb, but fast. Did I fuck my way up there?' She shrugs. 'I suppose I did. Ruined a couple of perfectly good men along the way. Got to the top, made movies, lived the dream, the Hollywood dream. Movie stars, drugs and sex. And then… everything comes in cycles, doesn't it? You go up, you get to the top, from there there's only one way you can go. If you want to stay there, when you see the start of the decline, and *everyone* sees the decline, you have to be able to fight it. You have to *want* to fight it. I didn't have the energy. But I'd lived the dream, twenty years and more. Decided to come home.' She wafts an airy hand around the room, and towards the great outdoors, the whole of Scotland her playground. 'I can do whatever I want now, just so long as it's not expect someone to give me a hundred million bucks to make a movie. And so I fritter away the days. Yoga and reading, and walking in the hills, and having drinks with friends, and occasionally speaking to one of my daughters on FaceTime. All terribly dull.

'I knew David Cowal from way back, and he asked me to help him out with the movie, and I thought, why not? It filled a gap in my schedule, you might say.'

'And it didn't bother you that it was never going to be released?'

'Not me, darling, of course not. Business is business. I mean, when one starts, when a project is mentioned, one always wonders... will this small, seemingly insignificant thing turn into *The Full Monty* or *Slumdog* or whatever. It's an industry of dreamers, after all. But I knew as soon as I read the script. It didn't really have anything about it.'

'Why make it then?'

'They needed a movie to meet their quota, they had money to spend, it was going to be a quick and easy shoot. And it was. Business, like I said, is business...'

'So, what, everyone bought into the programme? Everyone on the movie knew they were making this thing no one would ever see?'

'Of course, not everyone. It's the movies. People dream, and those dreams are big. Gigantic,' and she makes an exploding star gesture.

I take another drink of coffee. Even though we're coming to it, my concentration dips for a second, mind going in and out, realise as I lift the cup that the shake in my hand is obvious, which it must have been earlier, and now that I notice it, I notice her noticing it, though she will have already done so.

I stare at the floor for a moment, head somewhere else, then finally manage to look at her, and she's watching me with peculiar fascination, and she kind of smiles curiously, and it brings me back, and I say, 'Tell me.'

'Tell you what? You were away for so long there, I quite forget what it was we were talking about.'

'Who was upset about the movie not happening?'

'Ah, yes. A couple of the actors, of course. One of them's still bothering me. That little shit, Marvin. He's a creep. Making a movie with me that's never getting released, is about all the career he deserves.'

'We'll speak to Marvin.'

'Well, I don't know that you need to go that far. Anyway, I can... I'll get Marcie to fill you in on any information you need. The principal... perhaps, the one you should be most interested in, was the writer. Young woman, name of Leia Fisher. And yes, her parent's real surname is Fisher, and they named her after Princess Leia. Cheesy doesn't cover the half of it.

'It was her first script, it got optioned for sweetie money, but she was excited. Well, of course she was. Everyone is at that stage. Got her photo in the local paper, maybe even made one of the nationals, she was living the fifteen-minute dream. And then one day on set, one day when she was excitedly talking about film festivals and distribution and Netflix and award ceremonies, someone told her how it was actually going to be. And she had... she had a cow. She had a good old-fashioned movie set strop. It was like the ghost of Bette Davis. How wonderful!'

And she claps with delight at the memory of it.

'Doesn't sound wonderful,' I say.

'Oh, it was. I mean, I was there one day when Angelina Jolie ripped a poor AD to death on set. It was absolute murder. But she's Angelina, there's a reason she thinks she's queen of the world. But young Leia? Everyone thought it was hilarious.'

'How did it play out?'

'Well, she stormed off set and we never saw her again. There were only a few days filming left at the time, and of course, we hadn't actually needed her on set in the first place. The writing was done, it wasn't as though we had Russell Crowe demanding rewrites to his dialogue before every scene.'

'Did you hear from her again?'

'Did I? Quite the campaign she tried to mount. Spoke to people, wrote blogs, wrote e-mails, tweeted. You'll need to look her up. Now, I have to say, before you go sending round the SWAT team, body-slamming her into the dirt, and doing all that police shit that you do, I really don't think she'd have done all that, and then started murdering people.' She pauses, stares off to the side, and then continues, 'Well, maybe she'd have murdered David I suppose, she was really, really pissed at him. And if it is her, *I* should be looking over my shoulder. But this man Lord, and the bit part actor lady? That seems peculiar.'

'We spoke to James Crawford yesterday, he didn't mention anything about her.'

'Well, that's because he fucked her and was embarrassed. Ever since she went loco, he's been panicking she'll contact his wife.'

'She wasn't mad at him?'

'I think he was scared of her. When she found out the plan for the movie – or, rather, the total lack of a plan – James faked outrage so he could stay onside. It was hilarious.'

'What about you? Are you worried? D'you want to speak to someone about getting protection in place?'

'How sweet. I'll be fine. I have alarms, I'll make sure they're on, and I have Bobby.' A beat, then she smiles. 'But if you feel you have to move in here to protect me for the next week or so, I could put up with that.'

And then, naturally, she leans forward to pour some more coffee, even though she doesn't need to.

Must be on the lookout for husband number six.

37

I came away with a copy of the film burned to a CD. That'll be a fun eighty-seven minutes for us this afternoon at some point. Or maybe we can have a station movie pizza night.

Back along the M9, through Cumbernauld, take the cut-off down towards the M8 and the M74, and then off to Cambuslang, and I'm pitching up at the office in less than half an hour.

Took the pain au chocolat in the end. And another two cups of coffee. And some water. Even let her tell me a couple of stories, because she looked like she wanted to talk, and I was aware that the longer I spent there, the more normal I was beginning to feel.

Really liked her in the end. I hope she doesn't get murdered. If she does, the killer'll have to take care of Bobby the dog too, which would be a shame. And tricky. Although, when it comes to it, dogs are kind of dumb, and all that brute force can be fairly easily neutered with some aforethought. So, if someone goes there looking to commit murder, it'll largely depend on whether they've planned for the dog.

Walk into the station feeling the best I have so far today. Not as good as I was three days ago, but recovered from last night. No idea if I'm wearing last night's diet of alcohol, my *parfum du jour*, but the shakes have passed. Party celebration emojis all round.

Having called ahead, DI Kallas is sitting at Ritter's desk, looking at her phone, waiting for me.

'Hey,' I say. 'How are you?'

'I am fine,' says the robot, but the robot, of course, has had no small talk programming done on it, and so she quickly says, 'What did the producer say?'

'She has some stories to tell,' I say, settling down in my seat, turning on the computer, glancing vaguely at it as it whirs into life. 'And she conveniently laid a suspect in our path, which sounds much too easy. But we do need to look into it.'

'Who?'

'The writer of the movie, Leia Fisher. She was aggrieved about the attitude of the filmmakers. Fell out with them all, mounted an online campaign against them. I mean, we've looked the movie up already and haven't seen any of that shit. I'll get into it now, see how it looks.'

'You think perhaps the producer was giving us the writer as a diversion?'

'From herself? Entirely possible, of course, but I don't think so. Let me chase down the writer, I'll try to speak to her today, then we'll see where we are.'

'OK, that's good. Thank you.'

'You conduct any inter –'

'I spoke to Gill Blair again. I feel it was not a good use of time, but we shall see.'

'Nothing new?'

'I did not learn anything new. Did you say to her husband outright that we know she'd been having an affair with Cowal?'

I give that a second or two before answering, then nod at my own utter uselessness, and say, 'Not, you know, completely outright, but it was pretty obvious it's what we believe to be the case.'

'And do you think he already knew?'

'I would say he did, and he'd been lying to himself.'

'Wilful blindness?'

'Yes.'

'I think Mr and Mrs Blair had a discussion about her unfaithfulness last night. As a consequence, Mrs Blair was very tense, and not at all forthcoming.'

I lower my eyes, get the regular and familiar feeling of ineptitude, and as always seems to happen, Kallas sees right through me and comes to my rescue.

'You had to speak to him, and it would have been impossible for you to ask questions about David Cowal without awakening his feelings of resentment, regardless of how much he knows. If he did not already know, then we can scrub him from the list of potential suspects. If he did already know, then you do not need to feel bad about discussing it with him.'

Glass half full, eh?

I suppose I ought to take it. I nod, deciding the best course of action is probably to stop talking about it. I spoke to the guy, got nothing, she spoke to his wife, got nothing.

A phone starts ringing on the other side of the office, somewhere two of the guys are talking – still talking, three days later – of the miracle of Scotland winning a penalty shootout.

180

'Are you all right?' I ask, trying to avoid the silence, and asking a question with just enough of a veiled reference to what she told me yesterday evening.

'Yes, I am fine,' she says. 'You do not need to worry about me. You were drinking again last night.'

Nothing to say to that. I look around, thinking about Eileen. Haven't really been thinking about Eileen, because I've been too busy thinking about Kallas. I need to thank Eileen.

'Where are you on the case?' I ask, ignoring the alcohol observation.

A moment, then she accepts that this is where we are, and goes on to transmit. 'We have tracked down the manufacturer of the masks, now we are hoping to establish if a multiple buy was made from anyone in this area. The chances of success could, naturally, be inhibited depending on the amount of selling agents the product has. The company at least, alone in the world it seems, does not sell through Amazon.

'We are looking at cars that were caught on CCTV in the three areas where the murders took place, in case there is one that repeats. While they are all in Cambuslang, and it is not a large town, still it would be a significant coincidence for the same car to have been seen each time.

'We spoke, finally, to the director of Garrion Bridge care home. This did not go well, but I feel the conversation has moved on a lot since this item was placed on the to-do list.

'We have made calls and visits to most others involved in this film, *His Grey Return*. This is being coordinated by Eileen. She is in the ops room, perhaps you can go there and coordinate an approach to this Leia Fisher. It is possible someone has already spoken to her.

'So far, we have found no immediate connection between Mrs Malone and anyone dying of the virus, however it does appear that she was a virulent anti-lockdown protestor. She posted thousands of messages, and retweeted and liked messages on various platforms about ending the lockdown, the farce of it, how everyone should be left to make up their own minds. She promoted a lot of inaccurate science. She intimated that if and when a vaccine came, she would not be taking it.'

'That could be it, then,' I say. 'I mean, it's another strand, right, another way in which someone's ignorance put people at risk? The first victim put his own father at risk, and by extension possibly killed many others. The second risked the life of his family, and his wife died. And now this one was working against the community, and did who knows how much untold damage?'

'She had three followers on Twitter,' says Kallas. Deadpan. God, she's fucking wonderful. She'd absolutely kill it in a comedy movie.

'Not what I just said, then.'

'There is something in it, but for someone who tweeted over a hundred times every day, she can have had little impact. Her Facebook account is similarly deficient in follower numbers. Nevertheless, under the circumstances it still feels significant. We should not lose sight of the fact that this is the person she was.'

'I thought we should work on the potential next victim. I got the full list of people involved in the movie from Mrs Blake. Not just the cast and crew, who we have, but other subsidiary names, such as accountants and people involved in financing. It'll be tough, but we need to identify if any of them had a chequered history from the past few months relating to the virus. The kind of things we've seen with the others, basically.'

'Yes, very good,' says Kallas. 'Eileen is already collating that kind of information, but this augmented list with which you have returned should be of use. Perhaps you could take that in to her now.' She glances at the clock. 'I have a meeting with the chief inspector in four and a half minutes. Once that is done, I will join you and the sergeant in the ops room.'

We stare at each other, that familiar awkwardness, then she nods and turns away, and I watch her walk across the open plan, and I think of her walking just as easily away from me into the chill waters of the October Clyde.

'Fucking come on,' I mutter to myself, then I get up and walk through to the small ops room, where Harrison is sitting alone, her legs up on the table, staring at the information board, where all we know about the three deaths is laid out in a jumble of facts and buzzwords and photographs, and she's bouncing a small rubber ball off the desk, onto the far wall, back to the desk, back into her hand, with perfect control.

That there is impressive hand/eye coordination.

'Thanks,' I say.

'You're welcome.'

'I wasn't going anywhere.'

'The inspector was worried you would.'

I look at her, as she turns the ball over in her fingers,

nodding at the state of play.

'I don't deserve either of you,' I say. 'I don't deserve your concern.'

'Well, too bad you're cursed with it. We'll see you through, get you out the other side. Make something of you yet.'

We smile, I shake my head. She bounces the ball off the desk, wall, desk and back into her hand without really looking at it.

'Sorry, I ruined your evening.'

'You didn't.'

'No?'

'I told Sasha I had to work late. People are very forgiving of triple murder investigations, I find. Got to her place around midnight.'

I nod. Maybe I haven't stopped since the last time.

'Decent sex?'

'Ten out of ten.'

'Well, that's good. I don't have to feel bad. If you'd got there earlier in the evening when you were supposed to have done, who knows, it might have been three or four out of ten sex. But the wait was the clincher.'

'Yes, thanks, Tom, you saved the day.'

She rolls her eyes, she bounces the ball off the desk, sending it towards the wall.

And that, right there, that moment sticks in my mind, as being one of the last good ones before the shit hit the fan, and the whole fucking thing spiralled downwards into such a shithole of awfulness, it could have been part of the Sharknado series.

38

While most of the cast and crew and subsidiary personnel attached to this movie that none of us have watched yet have been contacted, no one can get hold of the writer.

Harrison was, unsurprisingly, already on to her. Fisher is a prolific writer and contributor to various websites; she has her own site to which she posts every single day; in the space of two and a half years, she's published twenty-seven novels, novellas, blog collections and poetry collections on Amazon; she vlogs, TikToks, and in general pounds the streets of online desperation for many hours a day. That was, at least, until it all stopped one week ago.

Ritter and Ablett went round to her address in Govan and got no answer. Ritter and Ablett effected entry to the property, and there was no one there. Nothing to indicate recent occupancy, as far as they could tell. A little dust on the kitchen worktop a clear sign. Everyone uses a kitchen worktop, even if it's just to lay down the bowl to pour the cereal in, or to dollop the Chinese takeaway onto a plate.

They noted, however, that there was no computer, there was no phone, there was no bag, no purse, no wallet. When she'd left the house, it was with intent. Impossible to tell if she'd packed a bag, and for all we know, she met a guy, she fell in love, she's spent the last week shacked up in a hut in northern Sweden, having Swedish sex, drinking lingonberry juice and spit-roasting whole elk over an open fire.

Nevertheless, we're thinking Thunderbirds Are Go on the writer. And it turned out her grandfather had died of Covid. People have different relationships with their grandfathers, but we found the blog she'd written about his death, and she was steaming. Blaming a lot of people.

You can see the problem. It's all too neat. When something falls this perfectly into your lap, particularly when someone else places it there, you'd be a fool to fall for it. On the other hand... sometimes things fit perfectly into place, because that's where they belong.

Cautious, but hopeful, we spend several hours on Leia

Fisher. Something unhinged about her. I love a nutjob. And every now and again, when she was in the appropriate mood, she posted topless selfies on her blog.

Great tits. There, I said it. Might as well tell it how it is. And that, after all, was why she posted pictures of them on the Internet. Using everything she had to try to make the breakthrough.

I wonder if it helped her career. Maybe she's not currently shacked up in northern Sweden, but doing the movie sex party circuit in Hollywood – if Hollywood hasn't burned down yet – the one Annabeth Blake frequented back in the day. In a week or two, she'll resurface, up to her eyes in fabulous stories, which she'll then tell breathlessly on her blog, with veiled references to such and such an actor, without naming names, and how he's got an enormous cock, or how he likes anal, or how he likes to recreate Hieronymus Bosch paintings during sex parties.

And, to be fair to the nutty girl, she can write. Has a turn of phrase about her. Prefer her to Hemingway to be honest, though I wouldn't say that on, like, *Front Row* on Radio 4 or anything. I'd be scorned.

Just after three in the afternoon. So far today, nine cups of coffee. Feeling good on it though, eyes racing across words on the screen, taking it all in, making notes, referencing items that might need looked at again, feeling like I've finally got last night completely out of my system, flushed out by caffeine, wondering if at last I smell more of coffee – man's acceptable addiction – than booze, which is, rightly, one of the many unacceptable ones, when I find myself giving a small celebratory punch in the air, long before I finish an article, and then by the time I get to the end of it my brain is whizzing, I've got hands raised a little, gesticulating as I talk to myself, and then I lift them briefly in the air, in a restrained gesture of triumph. Yes, restrained. One must celebrate these small moments of lucid and cohesive thought.

A scrunched-up piece of paper bounces off the back of my head and I turn to see Harrison looking at me with questioning shoulders raised. I look around the open-plan for Kallas, but I don't see her, and I remember she had to go back in with the chief for the third time today, and I've been glad to get buried in work, because Kallas has been a little off all day, and I don't know why, and then my phone pings as I gesture for Harrison to come over, and as she sits in Ritter's seat across the desk, I make the mistake of reading the message that's just come in.

Boom!

That pure, exhilarating joy of having a cogent thought is knocked out of me with a boot to the face and a boot to the stomach and a boot stamped into my balls as I lie on the ground, and suddenly, in the snap of a twisted finger, the buzz of nine cups of coffee, the buzz of actually enjoying my work for once, is extinguished.

'What?' she says, recognising that my mood changed as I looked at the phone.

I read the message again. It's short. Says what has to be said.

'What?'

I finally look up at Harrison.

I need to tell her this, but she'll be disappointed in me, and I don't want to. Instead, clutching at yesterday's news, I point at the screen.

'I found an article Leia Fisher wrote for the Rutherglen Chronicle. It never got published in the Chronicle, maybe they were waiting for *His Grey Return* to actually be released, but then… well, someone on the paper thought it worthy of just sticking it on their own blog. They credited Fisher, but it kind of implies it was never getting published.'

'What'd it say? And why did you look like Scotland had just won the World Cup, and now you look like England just won the World Cup?'

I smile ruefully at that, can't help it. Nice line. Perfect summation.

'You know we found lots of articles about the movie she'd written, and obviously didn't manage to place anywhere other than on her own blog. She must've realised the movie had a Cambuslang connection, that just by chance these various people from a fairly small town all ended up involved in it. But then I thought, what if that's her only part to play? What if she wrote the article, but then someone else saw it, and that's where they got the names? So, in fact, the killer himself has no connection to the movie. They have, however, the connection to Cambuslang. It *is* about Covid. The movie's the cover.'

'Why plant the masks, then? The masks are telling us it's about Covid.'

Shake my head.

'Don't have that,' I said. 'Maybe they want to instil the fear

---

186

about Covid, so that people who did wrong, or who may have been considered to have wronged, are bricking it. Meanwhile, they throw the police the curve ball.'

I shrug.

'That's all I've got.'

'Not bad,' says Harrison. 'Forward the article to the ops file, make sure Kallas sees it.'

'Already done it.'

We do that staring across the desks thing that I do with so many different women.

'Why the long face?'

I don't immediately answer. I don't want to. Real life is about to insert itself in my shallow existence, and I hate it when that happens.

From nowhere, as if apparating from inside the chief's office, Kallas appears beside the desks. And now it's Kallas and I staring at each other, and this time there ain't no elephant. This thing is going to have to be said.

I project disappointment onto her, because it's impossible to tell what she's actually thinking. Her face has gone full android.

'You are wanted in the Chief Inspector's office,' she says.

We hold the gaze. There's nothing for me to say, nothing else for me to do other than get up and walk in there. And it's not like I'm afraid of the chief, it's not like I particularly care about getting my arse handed to me, but two minutes ago I was working, I was having one of those rare moments of coherent thought, the thrill of the chase in my blood, and now, from the moment I get up off this seat, the path from here to me slumped on my bathroom floor, blind drunk and vomiting, is short and straight.

'What did the message say?' asks Harrison.

I hold Kallas's look for another few moments, then turn to Harrison.

'It's from Samantha Cowal.' I look at the message, reading in the mechanical voice of an Estonian. 'Told sis we fucked. She's pissed. Asked her to keep schtum, but she's gone to your chief. Sorry. I'll call later.'

Lay the phone on my desk, look at Harrison. Boy, do I recognise that look on her face.

'Friday?'

'Yep.'

She nods. We've been here before. When you've been somewhere because of addiction, it's only a matter of time before you return to it. So she's not disappointed, this was just what was going to happen. Sooner or later, round and round the maypole, the merry *danse macabre*, we all fall down.

'Come and speak to me when you're done.'

I nod, a last look, then I'm up, can barely look at Kallas, and I'm walking into the chief's office, Kallas beside me. So the interview is to be conducted beneath the watchful eye of my line manager. I have support.

Hawkins is doing that thing where she's looking at her computer screen, typing carefully, when I enter the room, and she takes a while before noticing I'm there.

Kallas and I sit in the two chairs by the desk, opposite the young woman who is about to punt my sorry excuse for a police sergeant's arse into the long grass.

She tuts at herself, brow furrows, types something else, makes another mistake, then pushes the keyboard a centimetre away from her and turns to look at me.

Well, at least my presence makes it hard for her to concentrate. I have that effect on women.

'A vulnerable young woman, a young woman whose father had just been brutally murdered, came to see you, and you got her drunk and slept with her?'

Not strictly accurate, of course. If I can read my women, and I'll give myself that ability if no other, she was not, and never has been, vulnerable. And she definitely wasn't drunk. And yes, I'm the officer and the older chap and all that, and I should have been the grown up, but that characterisation, quite possibly put in the chief's head by the sister, is completely wrong.

But all the caveats apply. Vulnerability, drunkenness and the very basic *who started it*, don't matter. I was wrong. Full stop. End of, as the wankers say these days.

'On what level is any of that acceptable?'

Jesus.

That's the trouble. I came in here knowing I'm in the wrong, happy to sit down and take the shit on the chin, get the fuck out of Dodge and go home and slide weakly into obliteration. The path was laid out before me, and I was pencilled in to meekly follow it. And then she comes out with shit like *on what level is any of that acceptable?* Fuck off, you pious cunt.

This, this is why Kallas is here. I wonder if she insisted she sit in on the interview. She's here to protect me, to make sure I don't say anything that'll make it worse. Because, really, I'm more than happy to say something that'll make it worse.

But not with Kallas, that's the thing. That still, calm presence beside me, the one with the beautiful eyes who I don't want to disappoint, that's what will keep the words buried, the hate and the bile and the anger, and will make me sit here in silence, not answering asinine rhetorical crap like *on what level is any of that acceptable?*

'Nothing to say?' she says. 'Typical. Just typical, Sergeant Hutton. The amount of your type I've seen on the way up, passing me on their way down.'

And here's me thinking I might be the narcissistic one.

'There will be proceedings, as ever. There are always proceedings with you, Sergeant, and for the life of me, reading your file, I have no idea how you've survived this long. Well, you cannot turn to DCI Taylor now, you cannot…'

She keeps talking, but I shut out the words. I don't want to hear them. I don't want to hear that I can't turn to DCI Taylor. I don't want reminded of that. Not by her, sitting in here.

The words stop abruptly, the flow of malicious, spiteful authoritarianism.

'Will you look at me when I'm talking to you?'

My eyes are closed. Clenched shut. Had done it without even noticing. I become aware of the tension in my hands, my fists, knuckles white, chest wound just as tight.

Open my eyes, take a breath.

'Go home. I'm suspending you without pay pending an investigation of your behaviour during the course of this investigation. I'm sure you are well aware of how the process will play out. For now, go home, *do nothing*, and wait to hear from PSD.'

She holds my gaze. My moment has passed. I will not explode, I will not speak at all. There's a twitch on her lips – I recognise that look in so many people – then she looks at Kallas.

'Anything else?'

Kallas too has nothing to say, and she shakes her head.

'Accompany the sergeant to the door. Right now. Do not let him linger in the station, do not let him look at his work computer. He is suspended and cannot legally be in the building.

———

189

Do not accompany him home, do not engage him any further than removing him from the building. This is now a legal matter.' She pauses, she looks at me like a cross schoolteacher reprimanding the kid who inked half the class. 'Consider yourself fortunate you're not being defenestrated. Now get out.'

And that'll do it.

Up, back turned, quickly across the office, and out the door, screaming *fuck!* loudly in my head as I go.

Stop at my desk. Harrison hasn't moved, still sitting in Ritter's seat, waiting for me. Guess she would've known I wouldn't be long.

I grab my phone, put it in my pocket, and move away from the computer before Kallas feels she has to tell me I can't look at it.

'I'm off,' I say to Harrison. My voice sounds funny. A weird, strained quality to it. 'There's something in that blog I didn't mention. There's a fourth person listed. You probably ought to get someone round there.'

'I saw it.'

'Right. I don't know how that makes any sense.'

'I guess the guy knew Harry Lord. Maybe they got talking, and he chose to get involved because of the producer being from Cambuslang. Small world and all that.'

I shrug. Either a small world, or an utterly ridiculous, unlikely coincidence. Right at this moment, still reeling from the metaphorical kick in the balls, I have no interest either way. Someone else's problem.

Last look, oh so familiar in tone and longing and apology and sympathy and, for me at least, that feeling of stupidity, an awareness of my total lack of self-control.

'See you.'

I turn and leave. Can't even look at Kallas, as she walks one step behind me. Past reception and good old Ramsey, ever present, jovially called a total cunt by everyone since his name was trashed on *Game of Thrones*, and I can't look at him either, and then I'm out the door, into a chill, grey October, the rain falling, not heavy, not light, not drizzle, just Glasgow rain, wet and bleak and relentless.

I stop, turn back to the door. I'm standing in the rain, feeling it on my head, and she stands in the dry, as still and composed and perfectly put together as always, her face similarly unreadable.

'Sorry,' finds itself to my lips.

She lets the word hang there, floating between us for a moment, and then she makes the killer play, says the worst thing possible.

'I'll come and see you later.'

She turns and walks quickly away, one second and she's out of sight, and now I'm just a fucking lemon standing in the rain, feeling about as abject as possible, lost and alone, ejected from the building like the shittiest wasted drunk from the pub at eleven-thirty on a Friday evening.

39

I'll come and see you later.

Brutal. Just brutal. And she knew it, too.

I sat in the room with that damned woman, the chief, and I thought, fine, do what you will. Throw me out. You think, you piece of shit in your Harvey Nichols, you think that two hours from now, when I'm fucking wasted, I'm going to give a shit about this? About you? About this job? About anything? You think I give a shit *now*?

Like I said, the road was short and straight. I wouldn't have thought there was an impediment that could be put in the way. And then Kallas tosses that into the mix. She'll come and see me. Simple and brutal. I really don't know what's going on, but there's something, and she's stuck the boot in. And it didn't need saying, of course, but it's a very basic tenet of the circumstances. I will not want to be blind drunk when she turns up.

And so now here I am, sitting by my jigsaw. Neptune. Average distance from earth, 4,459 billion km, temperature -220°C, length of year, 60,202 earth days. That's a long year, by the way, albeit only about half the length of 2020. The bottle of vodka I bought on my way home is sitting there, unopened. Here, too, sits the glass. The ice is melting. I didn't get as far as getting the tonic from the fridge.

Spoiler alert: I bought three bottles of vodka.

'Having a party the night?' said the girl behind the counter, smiling.

That conversation didn't get very far.

I swallow. The vodka, clear and crisp and expectant, calling out, the bottle glinting in the early evening streetlights, stares back at me.

'The fuck are you doing?' says the bottle of vodka. 'I literally don't understand what's happening here.'

'Fuck off.'

Neptune, feeling awkward, remains silent.

Close my eyes, lean forward, palm of the hand to my forehead. The tremble carries through my arm to the table.

I can hear the vodka laughing. That doesn't make sense. Vodka doesn't laugh. Anyway, why should it laugh? It's scornful, that's all. Mocking me. Sitting there, calling out, the fucking Siren. Just have *one*, it says. Stop the tremble. Maybe have another in a little while. Take your time.

Like there's such a thing as having one and then waiting. Like there's the slightest possibility I could have one drink, period.

I get up abruptly, hands at a shake, turning my back on Neptune, and the rest of his cohort. Fuck, fuck, fuck.

Brain screaming.

Do something. Do something that isn't taking a fucking drink. Do something that occupies your mind.

Fall forward on the carpet. On my knees, head in my hands. This is how it goes. This is how it plays out. I do this, I fold like a pack of cards, I drink vodka. Kallas comes, and I am ashamed.

What was it they called Hitler? Carpet muncher. Ha! Got a different meaning now. He was fucking mental, literally eating the rugs in his rage, so they said. Maybe some propagandist just made that shit up.

Head forward, face scrunching into a contorted rag of misery, crying invisible tears.

Drink, you fuck! Drink! Will it be fine? No, it fucking won't! But drink, and be damned! Drink!

'Drink!' cries the vodka bottle. 'Come on Hutton, you walking septic tank of human waste! You sack of shit! You colostomy bag of shame! You suppurating, pus-filled, rancid wound in the anal crevice of humanity! Drink!'

That is a mouthy bottle of fucking vodka.

Straighten up, straighten shoulders, look round at it.

You win. You win…

I need to give myself something to do while I plummet into the abyss. At least that. Please, at least that. Vodka, tonic, ice, lime, try to mitigate the ensuing disaster, hope that Kallas isn't too late.

She won't be late. She's got her kids to get home to.

Fucking jigsaw. Sorry, Rebecca, I can't do the jigsaw. It won't slow me down.

What was I doing before? What was the last useful thing I did *in my life*? The writer. That was it. Leia Fisher. The writer. Great tits. Sure, I decided she wasn't part of it, that someone had read what she wrote, but she's a starting point.

Anyway, she might be dead. Hasn't posted anything online in a week. How long ago was it that I found that out about her? An hour? Two? Five? What the fuck is the time anyway?

Jesus.

Lift the glass, into the kitchen, toss the old ice cubes into the sink, another three into the glass. Close the freezer door, open it again, put in a fourth ice cube, cut a slice of lime, grab the tonic from the fridge, pour the vodka, hand trembling, bottle clinking off the top of the glass, not too much, not too much, not too much, *stop!* Then the tonic, with the glass sitting on the table on a small mat, wondering how long I can leave it there, thinking I can go and get my MacBook, look up Leia Fisher, get into it before I actually take a sip, then I lift the glass, take a long drink, maybe a third of it, the ice cubes already at my lips, and Jesus, that is such a wonderful feeling, and I manage to lay the glass back down this time and go and get the computer.

Slow down, boss, slow the fuck down.

* * *

Sitting at the table, glass of vodka tonic to my left – my third – MacBook open on top of the jigsaw. The jigsaw is starting to irritate the fuck out of me. I need to get rid of it.

Bob playing on Spotify, coming through the small speaker I added to the apartment at some stage along the way. Spotify's random This Is Bob Dylan playlist, an endless stroll through Bob's career, back and forth, and absolutely perfect.

Have come at the search for Leia Fisher from a different angle. Could be wasting my time, of course. I have no idea what they're doing back at the station. Whether someone's doing what I'm doing now, whether they've already found her, whether they've found her corpse, victim of a thousand cuts, random parts of her skin flayed.

I have followed who she follows and who follows her, and have tracked their posts and their movements, looking for the picture that wasn't tagged with Fisher's name, the random clue to her whereabouts that crops up out of the blue.

God, it's pathetic, really, isn't it? Kicked out of work, set free to go and do as I please, and what's the only thing I can think of? Be a police officer. Fucking hell. And what do I care anyway?

It appears that I do.

——

194

The street buzzer goes. Kallas is not late. Not long after seven. I wait by the open door as she comes up the stairs, and then I stand back and let her in. I feel the discomfort walk in with her, then I close the door and the two of us are standing in the room, me and Kallas, Bob singing, with immaculate timing, *Tangled Up In Blue*.

We hold the gaze for a few moments – Jesus, I wish I could read it, or wish I could think of something to say, or wish she would say something at least, anything – then she turns away and walks to the window, passing the table and the jigsaw and the bottle of vodka.

'Can I get you something?' I ask. 'Cup of t –'

'Vodka tonic, please,' she says.

Hmm.

'Sure.'

I make the drink, I feel her presence all around me as I do so, then I place it in her hand, and we stand side by side at the window.

There are times I wished I lived by the sea, rather than on a dull little street in Rutherglen. This is one of those times. To be honest, every time I stand at the window is one of those times.

This is easier. We have an activity. We're watching the street, rather than looking at each other, waiting to see if the other person will have something to say.

'The chief will push for your dismissal,' says Kallas. 'I do not think I will be able to protect you.'

'That's OK. About time I was dismissed.'

'You are a good officer.'

'*Was*, maybe.'

'I did not work with you before. I work with you now. You are a good officer.' A beat. 'I like your theory that someone read the writer's account of the connection between the film and Cambuslang. It is a good theory, it makes sense, it requires no coincidence or contortion of the facts to make it work. I would still like to find the writer.'

I think I just found the writer, shacked up in a romantic liaison in Perthshire.

I don't say anything. Not sure why. Maybe I don't want to admit to working, or maybe I want to find the writer, surprise the watching audience by pulling something out of the bag, as if it might save me. As if I want saved. Which is stupid, of course, because if I obviously continue working, and subsequently

———

195

reveal my work, I'll be in even more trouble. I've been suspended, I need to keep my head down, keep the fuck out of everyone's way, and wait my turn to be kicked out the force.

'Did you go down to Troon and speak to Anderson again?'

It was Acting Assistant Secretary Anderson who was the fourth name listed in Fisher's article about having been involved in the movie, and connected to Cambuslang. Given that up until we read that, he'd been a guy who played golf from Troon, it's the kind of thing that leaps out and grabs you by the knackers.

'I did. He said Harry Lord was always talking about film financing. Not just film financing, though of course, film is something that people like talking about. Anderson heard about the low budget film, and because the producer was Cambuslang-based, even if the film was not, he got interested. He said he only invested fifty thousand pounds, and it was entirely for tax purposes.'

'You think his involvement could go much further than that?'

'I am not sure. I do not yet think so, but we shall see.'

'You put a man on his door in case he's next on the list?'

'We did.' And then, with barely a pause for breath, 'You are drinking.'

Her eyes drift to the bottle, and then back to the street outside.

'This is the first bottle you opened today?'

'Yes.'

Jesus, you'd know if this was my second.

'This is your second or third drink?'

'Third.'

'Your drink is a similar strength to this one?'

I nod, even though she's not looking at me.

'You will drink all night?'

'I have no reason not to.'

A beat. Uh-oh. I feel the awkward discomfort creeping back in, even though we're looking out of a window. This was supposed to prevent the discomfort. We have an activity, dammit.

'I would like you not to drink,' she says.

I let those words hang there, hovering in the room, over here, by the window, somewhere in between her and me. Did that mean that her not wanting me to drink is a reason I shouldn't be drinking? Because that, in its way, could be taken

———

as an acknowledgement of the elephant, and as soon as you acknowledge that fat grey fucker, the cat's out the bag.

'I can't promise.'

Now the clinking of the ice in her drink, as she puts the glass to her lips and more or less downs the entire thing in one go. I'm looking at her by the end of it, and holy fucking shit, that's sexy.

She lowers the glass, tips it back again to drain it, then sets it down on the table.

'You need to buy better vodka, Sergeant,' she says, and I can't help laughing. Kallas again with the kind of pitch-perfect delivery that made Bob Newhart's career.

'You're funny,' I say, which is something I regularly say to women when I'm hitting on them. I mean it this time, although I don't think it'll make any difference to her. Chances are Kallas does not consider herself funny. 'Would you like another? I mean, despite the vodka.'

I know she doesn't want another, just as she knows I know, so there's no point in her answering. The silence comes back, and together we stand there and look down onto the street. I still have most of my drink left, the ice slowly melting, diluting the vodka even further.

Lightweight.

A movement, and then from nowhere she touches my arm. A gentle touch, her fingers cool and soft. She doesn't look at me.

'I will come and see you again tomorrow evening. Try to take better care of yourself.'

She gives my wrist the slightest squeeze, and then turns away, and I can't stop myself, even though the words are stupid and wasted and pointless. 'You need to get home for the kids?' and she pauses, but does not look at me, and then finally she moves away, lifting her feet out of the sludge of the moment, heading towards the door.

Why did I have to come out with that? Really, Hutton, you abject pile of fetid putrescence.

She stops at the door. I have not followed her. I cannot stand beside her there, because I will want to stop her going. I will want to touch her and take her into my arms, I will want to embrace her, to bind her lost melancholy to my own.

'He took the children.'

This time, those words, they were not delivered in the usual monotone. How could they be?

She turns and looks at me.

'Anders took the children back to Tallinn. He has moved in with his parents. I'm sorry I lied to you yesterday evening.' A beat. 'They are gone.'

'Jesus. Isn't there something you can do?'

'I have spoken to lawyers. We wait and see.'

Holy shit. What a bloody awful thing to have happened, and she's in the middle of this shit, and then I go and complicate her life by being a dick.

And now we're standing here.

Except, the reason we're standing with things complicating by the second, isn't because I had sex with the victim's daughter/potential witness/potential suspect. It's because of the thing. The *thing*.

'Stay for another drink,' I say, at least managing to stop the words, *there's no reason not to*.

There's always a reason not to stay at Hutton's house!

A beat, another, a long look across a short room, then she says, 'No,' her voice soft and low, just that, all that needs to be said, and she opens the door and is gone.

40

Heading to Gleneagles. Have never been before, will be happy to avail myself of a cup of tea and a sandwich or two while I'm there. Not on duty, of course, so nothing to rush back for.

One presumes that the woman Leia Fisher has come away with has the money in the relationship. Fisher may have made the odd penny or two from her writing, but the desperation with which she produced, and the bitterness of much that she wrote, suggests that a living was not really being made.

And now she's gone quiet, and perhaps it's for the simple and basic reason that she's found money out of nowhere. Or, at least, she has found someone with money, someone to spend some of it on her.

Into the hotel car park, and then quickly out the car and it's only a couple of seconds before I'm accosted by an eager young chap in tartan plus fours.

'Can I help you with your bags, sir?'

Now, in her rush the chief made a crucial error. She obviously doesn't have too much experience of suspending people. Never got me to hand over my ID. And sure, perhaps it'll go out on the wire, do the rounds of police stations, Detective Sergeant Hutton is a leper, do not go near him, nor let him near you!

Makes no difference. It's not as though they can either tell everyone on earth, or make my ID vanish by remote control.

'No bags,' I say, flashing my ID, not stopping to talk. 'I'll only be half an hour,' and he smiles and nods, and I notice that flicker in his eyes, the one that caught the whiff of alcohol. Such a familiar flicker. Then I'm inside, and as I enter I take the mask from my pocket and slip it on – more about limiting my projection of stale booze than either common sense or the notice at the door – and up to reception, and aware enough to stand back a little from the desk, rather than lean over and pour my be-masked alcoholic's stench over the two ladies and two men sitting back there.

Hey, I didn't have anything to drink this morning, so there's that. And I was only sick once last night. Might have

———

199

cried once.

I cried once.

Today's good humour is very delicately balanced.

'Detective Sergeant Hutton,' I say, ID extended.

'Sir,' says the young chap. 'I'll get the day manager.'

'That won't be necessary. There's really no issue, I'm just looking to speak to one of your guests. It shouldn't take long.'

'I'll get the day manager,' repeats the guy, and he's lifting the phone as he says it.

I nod, step away from the desk. Rummage about in my pockets, find the mints, work them from the small box without taking it out, then pop a couple a little awkwardly behind the mask.

Reception. What you'd expect. Carpets and wallpaper; photographs as art, of the glen and the golf courses; the deer's head, the open fire, the aroma of smoke and wealth, the comfortable armchairs; the busboys in plus fours, the girls in tartan waistcoats and tartan skirts; an American couple talking too loudly about Sunday afternoon's round, the guy laughing at himself, which doesn't seem so American, because Americans are incapable of laughing at themselves, even though they all, no doubt, think they laugh at themselves better than anyone else on earth, so maybe the guy's Canadian, and I take a longer look at him and his attractive wife – yes, she's attractive, bite me – and I'm thinking, yes, probably Canadian, and then he says, 'I cannot believe the ball stayed out the hole,' and the way he says *out* is the clincher, and I relax. Canadians I can take.

I once said to Taylor I was thinking of moving to Canada, to get away from all this shit, and Taylor said, 'Why would you do that? It's so boring. Canadians are like stunned Swedes,' and I laughed, and I think of that now and, as ever, as with every thought of Taylor, it brings everything that happened this summer flooding back, so that by the time the hotel day manager arrives, I'm standing in the middle of reception, my mind a hundred miles away, mired in self-hate and guilt, already thinking about the bottle of vodka that's waiting for me at home, wondering why I bothered coming up here, when I'm not even working for the damned police anymore.

'Detective Sergeant Hutton?'

'Hey,' I say, managing to switch on at the mention of my name.

I suppose one advantage of social distancing is that we

never get close enough to shake hands, and so there's slightly more chance of being far enough away for them to not notice the stench of booze. *Slightly* more chance.

'You have a guest staying here, Leia Fisher. I'd just like a quick word with her.'

The day manager, a women in her late thirties, the kind of woman who got her hotel management qualification at the best hotel school in Switzerland, and who eats other authority figures like me for breakfast, before spitting out the remnants and squashing them like dog shit, smiles in the only way she knows how. And doesn't say anything. The *why?* is implicit.

'It pertains to an investigation we're undertaking in Glasgow South.' A pause. She continues to look at me, a succubus, drawing more information without opening her mouth. 'There will no trouble,' I say, and my voice is beginning to head south. If she continues to look at me like that for much longer, I'm going to have to threaten to bring the entire force along. A threat I naturally don't want to make, as I'm the most one-man of one-man teams there is. 'She's not implicated in the investigation in any way, the interview is entirely for background. I'm happy to have a chat with her wherever she chooses, and –'

'Why didn't you phone ahead?'

That's not an entirely shit question. I suppose, really, it's an entirely obvious question. I choose to answer it with the kind of stony silence she'll respect. Sure, I can't call in the reinforcements, but she won't know that. She's unlikely to push this and phone the station to find out what's going on, and my silence just speeds up the time until she makes her decision. Who's she going to be?

We have something of a stand-off, her cold blue eyes burrowing into mine, stripping everything away, peeling back the skin on my face like the killer did to Margaret Malone, then she turns away without a word, speaks quickly to reception, the receptionist looks past the day manager's shoulder at me, then lifts the phone.

The day manager gives me a nod, and leaves.

I wander back over towards reception and await the verdict. There's always the possibility that Leia Fisher tells them she doesn't want to see me, in which case I then have the call to make. How far do I risk pushing it?

The receptionist puts down the phone, smiling at me like

we're old friends.

'Miss Fisher is happy for you to see her in her suite. She's in the east wing, ground floor. If you go through the door here to your right, along the corridor, first right, and then three doors along. She and Miss Champlain are in the Murray Suite.'

I nod, no other words required, and then I'm heading out of reception, mind back in neutral.

The Murray Suite. Named after Sir Andy, d'you suppose, or perhaps just after some old fart, an eighteenth century gentleman farmer, who sold his soul to Westminster for a pocketful of land, Sir Bufton Tufton Murray of Auchterarder, who left seventeen bastard children and died of rampaging gout on his forty-sixth birthday.

Eyes down, stepping on the lines in the carpet, the corridor wide and bright, lined with picture-perfect paintings of Perthshire, cattle and deer, mountains and lochs, babbling brooks and waterfalls, salmon fishing in the Tay.

Knock on the door, step back. Stare at the carpet.

The door is answered. Not Fisher, the other one. The lover. Champlain. The one who posted an innocent photograph of herself and Fisher eating lunch in the fifteen-star Michelin bistro. Smiling, wearing a long white shirt, and nothing beneath, I'd say.

Just what I need.

'Sergeant Hutton,' she says, smiling. 'You can take off the mask, unless you insist.'

I hesitate, she continues to smile, says, 'Really, we're OK. Young and foolish. Come in, be free!' and she laughs, and I, easy prey, take off the mask and thrust it into my pocket.

She stands holding the door, while I file past. This really is a suite. It has a corridor. I have literally never been in a hotel room that had its own corridor. What age are these women? Neither of them can be over thirty, and they can afford to stay in a place like this?

I decide, with an old-fashioned closed mind, that Miss Champlain must have one of those fathers who owns several diamond mines in Africa, as well as half of America's national debt, and he happily provides his daughter with anything she requires, and she closes the door, leads me down the short corridor into the sitting room, and now there's three of us in a large, bright, tastefully, tartanly Scottish lounge, and everyone's smiling and dressed to relax, except me.

There are two sofas, a low, elegant coffee table in the middle of the room. There are doors off either side, and straight ahead, double French doors, leading out onto a small patio, looking out over the hotel grounds, out across the golf course, to the Perthshire hills, shrouded in mist and rain, beyond. To the right of where I'm standing, the blank screen of a large television, and a bar. Behind the sofa on which Fisher is currently sitting, beneath another large window, a writing desk with a leather top.

Fisher is wearing light cotton pyjamas, drinking a vodka and tonic, or a gin and tonic, or a Bacardi and lemonade. Impossible to tell. I just know it's not lemonade, it's not sparkling water. Champlain slumps into the sofa beside her, and, since she's wearing a shirt and nothing else, I get the glimpse of pubic hair she intended me to get just before she crosses her legs.

'It is you,' says Fisher. 'I wondered if it might be.'

I mean, really... All I wanted... I just wanted to come up here and sit in a café, or on a bench somewhere outside, looking at a distant mountain, ask a few questions, get a few answers, maybe find out something useful I could pass back to Kallas, try to finagle my way back into her good books, although her good books are not what I've been ejected from, and then get the fuck out of Dodge. It sounded so straightforward.

Instead, I walk into the sweetest of traps. Alcohol and gorgeous lesbians.

Ha!

'What does that mean?'

'I was telling Georgia about your sex video,' she says, smiling. 'The talk of all Glasgow.' She takes a drink, the ice tinkling beautifully in the glass.

I feel the weight of my jacket and tie, my collar tight against my neck, I feel the weight of non-responsibility, something in my head keen to point out that I'm currently suspended, so why not throw off the shackles and go along with the vibe.

'Now here you are in person,' she says. 'How exciting. A police officer who's not afraid to drink and fuck while on duty.'

'Can I get you anything?' says Champlain, springing to her feet, then downing the rest of her glass in one.

She holds the pose for a moment, her raised arm lifting the shirt slightly, allowing a more generous view of her thighs, then she lowers the glass and says, 'Vodka, that's what you drink, right?'

Vodka. Jesus.

I stand there like a fucking lemon, trapped between lust and the last vestiges of common sense and self-respect.

You know, you can only hate yourself so much, then finally you just give the fuck into it and accept you're a useless, pathetic piece of shit, who belongs in the waste bin of history.

Perhaps when Kallas comes by tonight I should go all out to be as drunk as possible. I can come on to her. Try to get her into bed. Be a colossally massive dick to her, and it really wouldn't be too much of a step for me to be *that* much of a dick. Drive her away. She is, after all, far too good for me. What's in it for her, all these tortured silences, this fucking chemistry with which we've been blighted? What possible good could come of it for Kadri Kallas?

'You know why I'm here?' I say to Fisher, and she takes a moment, finishes off her glass of vodka or gin or whatever, kind of smacks her lips as she lowers the glass, then leans forward with a smile.

'I wrote a piece about the connections between Cambuslang and *His Grey Return.* I mentioned four people in that piece, and three of them are dead.' A pause, and then, 'Or is it now four?'

She stands and walks over beside Champlain, lays the glass down, nods, mouths thanks, then returns to the sofa. Thought for a moment she would do that thing where they kissed lustfully for my benefit, but they didn't. I would have loved it and scorned it in equal measure.

'Of course,' she says, having enjoyed me watching her move from the sofa to the bar, back to the sofa, 'I can't be the only one who made the connection. But I get that you might be curious enough to need to talk to me.'

'You never published the article yourself?'

'Nah. I gave it to the Chronicle, and even they didn't bother running it in the end. There must've been too much interesting shit going on in Rutherglen and Cambuslang that week, eh?'

Champlain holds a glass in front of me, and then it's in my hand, ice cold on my fingers.

This is monumentally stupid. I have, at the very least, to drive back down the road. I'd be an even bigger fucking idiot to add drink driving to the list.

Maybe I could kill myself in the car, that might work.

Too liable to take another driver out with me.

Just the one drink.

Just the one.

'Who runs the blog that published it?'

'Derek, a guy at the Chronicle. He's sweet. He felt bad for me that no one would take it, so he said he'd put it up on his thing. Maybe he thought he'd get to sleep with me out of it, but sadly for Derek... Anyway, I was so pissed about the whole experience by then, I just thought, fuck it, you know? That was a decent script. Better than decent. Those fuckers just shat it out, straight into the sewer.'

'You must've been annoyed?' I say, sounding like, I don't know, a deadbeat, average, every-word-is-written-by-a-hack detective, with barely an original thought in my head.

'Sure,' she says, and she and Champlain exchange a glance that stops just short of an eye roll, and she adds, 'so pissed off I decided to kill everyone involved. But just those who live, or lived, in Cambuslang. I mean, personally I've never even been to Cambuslang, but I can see that coming from there, you kind of deserve to die just for that.'

'You missed one, by the way,' I say glibly, in response to her glibness, and she smiles in a way to say that she really, really, doesn't care.

So, there's a drink in your hand. My lips and my tongue and my throat are saying, *There's a drink in your hand. What are you waiting for?*

'Do you have sex with everyone you interview?' asks Champlain.

I stand with my drink, holding it before me as meagre protection. Like looking out of the window while standing beside Kallas, it is an activity.

'Would Derek be able to tell who'd read his blog?' I say, ignoring the sex question, trying to maintain the tenuous hold I have on the interview.

Champlain crosses her legs. Fisher smiles, then takes a slow drink.

'Not if someone just stumbled across it,' she says eventually. 'You know this already, sergeant, you know how it works. He does, however, have a small list of subscribers, so perhaps that might help. If he's willing to hand it over, which...'

---

and she finishes the sentence with a small shrug and a doubtful look.

'Would you ask him for me? In fact, could you just ask him, don't say it's for me? Make up some shit.'

'Interesting. Why would I do that?'

'Because if I ask him, it's possible I get the full-on, infringement of society, anti-police crap, and there's no way I'll get anywhere near it without a court order, and even then, with him working for a newspaper, regardless of which one and how small, he'll come at me, come at the police, and the mainstream press will be his willing accomplices, and then suddenly it's some shitshow or other.' A pause so that I calm the fuck down, because just the thought of Derek being a dick about it – even though he'd be absolutely right to be a dick about it – gets my back up, and the two of them are sitting there smiling throughout, and then I say, 'But if *you* ask him, and if I can gauge Derek, you don't even have to promise him anything, just leave it dangling there, the idea there might be something in return, you'll have it off him within five minutes.'

'That doesn't really answer my question, Sergeant,' she says, and she stands, and as if following the actions of her leader, Champlain stands with her, and they approach me across the short distance to the middle of the room. 'I get why you want me to do it. But why *should* I do it? Why should I lead poor Derek on like that?'

They stand either side of me. Champlain in her white shirt, top three buttons undone. Fisher in the light cotton pyjamas, calf length, thin top, her nipples pressing against the material.

'Because three people have been murdered,' I say.

I hold her gaze. Do my best. Can feel my hand shaking, the ice in the glass starting to rattle. Fuck, fuck, fuck, get a fucking grip.

'A fourth could be in danger, and then, who knows?' I force from my lips. 'Who knows how many more? Who knows who?' Swallow. Can feel my cock getting hard, know that it will be obvious soon enough. Jesus, I'm so easy, so sad. 'Could be you next.'

'Ooh, that's exciting,' she says, with the thrilling assuredness of someone who thinks they're untouchable.

'It's really not.'

She moves closer. They both do. A hand settles on my stiffening cock. I close my eyes. Now my resolve crumbles, and as ever, I'm swallowed by the moment, taken by the impulse, self-control set determinedly at absolute, hopeless zero.

I lift the glass to my lips, take a long drink. Vodka. Cold and sharp and smooth and wonderful, fuck it feels so good going down, delivering an instant kick of relaxation, and my cock twitches at the touch, and I moan softly, then the glass is taken out of my hand by one of them, then there are lips on mine, and I give in to it completely, a face pressed against me, the cool, moist lips, the tongue edging its way into my mouth, the hand pressed against my cock, and then the other one is back, having placed the glasses to the side, and she presses her hand against the hand that's on my cock, grabbing my buttocks at the same time, and her tongue is on my neck, and it feels glorious, and then the tongue is running down my neck, and she's ripping my shirt buttons open, down to my waist, belt undone, zipper down, and then my trousers lowered, boxers pulled down, and my erect, already damp cock springs free, and straight away there's a tongue on it, and then lips around it, and I slide it into her mouth, and Jesus fucking Christ it's so good, and I kick the trousers and underwear off my feet, and hurriedly remove the shirt and tie, and it's Champlain who's still kissing me, and I whisk her white shirt up and off, and then I'm taking her breasts into my mouth, and as I lick the nipples, I notice she has bite marks all over her breasts, and I feel those same teeth against my cock, and I jerk, and I slide wonderfully, deliciously, happily, with total abandon into the moment.

41

Some time after the sex was over I thought to look around to see if there was a phone set up to film the event. Sometime after the three of us had fucked on the couch. Sometime during the third vodka and tonic. Sometime before we had sex again. As I'm the most transparent fucking moron that ever walked the earth, they knew what I was doing, and they told me to relax. I said that's exactly what they would say, regardless of the situation, and Champlain said her father was paying for the whole thing, which was fine, but he thought she was here with a guy called Tyler, so really, there was no way she or Fisher were filming anything, fun though it would be, and I said well why did you post a picture of you and your buddy here in the restaurant, and she pointed out that she'd also posted a lot more pictures of her and the guy they'd roped into having sex three days previously, so that her dad would think he was the aforementioned Tyler, and I said that more than likely her dad wasn't stupid, that he would know exactly what she was doing, and that, for about the only time during the two and a half hours I was there, managed to put a dent in that knowing, smug air they had about them, and I felt bad about puncturing the hedonistic feeling of invincibility, and I apologised, I actually fucking apologised, and soon enough everyone was laughing again, and they were kissing, and teasing me, and there was fanciful talk of me going again, but somehow I got the feeling that maybe, despite the sybaritic atmosphere, and the alcohol and the orgasms, I wasn't the only one haunted by melancholy and self-loathing, and when I departed, as the afternoon was beginning to grow dim and finally concede to the inevitable sweeping rain from the north, the only thing I really left behind, was a miserable sliver of my sadness.

And now, here I am, back in position. Boo-yah for Hutton. Me, my jigsaw and my vodka. Good to be home.

And what point was there in my trip to the Perthshire countryside? Utterly moronic of me to go up there in the first place. The sex was just about all I got from it.

So now I'm sitting here, waiting for my phone to ping, a list of names from Leia Fisher. Time, like the spider that sits in the corner of the room, never, ever moves. Time as still life. Time as a non-existent entity. Time as an illusion.

Feeling drunk. Also waiting for the doorbell to ring. Kallas. Dark outside, gone seven-thirty. She usually doesn't work too late. Hoping she calls, hoping she doesn't. Don't want her to see me like this. Not sure I'll be able to speak at all coherently. But, despite the sex and the whatever, I can't think of anything I want to happen more than seeing Kallas this evening.

I can't do what she asks, I can't change my behaviour to accommodate my feelings for her. Nevertheless, I want her here. I don't know what I would do in her presence, and I can't even dream of an outcome that goes well, but I want to see her, just as much as I know I don't deserve to see her, and she really, really ought not to come anywhere near me ever again.

Drain another glass, let the ice cubes rest against my lips, look down at the jigsaw, which probably also thinks I'm a useless waste of space, so little productivity do I have for the amount of time I sit here.

The doorbell goes.

I don't deserve this woman. *Look, Inspector, I know I'm drinking and you asked me not to, not to mention those women this afternoon, but that was just a little trifling thing we can ignore, because I've really fallen for you…*

'Hey,' I say into the intercom, head leaning against the wall.

'Sergeant Hutton,' says the crisp, business-like voice from downstairs, a slap across the face, a sharp rap on the cheek, a poke in the eye with the mercurial sharp stick, the vicious kick to the balls.

Hawkins. The Chief.

I don't speak. I buzz the downstairs door open, open my front door, and then turn my back on it and return to the table. Tempted to pour myself another drink, but I just sit there, shoulders rounded, a shadow of the intrepid stud-like figure who heroically bedded two women this afternoon, awaiting my fate.

I listen to the distant call of her footsteps on the stairs, gradually growing louder, then the brief hesitation on the landing outside, and then the door being pushed further open, then the door closing, then the gentle pad of footsteps across the wooden floor and the rug, and then she's standing to the side of me, a couple of yards away, the way we've all been standing away from people since the spring.

She waits for me to turn to look at her, but I can't. Head stuck, staring straight forward, and down. Jupiter, on average 691 million km from earth, temperature -145°C, a year lasting 4332.6 earth days.

'Give me your identification card,' she says.

I don't have far to go. I reach into my pocket, take out the card, keep it in my hand for a moment, turning it over. End over end over end, slowly, end over end. I stop, holding the card upright, looking at my three year-old picture. Detective Sergeant Thomas Hutton, Cambuslang Station. Number L1983007.

'There was never a time when I was fit for this,' I say. 'If I could look at all the ID cards I've held over the years, there wouldn't be a single one of them I could look at and think, it was good back then. *I* was good. I was struggling from the first day.' A beat. 'Until the last,' I add after a few moments.

She's not saying anything, but I can feel her hand still outstretched towards me, as though lowering it will be giving in, letting me keep the card.

I turn, look at her, extend the card into her fingers, and she takes it from me, does not do me the small honour of trusting me, takes the time to check that it is my current police ID, then she places it in her pocket.

'What did you find out?' she asks.

'Nothing.'

I shake my head, turn away. I can feel the drink calling.

'I was informed that you stayed at the hotel for a little under three hours.'

That long, eh?

'You learned nothing in three hours?'

An explanation of the course taken by the afternoon is on my lips, but I manage to keep it to myself. Chief Inspector Hawkins does not want to hear it, of course, so I'd only be saying it to spew spite at her. I'd be throwing it at her, like one of those fucked off chimpanzees in a zoo who masturbates, and then tosses the sperm at the lower lifeforms lined up to watch him in his cage.

I really ought to be a higher lifeform than a chimp, although sometimes you have to wonder.

I look away. I look at the vodka bottle.

'She had nothing to say about the murders, other than that she knew about them. However, she does have the very solid alibi of having been up at that hotel for the last week. If you want, you could check their CCTV to see if she came and she went, but she and her partner both said she hadn't left.

'A friend of hers placed the article online. His name's Derek and he works at the Chronicle. She said she'd try to get him to send her his subscriber list. If he's done that, she hasn't passed it on to me yet.'

It may have been just under three hours, but that was literally all I got. In relation to the investigation, at least.

'Derek?'

'Didn't get a second name,' I say. 'He's all yours. If I get something from her before tomorrow, I'll let Inspector Kallas know.'

'You will let me know,' she says.

No further explanation looks to be forthcoming. That, at least, does not make sense, as the Chief Inspector, ball-busting young dude that she may be, is not a detective.

'What happened to Kadri?' I say finally, when the silence looks like it might become interminable.

'She's gone.'

'What d'you mean?'

'That's all. She's gone. Detective Constable Ritter is now the highest-ranking detective on the investigation, pending the arrival of a replacement for Inspector Kallas from Rutherglen. Until then, I will be working with Emma. Should you come into any information pertinent to the investigation, you will please pass it on to me first. I do not want you dealing directly with Detective Constable Ritter. I do not want you speaking to anyone at the station. And now that I have corrected my oversight and taken control of your ID, do not, under any circumstances, attempt to pass yourself off as an officer of Police Scotland, as you are not currently one, and more than likely won't ever be again.'

Another beat, the look growing steelier by the second, and then she turns to leave.

'What happened to Kadri?' I say to her back.

She gets to the door. Finally, I'm drawn from my seat, walking after her, aware that if I get too close I might do something stupid, might grab her, might fucking explode, and I stop in the middle of the room as she's crossing the threshold.

'What happened to Kadri?' I repeat, more loudly this time.

She pauses, her back still turned, and then she closes the door with a sharp rap, and the sound of her footsteps ring out more loudly in the hallway on her departure than on her hesitant arrival, and she is on her way.

42

The rain is tipping down, the weather these days deserve, and I stand across the precinct, beneath the cover of the walkway, watching the front door of the station, waiting for Harrison. I could have texted, I could have called, I could have sent a fucking pigeon, what difference would it have made? I need to speak to her, at some point she will emerge, and I know from the way Eileen works, she will not already have done so.

Found an empty small bottle of vodka lying around, tossed into the bottom of a cupboard. I don't know why it was there. Somehow it had escaped the fortnightly glass recycling collection. It must have known it had a purpose to serve, and that purpose is now, as I filled it to see me through the evening. I take a shot, then screw the lid on, and put it back in my pocket.

Already halfway through it, and I wonder how long I'll survive out here if Eileen doesn't come soon. Do I really want to be standing in the sodden cold, inappropriately dressed (of course), without booze? Trying to limit the frequency of slugs from the bottle, trying to limit the amount taken each time, trying to spin it out.

Look at my phone every now and again, part checking the time, part checking to see if there's a message from Kallas, maybe from Eileen. *I see you standing over there, Hutton. Go home!*

What's the plan? No idea. I've got nothing. I'm going to speak to Eileen, she's going to tell me whatever she feels like telling me, and then, I don't know. Sure, I want to saddle up, ride off to the rescue, save Kallas from the jaws of the beast – assuming she's in the jaws of a beast, and hasn't just gone back to Estonia to try to rescue her kids – but really, how practical is that? They're in there, at the station, working their arses off for her. They're not waiting for me. No one's thinking, if only our hero Hutton was here to save the day. And certainly, no one's looking out the window anticipating the arrival of Drunk Hutton, that even bigger arsehole. Drunk Hutton, only ever one sentence away from being a complete prick.

Another drink, another shiver in my wet clothes, another

regret at not wearing a waterproof coat or bringing an umbrella, except I don't own an umbrella, because I've never, in all my life, displayed the common sense required to buy one.

Another drink. And another.

Beginning to feel shitty. *Beginning!* Too much alcohol on an empty stomach, too much time spent walking through the pouring rain, too long standing still in the chill of the night, as the grim darkness seeps into me, my clothes having long ago given up any pretence at protection.

All my weight against the wall, eyelids beginning to droop regardless of the discomfort. Eyeing the ground, damp despite being undercover, and wondering if I might just sit down. It'd be so much easier. Or lie down. I could lie down, wait for Eileen like that, dosing, half an eye on the station door, leap heroically into action when she emerges.

God I'm tired. Tired and cold and old.

I can't lie down, I'd be asleep in seconds. Half an eye? Seriously… But sitting down, that's another thing. Clothes already soaking, what's a little more dampness?

And so I slide down the wall, settle on my hard, bony arse, ease it forward so I'm leaning back, marginally more comfortable, vodka bottle out the pocket, tip it back, not as much left as I thought there was. Sit it out, sit it out, maybe the phone will ring, maybe the phone will ping, maybe everything will come together, maybe Kadri is already home, maybe her husband called and asked her to meet him in Estonia, maybe I could go to Estonia, maybe I could fly…

* * *

'Tom!'

Gnawing, cold confusion.

'Tom!'

A disembodied hand on my shoulder, pressing, shaking, pushing. A horrible sense of bewilderment, my brain coated in thick, dark sludge.

'Tom! Wake up!' A beat. 'Jesus.'

Open my eyes.

One. Two. Three.

Fingers snapped in front of my face.

'Jesus. I'll call an ambulance.'

She stands, moves away from me.

'Stop.'

The daring, exciting, exhausting rush of reality. Eyes coming in to focus, I see her turn. Behind her a wall of rain. Why does it always rain?

Need to get up. Try to force myself off the wall, don't get very far, slump back with a grunt.

Fuck. Head feels like shit, mouth feels like shit.

'Is this all you've had?' asks Harrison, holding the small, empty vodka bottle.

Did I finish it? I don't remember finishing it. Must have spilled some.

'Yes.'

How easily the lies spill from the lips of the drunk.

Rub my hands across my face, tense the muscles in my upper body, arms and shoulders and neck, prepare properly, then force my body up off the ground, stagger to my feet, lean against the wall.

I could use a drink. She sees me looking at the bottle.

'We need to get you home.'

'Tell me about Kadri.'

'Really, Tom?'

'Where is she?'

'She's missing. We don't know. Now come on.'

She reaches to take my arm, and I pull away from her. A misstep, a stumble, catch myself, steady against the wall. Shut my eyes for a moment, take the time to reacquaint myself with a clear head, as though there's the slightest possibility of that.

One. Two. Three. *Mind in gear, Batman!*

'What's the story?'

'I'll tell you on the way home.'

'I'm not going home.'

'You're going home, you're going to bed. Come on.'

'What happened with Kadri?'

She grits her teeth. I, in turn, grit mine.

'We're working on it, Tom. And what d'you think you're going to be able to do? Look at you. Look at you!'

Her voice is raised, close to shouting, then I realise just how much noise the rain is making. One of those torrential downpours, timed by God, that total bastard, to coincide with stress and worry and panic and a need for action. A need to do *something*.

'Tell me about Kadri.'

215

The phrase *don't make me choose* stupidly comes into my head, and somehow I stop myself saying it.

'Fuck it,' says Harrison, shaking her head, glancing up at the station, then turning back. 'She went out around two this afternoon. Went to see Gill Blair,' and she finishes with a head shake, hands hopelessly tossed to the side.

'That's it? She hasn't been seen since then?'

'No.'

'You've been round there?'

'There's no one.'

'What about the husband?'

'Gone.'

'So, what? It's Blair? It's the husband? What?'

'We don't know, Tom. Now, you need to –'

'Why did she go on her own?'

'Really? She went on her own, Tom, because that's what we do often enough when we're stretched. We're stretched, you know we are…'

She stops herself, she shakes her head.

'Go on, say it.'

'I'm not going to bother, Tom. We both know. Now, come on, you need to get home. You're a mess.'

She looks up at the station, obviously thinking about calling for assistance.

'Oh, fuck off, Eileen,' I say.

Fuck Off Eileen, Dexy's ill-remembered follow-up.

'You're going home, Tom. You shouldn't be here, and certainly not like this.'

'Have you got an alert out for her? For them? Is it –'

'Emma's all over it, the chief's inserted herself at the top of the tree, we're waiting for Collinge to come up from Rutherglen tomorrow –'

'Collinge! That guy's a fucking mor –'

'It doesn't matter, Tom, doesn't matter who it is, and especially not to you. You removed yourself from the investigation. I know you can't help it, I –'

'Just, fuck off! Fuck off, Eileen.'

'Come on, you're coming home.'

She reaches out to take hold of my arm, and I slap her hand away, catching her hard. The anger flashes across her face, she grits her teeth. I know the look, I know how close I am to getting rid of her. And I don't want her here, I don't want her help, I

216

don't want her stopping me doing whatever the fuck it is I'm about to do now.

Of course, I have no idea what that actually is.

'Leave me.'

'I'm not leaving you.'

'Fuck off, Eileen, really. Fuck off. You're not my fucking mother. I release you from whatever obligation you feel.' A pause, we stare at each other, I can feel her resistance breaking. At some stage you have to let the fool and his determination to self-destruct have its way. 'Just get out of my sight,' I toss into the rainy night, and she scowls, takes a couple of paces away, stops, fights the competing urges, and then walks quickly away to her right, back beneath the station, towards the car park.

I watch her for a short while, and then decide to move quickly. She might come back. She *will* come back. I know Eileen. She'll get as far as the car, she'll be hating herself, she'll think about the fact that we might well have lost Kallas, and she can't be losing me the same day, and she'll be back.

I'm out into the rain, across the precinct at a run, keeping out of the low lights, running in the shadows beneath the main street. If I wasn't already damp, I'd be soaking in five seconds. Aware, as I run, of just how terrible I feel, out of breath in an instant, all that vodka swilling in my stomach, looking to come splashing back up, like waves in a storm on the rocks.

The thought of being sick makes me feel worse, makes the vomiting more likely.

I stop beneath the shadow of the tower block on the east side of the precinct and look back. Nausea rising, the sound of the rain thunderous, the noise all-consuming. Heavy summer rain in early October, the deluge of a long hot day, having not troubled us with the long hot day beforehand.

I see her now, hurrying back, slowing as she realises I'm not there. I lurk in the shadows, so she doesn't see me, and as she hurries on, round the far corner, I turn quickly away and run beneath the tower block, and then across the car park.

Don't get very far, and then I'm in between two cars, on my hands and knees, spewing up that evening's booze. One retch, then another and another. The pause, but I can still feel it, and I'm panting, and desperate, feeling like absolute shit, and then another splurge of sick rises within me, and I spew it out, as the rain bounces off the cars on either side of me.

I stay in that position, head hung forward, nose and mouth

217

hovering over my own sick, waiting to see if there's going to be any more, but that's all for the moment. However it is the strange vomit mechanism works, it's done its work for now, and finally I move a yard or two away and slump against the car, my head back, letting the rain wash my face, letting the rainwater into my mouth.

I spit, and repeat, and spit, and repeat.

I can apologise in the morning, that's what I'm thinking. Because I'm a selfish bastard, and that's how selfish bastards think. You can say and do what you like, you can use your friends as a punching bag, because when you've calmed down or sobered up or done whatever it is you need to do, you can apologise and they'll still be there for you, no matter how many times you do it, because you, you selfish, narcissistic prick, are what matters.

God, I need a drink.

Phone starts ringing. Eileen. Has to be Eileen. And she'll be somewhere, somewhere hereabouts, listening for the ring. I clip the ringer off while the phone's still in my pocket, and only if she's on the other side of the car would she have heard it, then I take it out, glance at it, end the call.

No other messages. Nothing from Kadri. Two minutes past midnight. Jesus. Eileen worked late. And I slept a long time, lying against a wall, a drunken bum.

The rain and the vomit sobers you up fast enough.

How long does it take to walk home? Forty minutes on a good day. In this state, in this weather, call it an hour. God, that sounds awful.

I'll need to find an open bar in between here and there. What are the chances? Think along the route, head resting back against the car. Zero, the chances are zero, because all the damned bars will be shut! Then, when I straighten my shoulders and look straight ahead, divine intervention.

A thought forms and spirals in a second. One tick of the clock to the next, three quick snaps of the fingers, and I burst out laughing. I mean, fuck it, why not?

St Stephens is right there, waiting for me. The house of God. Every useless bastard welcome! And the minister has her stash of booze.

That's too funny. Break into a church to steal the communion vodka. That's the stupid thought that forces itself into my head, and then I'm literally lolling to the side, laughing

---

218

at the phrase *communion vodka*. Like that's a thing.

Come on then, get to it. Break into the church. Steal the booze. God won't mind. I mean, one of His son's most famous miracles was helping folk get ratted at a wedding. Christianity loves drink. That's why communion exists, for fuck's sake. Blood of Christ, my arse.

Still laughing to myself, I crawl out from behind the car, and look back towards the precinct, towards the last place I saw Eileen.

No sign of her, no sound. I put my fingers to my lips, shooshing myself, even though I'm not making any noise, and, still giggling like a schoolboy, I start crawling in between the cars.

43

I stand still in the dark of the nave. The lights from outside, low at this time of night, dully illuminate the colours of the stained glass, allowing the most meagre of light into the church.

Every corner is dark, every pew enveloped in secrecy, the space a giant shroud, engulfed in silence as much as in shadow. Here now the quiet of the grave. The only sound had been my damp shoes, squelching down the carpet, and now that I've stopped walking, the rainwater drips from me, the sound of it hitting the floor cacophonous.

I take a seat, intending it will just be for a moment. That hilarious idea I had of breaking into a church suddenly seems stupid. Juvenile. Here it is, here it comes, the regret and the self-loathing, feelings that are only ever just around the corner. Sometimes they wait for morning, and sometimes they slap you right in the face at any time of day at all.

Tony Blair. Really? Should I just have let him lift his shovel, turn his back, and walk away? Maybe he didn't commit those first three murders, but then I blundered in to more or less tell him his wife was an adulterer, and he decided to take his revenge, sweeping Kallas up in the tumult as he went.

But really, a killer called Tony Blair? Ha! Just another name on a list, another herring in the net.

I lean forward, rest my head on the pew in front. Fucking idiot. Fucking loser. Fucking fool. Where's Jesus now, laughing with me as I bust the lock on the door, and enter His house to plunder His sacred booze?

Fuck it.

Straighten up, look around, eyes becoming adjusted to the dark.

Yep, it's kind of fucking creepy, I'll give it that.

I get up, force myself to be positive, stop for a second while I could go either way, and then turn and walk down the aisle towards the altar, or, more precisely, the door to the side of the altar that leads to the vestry.

The corridor is pitch black, no light shining from beneath a door. I did wonder if she'd be here, my delinquent minister, slowly getting hammered. As I take my phone from my pocket and walk down the corridor, leaving the door to the nave open behind me, I can't help feeling the utter childish stupidity of this.

Clink!

A funny little noise. I turn quickly. Heart suddenly thumping, I swallow. Look back into the nave, then lift the phone and shine the inadequate torch towards the cavernous gap. The torch picks up nothing.

It was a small sound, a safe sound, though I can't imagine what it was. Not a heavy footfall, not someone bumping into something, not someone creeping around behind me.

I swallow. Body tense, ears attuned to any disturbance in the silence, but there's nothing. The sound, whatever it was, came and it went.

I suddenly think of the dark corridor behind me. Hesitate before turning, and then I swivel quickly, torch shining into the small dark space beyond, and there's nothing. No one. No sound.

'Jesus,' I mutter quietly.

What in the name of fuck made me think *this* was a good idea?

I try the vestry handle, and the door opens. Shine the torch in, and the room stares blankly back at me. The chair is empty, the desk is tidy, the minister is not here.

I close the door and turn on the light, an internal room that will not betray itself to the outside. Here we are, the detective and his prey, a quiet room with a drawer containing vodka. What else could anyone need?

And what now? No point in stealing the drink and heading home. You have drink at home. No point in doing nothing.

This would be a fitting end to my career. To be found asleep and drunk in the vestry by the local minister. Or better, she sees the locks have been busted, she calls the cops, and over we troop from a hundred yards away, and I'm found in all my hopeless, plastered glory by a couple of my subordinates.

That has me smiling for the first time since the car park, and then I wonder if I should do something else stupid. Throw caution to the wind. To be found not just drunk, but naked! Naked, and having done something wonderfully and grossly vulgar, like masturbating into the vicar's gown.

I slump down into the seat, aware that I'm infecting everything with dripping water. Pull open the large desk drawer on the right, and there it is, splendid and perfect and delicious, just waiting for me. A half-full litre bottle of Absolut. I lift it out, then clink the two glasses together lifting them with my thumb and forefinger, and place them on the desk, then pour a healthy shot into both of them. Perhaps the act of pouring the second glass will summon company, in this house of miracles.

My phone vibrates, the sound still turned off.

I take a sip, what was meant to be a sip, but the glass doesn't leave my lips until it's tipped all the way back and it's been emptied.

God, cutting through the ugliness of the leftover vomit, it tastes wonderful. More, vicar, more!

I pour another glass, I clink it against the glass on the desk, as though my other half is here, and take a quick drink from the second glass.

Kallas. I was supposed to be thinking about Kallas. Where she'll have gone, and my part in her rescue. Except, of course, it's liable to be far too late to make the rescue. If she's been taken by Tony Blair, or Gill Blair, one of the Blairs! if one of them really is the killer, and Eileen sounded reasonably sure, then there's little chance of Kallas being found before it's too late.

Why keep the police officer alive? It just encourages them. Makes them think they're on to something, that they've still got a chance.

Look at my phone. It's not from Eileen as I'd assumed. Instead, Leia Fisher.

The text reads simply: **We're here all week if you want to do that again.**

Have barely given her any thought since leaving the place, but now that the suggestion is there... holy shit, that might not be a bad idea. Might as well make the most of my suspension. All in on the downbound train! Toot toot!

The phone goes again. Leia Fisher again.

Derek sent me the list. Seventy-nine names. Here you are. See you later! :) xx

Fucking hate that smiley thing. And *see you later*, the fuck does that mean?

She's copied the list of names into the message, and I scroll down, a quick look through, glass of vodka in my hand, a sip corresponding to roughly ten entries. Trying not to rush, don't want to miss anything, knowing that it might, in any case, be utterly meaningless.

What does a name on this list mean anyway? The person is interested in niche Cambuslang and Rutherglen news? Big fucking deal. I mean, it's sad, but it's barely of significance.

I stop.

Blink a couple of times. Drain the glass, lay it back down, don't immediately refill.

Scroll through the rest of the names, all bland and unrecognisable, and then go back up to the name that stopped me in my tracks.

There are no coincidences, that's what Taylor and I used to say, right?

Don't think about Taylor.

Everything happens for a reason, everything you do, every decision you make is for a reason. And now, here I am, sitting in the vestry of the church of a fucked up, distraught and overworked minister, who's had the year from Hell, and her name pops up on a list.

No way, no way, I can hear some detached voice in my head.

Of course the minister's on the list. Why wouldn't the minster be on the list? She needs to know what's going on in society, she needs to know what's going on with her parishioners, and she can't get it all from gossip at the bake sale.

If it's nothing, explain that uncomfortable feeling in your stomach, then, you fuck.

I open the drawer again, start raking through the papers. I don't know what I think I might find, but I'm looking for it anyway.

Nothing in this side, open up the large drawer on the left. Jesus, an unopened litre bottle of Glenfiddich. Classy. You've got the moves, babe.

More paper, more church business, a book with a list of addresses. Now the two shallow drawers at the top. A Bible, and pencils, pens, a hole punch and a stapler, and the standard detritus of office life, and I rummage around and there's nothing there, not even anything that's slightly scandalously interesting, nothing filthy like I would imagine this vicar possessing in her office drawer.

Push the chair back, open the large cabinet to the right, the only other piece of furniture in this small room, bar the desk and chairs. Where's the box of plastic face masks, where's the box

———

223

of crippling evidence?

Not in here. Gowns, three different colours, and other ceremonial garments. Jesus, I didn't realise a Church of Scotland minister wore all this crap. Maybe she's a secret Catholic. Ha! There'd be plenty around here who'd think that worse than being a secret serial killer.

I close the cupboard door, look over the small room. Stare at the vodka bottle. For the first time in I don't know how long, I don't want any. The thought of it tastes sour in my mouth. Look at that. *Drinker Has Had Enough Shock!*

Bollocks. I'll be pouring myself another glass in about five minutes if I'm still here.

Hands thrust in damp pockets, as I look around the room. What do I have to show for my brilliant plan of breaking into the church?

Fuck it, I got the booze, that was why I came in here, right? I didn't know the minister was on the list, I didn't come here expecting to find a vital piece of evidence, or a thing, or Gill Blair tied to a table, or Kallas sparked out on a chair, waiting in line in the laceration queue. I came for drink, I got it, and now what?

I'm freezing. With the end of the game for the evening, comes the cold, and the shiver, and the awareness that I still feel like shit. Funny how drinking vodka on top of an on-going drunken hangover doesn't make you feel any better.

I look at the still-full second glass, all of thirty seconds after deciding I didn't want any more.

Thirty seconds. You lasted that long, eh? Jesus…

Rub my hands across my face, damp and cold, notice my fingers are starting to turn white.

The phone goes again, even the vibrate on the table loud and grating in the late night silence. Leia Fisher: **Did you find what you were looking for?**

I read it without thinking. Brain not really firing, after all.

Try to switch on. Why does she care? Why is she looking for me to text at midnight? Then I have a *wait, what?* moment. Wait, what? What does it actually mean?

Your mind creates stories when it's in this fractured, late night state.

Does she really mean did I find a name on the list, or does she know I'm here, searching through random drawers?

How could she?

_____

See you later.

Lean forward on the desk, head racing – insomuch as any head which has taken this much abuse can race – trying to think of their set-up at the hotel in Gleneagles. How easy would it be for her to sneak out of there, late at night, without anyone from the hotel noticing?

A ground floor suite. The double doors. She could walk out of there in a second, through the woods, nip across a fairway, she'd be at the main road in a few minutes, and she could have a car parked. No record of her leaving, all the time in the world, leaving behind the perfect alibi. We can't know the depth of their relationship, but she certainly knows plenty about Champlain that Champlain doesn't want widely known, so she'd have that threat to dangle over her should she refuse to cover for her. The lover doesn't need to know what Fisher's doing.

Dammit. I should've handed it over to Kallas last night, when I had the chance. Now here I am, always the last clown left sitting in the clown car.

So, could Fisher have followed me down? Planted a tracking device on me? Maybe they opened my phone when I was in the shower. Could I just open some fucker's phone? Not a chance, but it doesn't mean she couldn't. If she's capable of everything we've seen so far, she'd be capable of that.

The light goes out.

Breath catches in my throat. Heart stops. I fumble for my phone, fumble like a fool, bring up the wrong screen, and again, finally open the torch app. Shine it at the door.

The door stares blankly back at me.

Then, from somewhere in the church, there is a loud, single clang. Deep. A sound that booms through the building, and echoes off into the far distance.

Then, nothing.

44

Jesus, this sobers you up faster than a bucket of ice water.

I stand by the desk, phone held up, light on the door. Every muscle tensed, straining to hear any sounds from the building. An approach from along the corridor, the scuttle of feet.

A sudden thought that maybe it's just the police. A couple of plods from our place, investigating a reported break-in. Maybe I tripped a wire. Maybe they killed the lights to throw the robber off his game.

Maybe, fucking maybe.

Grit my teeth, ignore the reflex to get a shot of vodka before action, then walk to the door, slip my phone into my pocket. I don't turn off the torch, just place the light against my leg so that it's not visible, yet easily accessible if required. Fingers on the handle, final steel of the nerves, and then I slowly open the door.

Braced for there to be someone there, but I'm greeted by darkness, no sense of anyone else.

Another pause, another swallow, another moment before stepping forward into the fire.

'Come on Hutton, don't be a pussy,' I murmur quietly to the night, and then I'm out of the vestry and into the short corridor, and walking towards the nave.

Wondered if I might see torchlight all over – that would likely be the case if this was the coppers – but the nave greets me with the same darkness as it did earlier.

Altar at the front, next to a low pulpit, the rows of pews stretching beyond, with two small side sections, and a large central area. So much shadow and darkness. So many things hidden.

I start walking back down the left hand aisle. What's the plan now, Genius? Get the fuck out of Dodge? Call the cops? Really? Or wander around like a lemon in the dark, waiting to get jumped.

I feel completely owned by the situation. It's dark. Impenetrable. I could hide, I could wait, I could be the deliverer of the jump scare; but here I am, on the back foot, wandering,

226

searching, hoping.

Freeze. The noise again.

Clink!

What *was* that? Something tapping against metal? Water dripping onto a pipe? Just water. A drip, echoing through the silence.

Or blood. It could be blood.

Calm the fuck down.

But suddenly I can smell it, sense it, sense the other person here in the nave, lurking somewhere in the shadows.

I stop, turn, look around. No one behind, creeping up on me. Heart pounding. Imagination rampaging through the night. Damp clothes sticking, cloying, clutching, starting to feel warm, uncomfortable.

Phone vibrates again. She's fucking taunting me. Phone out, bring the message up.

Leia Fisher: **You're no fun, Sergeant.**

Jesus, what does she want me to do? Where does she want me? I'm staggering clumsily around, lost in the dark, the beam from my phone a giant target on my head. Fuck me.

Heart galloping, breath catching in my throat, constant movements of my head, not wanting to be blind-sided. Fearing the scurrying attack from behind. From the shadows of a pew. From the balcony looming ominously above.

I need to stop, stop moving, but I can't do it here, now, in the middle of the nave. I have to get to a wall, set my back against it, wait for the attack, the torch sweeping back and forth.

My breathing sounds so loud now. Horrible and gasping and desperate in the black pit of this place. I can feel the uncomfortable stir of nausea in my stomach, up my throat, driven by too much alcohol and tension, adrenaline and fear.

The phone vibrates again!

You fucking bitch! Enough! Just come at me, for fuck's sake!

Throat dry, yet tickled by the threat of sick, hand shaking.

A photograph. Leia Fisher on the bed, Champlain beside her, head turned away so her face isn't in the picture. They're both naked, gorgeous, beautiful, teasing, promising.

They must have taken it earlier. That's my first thought. It's not true. Can't be true. Doesn't make sense otherwise, because she's here.

I swallow. Look up.

That's when I feel the stab of pain in my leg, the rush of it, as the vomit rises in my throat. I feel dizzy and discombobulated and lost, and I slump forward, phone falling from my fingers, reaching for the back of a pew, missing, slumping uncomfortably and painfully in between the seats.

45

Open my eyes. Blurred sight. Close them again. Open. Blink. Squeeze eyelids. Smell vomit. Close eyes. Gag. Swallow. Open eyes wide, try to move rest of face. Nothing happening. Try to move my arms. Nothing. Stare straight ahead.

Everything slowly beginning to clear, though it doesn't make sense. Women. Lots of women.

Lots of women?

Take your time, Hutton. Slow down. Think. Count. Break it down, woman by woman. There aren't lots of women.

Where's the writer? She should be here. Mental. Batshit. The batshit writer, messing with people's lives. Mine too. She messed with my life. We had sex. Me, her, someone else. Wasn't she supposed to be here?

I see the picture of her and the other woman in bed. When was that taken? Earlier. Wasn't it earlier? That's what I thought. A Blue Peter photograph – *here's one I prepared earlier* – to make it look like she wasn't in the church, stalking me.

My own fault for going to the church. Should've gone home with Eileen.

'Where's the writer?' I say, trying out my voice.

Voice still works, though I don't recognise it. Don't recognise myself. Maybe it's not me.

'What writer?'

Who was that? One of the women. There aren't that many.

Wait, I'm naked. Didn't see that coming. On a wooden chair. Neck feels sore. Must have slept funny. Can't move my arms, can't move my legs, maybe because of the duct tape. That'll be it.

My eyes fall on Kallas. A couple of feet away, also bound. Wrists tied together, ankles tied together, torso strapped to the chair. Eyes closed, head slumped uncomfortably to the side. Not a natural position. That'll hurt later. She's not naked. I wonder why that is?

So, who spoke then?

The minister.

The minister. My eyes fall on her. She's also on a wooden

chair. She's not naked either. Black pedal pushers, white tunic top. Flowy.

She's not bound.

Wait, she's not bound. And she just asked 'what writer?'

There's someone else, another woman, but she's on the table. Like a regular kind of a dining table, but long, long enough to hold the length of a body. This woman might be asleep.

Gill Blair. It's Gill Blair. The suspect.

Some suspect she's turned out to be. Never a good look when a suspect ends up a victim.

She's bleeding. Jesus she's bleeding. A lot of blood. Maybe she's not asleep. Maybe she's dead.

I watch her chest, blood covered pale skin, barely moving. No, not barely, there's no movement at all.

Her husband must have got to her. That'll be it. Where's the husband? Don't see the husband. Just women. Maybe the husband locked us all in here. He's off somewhere now, another part of the building or the house or wherever we are. Getting a cup of tea, going to the toilet. That'll be it. Kill someone, break for tea, kill someone else.

That doesn't make sense.

Look around you. *Look!*

There are just three women here, that's all. One bound, one dead, one free.

One free. A killer, Tony Blair or anyone else, would not have wandered off leaving one of his potential victims sitting happily on a chair, unbound.

Like I couldn't have seen this coming.

I'm waking up now, waking up.

Joy to the fucking world!

The minister. Jesus, it's always the minister. Seriously. The minister or the priest. They've got this respectable cover, under which they can do whatever the fuck they want. Same thing happened here a few years ago with the last fucking guy, or some fucking guy, maybe not the last minister. But *a* minister. A fucking minister. All that God crap, and they use it as camouflage.

I have a million questions. I think I do. I mean, I should have a million questions after all. And yet, now that I have the perpetrator here, assuming the one person in the room neither bound nor dead is the perpetrator, the first question that emerges, as she and I look each other in the eye, is, 'What?'

She's leaning forward, feet planted squarely on the ground, legs at ninety, forearms resting on her thighs, glass of vodka or gin or water or something in her hand. Let's assume vodka, it'll suit narrative consistency.

'What?' she says, mimicking my question, rather than asking what I mean.

'Got any more of that?' I ask.

She lifts the glass, asking if that's what I meant, and I nod.

She has no blood on her tunic. That's impressive. She's wearing a white tunic, she slashed the absolute shit out of poor Blair here, and yet, not a drop made it onto her white top. God, if that was me, I'd look like a butcher.

'I don't think that's a good idea,' she says. 'Ironic, really.'

'Why?'

'I offered it to you a couple of nights ago. You didn't want it. Now that your body's full of GHB, and I'm guessing, you already had too much to drink, and I'm thinking you're going to be a borderline basketcase, *now* you want it? Seems ironic. Anyway, you're not getting any.'

I glance at Kallas, head at an awkward angle, no sign that the sound of conversation might stir her into consciousness.

'So, what's happening?' I ask.

I could really use that drink.

Goodbody laughs, takes another glug from the glass, the way her face briefly contorts indicates she's drinking it neat, shakes her head.

'I just killed Mrs Blair here. Kind of pointless now, really. She deserved it after all, they all did, but now...' and she indicates Kallas, and she indicates me, then she takes another drink, this time unable to lower the glass until she's drained it, then she sets the glass down on the floor, beside the bottle.

'Where's her husband?'

She holds my gaze, looks troubled by the question, lowers her eyes, face a haunted scowl.

'He's dead,' is all she says.

Silence.

This woman is as damaged as I am. We would make a perfect couple.

'What's the plan?'

'Now look, Detective Genius Boy, I'm not getting into some Poirot, Scooby Doo type of shit, where I confess everything. She's dead, her husband's dead, the others are dead, now you're about to be dead.'

She looks at Kallas.

'I have no idea what I'm going to do with her, she's not supposed to be here.'

'Why am I?'

She's got the duct tape in her hand now. Seems she's keen to shut me up. This is where I'm supposed to think of something brilliant to say to stay her hand, to keep me and Kallas alive, until I can pull the great escape from the bag.

Something brilliant…

'Why am *I* supposed to be here?' I ask again, as it's all I've got. I don't like the quality of desperation in my voice. Not a good sound.

'You killed someone, didn't you, Sergeant? All these people, with their cavalier ways, their cavalier attitudes, with their careless and casual arrogance. Just a virus, just the flu, it won't affect me, and it won't affect you. Harry Lord killing his father, wiping out the people in the home, and Cowal… he might as well have put a knife in his wife's heart… Round and round we go. That bloody woman with her malicious social media shit, and poor Gill here… She knew Cowal was infected, she kept on keeping on, couldn't stop herself. Couldn't say no.' A beat. Her face drops, eyes deaden. 'Did she kill anyone? I don't actually know. But she… she was the problem. Her, and her type. Didn't care. Thought they'd be fine, and huzzah for them, they were fine. Nothing to worry about. But how many people did they infect along the way?'

She's just talking, and talking – so much for wanting to avoid the Scooby Doo situation! – though there's not much more to say, the words blending into the room, the stark, pale room, with plain walls and nothing to live for, and I'm included in this, and I know why I'm included, but she shouldn't know, she really shouldn't. How can she?

'How?' I say, interrupting her. I don't know the last thing she said.

I need to talk about this, but I don't want to. I don't want to think about it, because thinking about it makes me want to vomit. And it makes me want to drink myself to death, which is what I've been trying to do for the last two and a half months. And I would have done, if my fucking body didn't keep rebelling, spewing forth the invading alcohol at will.

232

She looks at me, almost pityingly, then she steps forward, stretches out the tape with a smack, and wraps it quickly around my mouth, back of the head, back round again a couple of times.

'Can't have you screaming,' she says.

'How?' comes crying from my lips, but there's nothing bar the dull, anguished grunt from deep in my throat, and then she's placed the duct tape on the ground, and she's lifted the knife, and without even thinking about it, without pausing, without calculating, she inserts the point of the knife in my shoulder, deep, then pulls it down and out, cutting the skin, while the blood oozes, and then flows.

Another useless grunt.

'Your buddy here really fucked this up,' says Goodbody. 'She wasn't supposed to be here, she wasn't supposed to walk in on me when I went to get this one. I don't want to have to kill her. I don't want that. God doesn't want it. Hah!'

Head shaking, she turns away. Jesus, if she's going to give me a thousand cuts at this rate... holy shit.

'Fuck it,' she barks from nowhere, then she turns back to me, squeezes the knife in behind the tape, with one harsh sweep she cuts it, and then she yanks it painfully away from my mouth, and this time my gasping groan is much louder.

'Tell me,' she says, and I can feel the blood on my cheek, the pain of the tape still fresh. 'Tell me,' she repeats, and she presses the edge of the knife against my forehead, just above my right eye.

'What?'

'Why you're here, Sergeant. Go on, tell me why you're here, you selfish, drunken fuck.'

I swallow. The thought of it, of why I'm here, is much worse than the knife and the cuts and the tape ripped across an unshaven face.

She leans in towards me, presses the knife harder so that it breaks the skin, and now her face is contorted with hatred.

'Tell me now, tell the fucking world, or I'll do to your face what I did to Malone, and first of all I wake up your friend here, and she'll have to watch, and she'll have to listen to you screaming.'

Close my eyes. Don't make me do this. Just fuck off. Leave me alone. Let me die. Stab me. Drive that knife into me. That'll do, Donkey, that'll fucking do. Come on!

'Just stab me, you coward.'

'Hah!'

'Stab me, come on. Do it properly. Just kill someone for once, instead of all this affected thousand cuts bullshit. Come on!'

'Fuck off, Sergea –'

'Come on!'

'Tell me what you did!' she shouts, and with it she flicks the knife, and it cuts a line across my forehead.

'Just fucking do it!'

'Tell me what you did!' again, and this time she slashes the knife across my face, and blood spurts, and now, *now*, she's got blood on her white tunic, the bitch.

'Come on!' I shout, straining at the bonds, and God I wish I could be free. I'd grab that fucking knife and stab myself with it and save her the trouble. 'Come on, you bitch! Come on!'

'What did you do?' she yells, and she slashes the knife across my thigh, and I wince and cry out, an ugly, loud sound, filled with the pain of the cut, and the pain of what she wants me to say.

'What did you do?' Knife jabbed into my leg.

'What did you do?' Knife into the leg.

'What did you do?' Again.

'What did you do?' Again.

'Fuuuuuck!'

'What did you do!' at a scream, again the knife, the point left in this time, then dramatically whipped out. Blood spurts.

'Fuuuuuck!'

'What did you do?' Another quick jab, higher up the thigh. 'What did you do?' Jab. 'What did you do?' Jab.

And finally, finally…

'I killed him!' comes screaming from contorted lips.

46

Blood covering my legs, pain shooting through my body, sweating, heart racing, blood in my mouth, *blood in my mouth?*, must have run in from my cheek, or maybe I've bitten my tongue or my cheek, the taste of it melding with the taste of sick, and now finally she pulls away, slumping down into the seat opposite, leaning forward, breathing hard, elbows on her knees, bloody knife held in hot, limp hands.

She lets the silence grow, lets the drama of the last minute subside, the pause before the next explosion of action or sound or confession. An explosion of confession. That's a moment in which we all belong.

I'm breathing hard, head down, gasps of air taken in through bloody pain, waiting for the endorphins to kick or for something to kick in, or maybe I just need to rile her more. She's already deviated from her normal practice, maybe I can get her to just hurry the fuck up. Get this all over with.

'How do you know?' comes uncomfortably from my mouth.

She watches me for a moment, leans back, lifts the bottle, takes a long swig of vodka, more or less thumps the bottle back down on the floor, steadies it, then once again leans forward into the silence.

Eventually...

'You told me,' she says, voice steady and slow. A beat. 'You confessed.'

'No.'

Wince, as another shard of pain from my leg suddenly decides to race through me, as though the knife had just been thrust into it once more.

'No,' I force out again.

'For God's sake. No one... not one of you will admit it, will you? You all want to think you played no part, as though this virus spreads itself. As though the virus doesn't spread because people are selfish. But you, Sergeant, you know what you did, and that is some fantasy you've created to protect yourself. It's not working out too well for you though, is it?'

She holds my gaze, a malicious look, contemptuous, then

she leans forward and swipes the blade suddenly across my knee, the cut shallow and painful.

'Fuck!'

'Tell me about DCI Taylor,' she says, and my contorted, bitter and twisted face falls, and the hurt of it, the hurt of the name, the hurt of her knowing, the hurt of her using it, beating me with it, torturing me with it, is worse than the jabbing, screaming pains in my legs.

'Tell me!'

'You said I already confessed,' I manage to squeeze meagrely, abjectly from my lips.

'You talked about him as though he was still alive. That's what you do. That's how you think. But you know, you *know* that I know he's dead. I took his funeral for God's sake.' I can't lift my eyes to her. 'That, then, was your confession. The pretence wasn't about being unable to live without your beloved former boss. It was guilt. Guilt that the chief inspector died of Covid, guilt that you might have given it to him. How does anyone really know where they got it from? But you... you think you passed it on to him, don't you?'

Bile rises up my throat, the tears rise in my eyes. They both stall, and the dry sob belches uncontrollably from my lips.

'Do you *know* you gave it to him?'

Nothing in the question but scorn. I don't answer.

'Do you *know*?' she spits out.

'Of course not,' I spit back.

'But you had symptoms and you came to work, and you didn't... give... a fuck who you hurt.'

Sounds formulate in my mouth, but I have no words, and all that comes is an anguished cry.

'Jesus, you people. All the fucking same.'

She stands up quickly, pushing her chair back, taking a step or two away. Then she bends, lifts the vodka, takes a swig, pauses, another, then settles the bottle back down.

She turns now, regards me with the same look she's held for the past few minutes.

'We are kindred spirits, Sergeant,' she says. 'I suppose you'd like me to finish you off quickly.'

Stare at the floor, sweat and blood and fuck knows what else runs off my face.

'Do what you fucking want,' forces its way out.

Feeling tired all of a sudden. Wait, wait, that wound in my

leg, the worst one, the one that hosed, it's still pulsing blood. Slowly now, but it's coming, and it's not the only one. Ha! I'm bleeding out. Hallelujah! I'm bleeding out, you fucker!

'Maybe I want to cut up your little friend here,' she says. 'How d'you feel about th –' She laughs, laughs in my face, as my head shoots up, a darting glance at Kallas, before turning quickly back to Goodbody. 'Ooh, what was that?'

Grit my teeth, lips clamped shut, nothing to be done about the malice shooting from my eyes.

'That wasn't just not wanting to lose another boss. That was... do you have a thing for your inspector, here? Do you, Sergeant? How romantic. The drunken, wasted piece of shit sergeant has a crush on the girl. Well, well, well... we're practically in a Doris Day movie.'

I can't look at her. Can't look at Kallas either. How easily I betray myself. So I stare at the floor, inept and bleeding and condemned.

'Cat got your tongue, eh? Well, here we are, in a fine pickle.' She picks up the vodka, drinks, settles back to stare at me. 'I didn't really know what to do with the girl, to be honest. Stumbled into each other when I was taking care of this clown and her husband. Had to bring her along. Obviously, I can't let her live, but... I don't know anything about her. No reason to inflict particular punishment. Now, however, now that the sergeant has shown his hand...'

'Leave her alone.'

'Ha!'

'Leave her!'

'Such desperation. How sweet. How loyal. Do you love her, Sergeant? Do you? That would be very, very romantic.'

Close my eyes, face tensed, bracing against the pain and the moment.

'I asked you a question, Chipper,' she says, and her voice is much closer, and when I open my eyes, her face is only a few inches from mine. 'I asked you a question, *Chipper*,' she repeats.

'Fuck off.'

She jabs her finger into the open wound in my shoulder, moves it around inside, as the tortured howl comes roaring from my throat.

'What d'you think, Chipper? I asked a simple question, that's all. Easy enough to answer, isn't it? A simple yes or no will do. No need for us to be uncivil, is there?'

237

She pulls her finger out of the wound, suddenly, brutally, and I yelp with the pain of it, and then there's instant relief that her finger's not there anymore, but still the gnawing, nagging, underlying hurt of the invasion of the wound, and the word 'fuck' escapes my lips, and she says, 'Let's do that again!' with the mock enthusiasm of a children's TV presenter.

'Yes!' I cry, 'Yes, I love her, Jesus!'

'Ha!'

'Happy? Just… just let her go.'

'Really, Chip? Really? This isn't some kind of science fiction bullshit. I can't erase her memory. She's dying.'

I struggle hopelessly against the bonds, and then, because it's all I can do, and I'm so full of anger, I spit blood across the short distance, onto her already stained white blouse.

'Oh, for God's sake,' she mutters, head shaking, then she takes another mouthful of vodka, barely seeming to even notice the latest bloody mark on her top.

'I've got nothing against her,' says Goodbody. 'I mean, fuck, I don't know her. But you, Sergeant. You're the problem. You, and all the rest like you. You brought so many people, so many families, so many businesses and institutions to their knees, because you were a selfish… fuck,' and she spits the last word. 'You're a selfish fuck.'

'Kill me then! Just do it!'

Another drink, bottle tipped far back, coming to the end. God, she's got guts of steel.

'Your girlfriend's going first. You get to watch.'

'Fuck!'

'Thought you might enjoy it. Tell you what, I'll give you a thrill. I'll undress her for you. I'm guessing what we have here is one of those unrequited things that people make movies about, so you two won't have, you know... You're not going to have banged the boss, and certainly not after what you did to the last one. I mean, you really fucked him, right?'

Can't even bring myself to ejaculate a profanity towards her.

Now, for the first time since I've woken up here, she turns her attention to Kallas, who has sat unmoving and unconscious throughout. Goodbody leans forward, elbows on her knees again, knife held loosely in her fingers.

She studies Kallas for a while, watching her breathe. I become aware that the only sound is my own heavy, gasping breaths, the drip of blood from my legs to the carpet.

'She's so beautiful,' says the minister, her voice suddenly altered. Softer, quieter, the edge having gone. 'I mean, when you really look at her like this. She's beautiful.'

'Let her live then,' I say, as though all Goodbody's been waiting for to change her mind is a sign of God's hand at work.

'I can't,' says Goodbody, her tone unchanged, her anger dissipated. 'You know I can't. Anyway, all things must pass, everyone has their time. And time has come prematurely for plenty of people this year. What's another one or two?'

Her eyes haven't left Kallas, and then finally she turns to me, holds my gaze for a moment, smiles and says, 'Let's see what lies beneath, shall we?' and then gets up out of her seat.

'Come on, you fucking coward,' I spit at her, but the words have nowhere to go.

'Let's just make sure she's as out as we all think,' says Goodbody, and with that she brutally strikes Kallas across the face, open hand, a loud, perfectly timed slap.

Kallas's head jerks to the right, her body pulls against the constraints, and then she settles back into position.

'Ha! Look at that,' says Goodbody, 'Well, you don't mind if we don't try to wake her up before the big event, Sergeant?'

She steps forward again, begins to cut the tape around her chest that binds her to the chair, then she pulls it away, and it lifts Kallas's black blouse, pulling it tight, and then it comes away and Goodbody scrunches up the tape and tosses it aside.

'Think we'll leave the bonds on her wrists and legs for the moment,' she says, her tone again like a children's TV presenter, explaining how to make a telephone out of two tin cans and a piece of string. 'Can't be too careful.'

She turns and gives me a strange smile, as though we're all in this together.

'You engaged, Sergeant? You ready for the big reveal?'

Her eyes are wide, the intoxication showing, then she turns back to Kallas, holds the knife to the side, so that the blade is coming out of the bottom of her fist, grabs either side of the blouse and rips it open. Beneath, Kallas's pale chest, her small breasts in black lace.

'Ooh, look at that,' says Goodbody. 'What d'you think, Chipper?' She turns to give me another smile, and then looks back at Kallas. Now, the knife placed almost gingerly in the join between the cups in the bra, she pulls it tight, and then whips the

239

knife through it.

Her breasts are revealed, the bra falls to the side, and Goodbody pushes it beneath Kallas's arms out of the way. I'm expecting her to turn, insomuch as I'm expecting anything, because fuck it, I'm feeling tired, I really am, and sleep would be so nice, but she doesn't. She doesn't turn.

She's held there for a moment, captivated by Kallas's beauty, and then she reaches out, a tentative finger, and slowly runs it over the skin of Kallas's right breast. Across the nipple, which does not react to the touch, and around and down across her taught stomach.

'Jesus,' mutters Goodbody. 'I never looked this good in my life, even when I was eighteen.'

She turns to look at me now, her pupils seriously dilated, the look on her face this strange mixture of hate and wonder.

'How does it feel?' she says. 'To get so close, and yet –'

The movement, when it comes, is quick, brutal, instant. Kallas lifts her bound hands, up, over Goodbody's head. There's time for the shock to show on her face, but that's all. Bound wrists around Goodbody's neck, Kallas uses the purchase to force herself up off the seat, and then her weight is on the minister, driving her back, then the two women are falling, and Goodbody smacks her head off the table and hits the ground with a thud, the knife skittering from her fingers across the floor.

Kallas kneels on her back, pulls the chokehold tight, forcing her hands together behind Goodbody's neck.

The last thing I think, before finally blacking out, is that Goodbody is already knocked out or dead, but Kallas is here for the fight, and does not relax.

And that is all I can remember.

47

'You're like James Bond,' says Harrison. There's a flippancy to her words, but not her tone. 'Seriously, what is it with you?'

I smile, and discover that it doesn't actually hurt to smile, which is good because it hurts to do pretty much everything else.

'I do what I can,' I say, weakly.

'Most of us manage to solve crimes without too much drama... but look at you. Sex with as many women as possible? Check. Invariably end up in hospital? Check. Constantly on the point of getting kicked out of your job? Check... Bond. James Bond. You're a piece of work.'

Outside there's one of Springsteen's unbelievable blue skies. Inside, white sheets and magnolia walls, the antiseptic sterility of a hospital ward. I'm sure I usually get my own room in these circumstances. We must be making cutbacks. There are three other occupied beds, two old guys asleep, another bloke talking to his wife.

I close my eyes for a moment, rest my head further back against the pillow. Lost a lot of blood, they say. Nearly bled out, they say. Stitches in my shoulder, on my legs, on my face. Going to have scars to remind me, and plenty of them.

Mouth dry, reach out, lift the cup and straw without opening my eyes, take a drink, place it back on the table.

'I think maybe I'll be getting kicked out anyway,' I say. 'About time.'

There's a pause, a silence, the peculiar kind of silence that sounds like it ought to be filled by something, and I open my eyes.

'Not what I heard,' says Harrison.

I straighten up, finally manage to prop myself a little further up in bed.

Eileen looks as wonderful as ever. A heavy winter jumper – must be cold out – high neck, blonde hair down over her shoulders.

'I'm sorry about the thing,' I say.

She holds the look. This is a conversation we've had before, earlier this year, previous years, a multitude of times.

241

Feels a little different this time.

One of these days, I always think, she won't be so forgiving. I think it, but don't really believe it. I think it, but there's another thought – the narcissist's crutch – that says everything will be fine. Sorry, so easily spilled from one's lips, will be the cure-all.

She doesn't speak. She kind of nods, just a small movement. An acknowledgement that I spoke, but not necessarily an acknowledgement that the apology is accepted.

That's all I'm getting.

She possibly thinks this isn't the time to have the conversation, and I'm not man enough to start it. And anyway, what's there to say? Words are meaningless. All that's left is time, and the time needs to be filled with the guilty party – me – not doing what it was that's created this atmosphere in the first place. Me, going days and weeks and months and years choosing to be a friend rather than an asshole.

The prospects don't look so great for Sgt Harrison and I.

'What d'you mean?' I ask, to fill the void.

'About what?'

'That I won't be getting kicked out? The chief's gunning for me.'

'I believe the inspector might have come to your aid. Like Theoden turning up at Pelennor Fields.'

Smile at that, but then, Theoden dies.

'Kadri's all right?'

'Sure. Not a scratch on her. Looks like she can take care of herself.'

OK, that was the nagging worry at the pit of my stomach. I hadn't thought about it enough to have located it yet, but now that I hear Kallas is fine, my stomach relaxes.

'She shouldn't be protecting me,' I manage.

'She's your boss, it's her job.'

'I didn't do anything.'

'To hear her tell it, she would've died if you hadn't been there.'

I hold Harrison's gaze, searching her eyes for the joke or the teasing or the disbelief, but there's nothing there. Literally nothing there. Harrison is here, sitting by my bed because she feels she should be. It's what friends do.

I smile wanly, tiredness beginning to sweep back over me. Try to recall the evening. Which evening was it? Last night? The night before? Time is lost.

Maybe Kallas is not wrong. If I hadn't been there, perhaps she would just have been killed. There would have been no showmanship, no drama, the minister wouldn't have had time to get drunk.

'Is she dead?' I ask.

A moment, and then, 'The vicar?'

Go to reply, but the word stalls on my lips, and I nod instead.

'No. Knocked unconscious. She's in hospital, under guard. Not this hospital.'

I want to ask what was going on, what was her motivation, but there's nothing there. No more words to be spoken. Anyway, wasn't her motivation clear? Revenge on a society that had failed itself. A society that couldn't cope with inconvenience for too long. Here I am, hand raised, one of the many to blame.

My eyes are closed. The sounds of the ward, of the hospital, of a distant road outside, blend slowly into one. I feel Harrison's soft lips on my forehead and feel no more.

* * *

When I wake up there's someone standing at the window. Dark out there now, the blind is raised – though I'm sure I saw a nurse lower the blind at some point – and the lighting in the ward is low. Night lighting.

He turns, seeming to feel that I'm awake, then he nods and comes to sit down beside the bed.

'Hey,' he says.

'Hey,' I reply.

It's hard to look at him. I'm not sure I can do it without crying. I don't want to cry.

'Pulled another one out the bag by the skin of your teeth,' he says with a smile. 'You have a way about you.'

I make some kind of rueful noise as a substitute for words.

I don't know what to say. The last two months I've had no trouble talking to Taylor. The idea of him. Me and Dan, huddled over a bottle of vodka, talking through the case, talking about anything. He didn't need to know what happened. He didn't need to know my part in his downfall. No one did.

And then I blurted it out, because that's who I am, always totally fucking useless under pressure, always selfishly spewing forth the inner me – some fucking James Bond I'd be – and now it's out there. The secret is revealed. And it's not just that I said it to the minister, and not just that Kallas was presumably awake throughout and will have heard. It's *out there*, dammit. That's what matters. It's not just Goodbody and Kallas that know, the Universe knows. *Everyone* knows.

Taylor knows.

I wanted to say to him when he was in hospital, but of course, of course, none of us could get to see him.

'I'm sorry,' finally appears in my mouth.

I open my eyes. He's leaning forward, elbows on his knees, head down, and then he looks at me, feeling that my eyes are open.

I want to say it again. I want to be able to give an explanation, except there isn't an explanation to be given. I am sorry, that's all. And I've said it. Anything else would just be talking, talking for the sake of it. And it wouldn't be about him, it would be to make me feel better. Just like the entire conversation itself.

'You don't have to apologise,' he says after a while.

'I do.'

'Tom…,' he begins, then he smiles, his eyes with an old, familiar look, 'I'm not going to blow sunshine up your arse or anything, but we were both out there doing our thing. Doing our jobs. I was in contact with people all spring, all summer. God knows where I picked it up. And sure, it might have been from you, and you shouldn't have come to work, and I know you came… I know you came because you didn't want to sit at home any longer, and there was selfishness there, but Jesus, son, you're not alone. Won't say everyone was doing it, but thousands were.' A beat. 'Tens of thousands.'

'It doesn't matter,' I say. 'I did it, you're dead. That's all.'

'And I might be dead anyway.'

A sob chokes in my throat, but I manage the words, 'That's a pretty big fucking *might*, by the way,' and we both laugh. Laughing at bringing the word *fuck* to the discussion, like it's actually funny anymore. Like me saying 'fuck' could possibly be funny, ever.

'I don't have anything for you,' says Taylor. 'It happened. Life goes on, or not. We all die at some point. You will one day, and the way you're going, one day pretty soon.'

'I can hope.'

———

'Don't say that.'

'What does it matter?'

He doesn't answer. We hold the gaze for a while longer, eventually the look slips away, and now we're just two guys sitting together, him staring at his hands, me staring blankly at the end of the bed, in the half-light of a hospital ward in the middle of the night.

'You'll come back,' I say eventually.

Maybe there'll be a time when we can get past this, move on, back to the old conversations.

'I can't,' he says.

I wait for the addition, the words tagged on to the brutal truth. This isn't real. None of this is real.

We look at each other again. I'm so tired. Tired and sad, and it feels so real, like it has a physical form, this amorphous mass sitting on me, crushing me, and all I can think to do is sleep, because that's the only way I can ignore it, the only way for it not to be here.

'Will you be here when I wake up?'

Feel like a kid asking his dad if he'll stick around. Watch me while I'm sleeping.

'No,' he says.

Swallow. Choke it back. Choke back the hurt. Choke back the self-loathing, that other entity with whom I exist.

'That's just the way it is.'

Those words are spoken, they're there, somewhere, in the air, hovering over the bed, existing somewhere in the room, and I don't even know who said them. Maybe it was me, maybe it was Dan. Last thing I'm aware of before I fall asleep. The last thing I remember having been said when I wake up.

* * *

And when I wake, it's morning, and the chair beside the bed is empty, and the first thing I think about is that Taylor is dead, which is the same thing I've thought every morning for the last two months, and the pain of it is so visceral, so aching, so real, that I can barely move.

There's a nurse, and she's young. Tall, beautiful, Somali origin maybe, but her accent is finest Glasgow.

'You feeling all right, Tom?' she says. 'You were restless in the night.'

245

epilogue

Soon enough, back at my desk. Compiling the case. Ducks in a row, everything that needs to go to the procurator's office.

Detective Inspector Kallas did her bit. Told her tale. Seems she neither lied nor even exaggerated, but made the point that if I had not suspected the minister, had I not therefore gone to the church, then the minister would not have been alerted by the alarm app on her phone, allowing her to apprehend me and bring me along to the death party in the old abandoned village hall on the Halfway Road. And then, more than likely, Kallas herself would just have been killed without ceremony, along with Gill Blair. In short, were it not for my actions, she would be dead. Shorter; I saved her life.

One way of putting it. And all true apart from the bit about me going to the church because I suspected the minister.

Either way, my job got saved. Again. Always landing on my feet, said the chief, which was weird, because I thought I always ended up on my knees.

Sometimes the accused sing and sometimes they never open their mouths. The Rev Goodbody is, mundanely, somewhere in the middle. Boy, how much of myself I see in her own self-contempt.

She's already admitted guilt, and is cooperating, so there's that. There will be no drawn out court case, no day-after-day trial, the details poured over by the media.

The church in Scotland is floundering, we all know that. Was before this started, and now, in the midst of a pandemic and several thousand deaths, and all the associated crap that's gone with it, it's possibly received its death knell. The slow decline just got that bit faster. Nothing to be done but pray, and we all know where that gets you. And so the Reverend Goodbody, faced with week upon week upon bloody week of funerals and death, finally cracked. Took her revenge. Identified people in the area who she held responsible, either for specific deaths or just in general, and went after them. Tony Blair was just a random victim on the path, just a someone who got in the way, as Kallas could have been, had I, the hero, not turned up to inadvertently affect events.

Goodbody selected Lord as her first mark. Sucked him in with a faked flirtatious personality. Bizarrely ended up in his attic, neither intent nor pre-planning involved on her part. Over dinner he'd said it was the only place in his house he'd never had sex. So they went up there to fuck. Men... Well, he got fucked all right. The only time in all my dealings with her where I've seen any kind of light in her eyes, was her retelling of having to creep down from the loft in the middle of the night, trying not to wake the wife. Called herself a cat burglar, even got the giggles when she invoked David Niven in *The Pink Panther*.

Why leave the masks? She wanted everyone to know why the victims deserved to die. Why then construct the cover story around the movie? She initially said she thought it was fun, then retracted that because, perhaps, she realised it made her sound psychotic, rather than pissed off and driven to ill deeds by circumstance. She had another distraction lined up, a link between the members of a choral group, who had, it transpired, secretly rehearsed in the choirmaster's house. The choirmaster had been fined for holding the meeting, though he never got the chance to pay the fine. Dead now. So are three other members of the group, with who knows how much mayhem spread around the community as a result.

The minister was onto it, the next hit list in her diary. So, hey, look at us, we saved some more lives...

Kallas and I, stuck on the same awkward merry-go-round, are stopped for coffee on the way back from the procurator's office in Glasgow. Her husband came back when he learned of her brush with death. Brought the kids. Happy family. I have no idea if he's staying.

'I never suspected her,' I say, as ever the one drawn to talk by one of the silences.

The inspector looks at me over the top of her flat white. She takes a sip, her tongue elegantly removes a little spot of froth on her lips, she lays the cup back in the saucer.

'The minister. I never suspected her. I went there...'

I don't get the words out. Seems pointless saying them, and they drift away. I don't even lift my coffee, just stare across the shop, looking at the two women sitting at the window, laughing over something on a phone.

'You knew she had vodka.'

'How did you know that?'

'Your DNA was on the bottle and both glasses. We knew it was you who'd been drinking in the church vestry.'

I nod, the nod becomes a head shake. That was pretty obvious.

'It will remain in the report that you went there because you suspected her.'

'You don't have to do that.'

'I cannot change it now. That would not look good for me. You have to stick with that story for my benefit.'

Well there's a sharp piece of legerdemain, turning this in to me somehow helping her. What can I say to that?

Another one of those silences, this one accompanied by an uncomfortable look across the table. Choosing to leap into the fire, I decide to address it, having practiced this conversation while lying in bed, wide awake, at four a.m.

'You were awake the entire time I was talking to the minister?' I ask.

We all know where this is going, but there is at least marginally easier footing to begin with.

'Yes.'

'How did you even manage that? Didn't she give you the GHB?'

'She did, but we know from working the case she varied the dose. She administered what she thought was required. She took me by surprise at Gill Blair's home, she incapacitated me with a small dose. This knocked me out, although not for long. However, even though I pretended to still be unconscious, she later gave me a further dose. Again, I was not out for long, I do not think. I awoke while she was killing Gill Blair.'

'She didn't notice?'

'I barely opened my eyes. It was apparent Mrs Blair was already dead, so I elected to play the part, rather than reveal myself. I wondered if a more suitable moment might arise.'

Something in her eyes, a shadow I don't recognise in her, but which I instinctively know is guilt. I wasn't expecting that, but, of course, I've thought that evening through often enough in the past couple of weeks. She picked her moment, but the moment was after I'd been stabbed and slashed. Sure, Goodbody wasn't trying to kill me at that point, but it was entirely to chance that one of those knife wounds didn't do the job nevertheless. She was drunk and out of control by then.

'There would have been no point in you reacting before

———

248

you did,' I say.

She blinks. Even that seems a significant and rare deviation from the normal. Everyone blinks, but that was a *blink*. A guilt blink.

'What were you going to do? If you'd spoken up, we'd both have died.'

'I was lucky. I should not have been so helpless as to have left something to such chance.'

'We all walked into it.'

'That does not make me feel any better.'

'You can't feel guilty about it.' She still looks guilty, so flippant words find their way, to no one's surprise, from my lips. 'Letting me get repeatedly slashed, so that I look like Al Pacino in *Scarface*, times a thousand, was really your only option.'

That doesn't really get much of a reaction. We need to work on her flippancy-recognition skills. Maybe the chief can send her on a course.

'I have not seen that film,' she says, and I can't help the small laugh.

'Well, Inspector, it worked out. You couldn't save Gill Blair, you saved the only person there you could, and you got out alive.'

She has nothing to say to that. She takes an evasive sip of coffee. Perhaps she's contemplating the fact, as I already have, of just how fortunate we were to wrap the whole thing up when we did. We stumbled upon the killer. Nothing we did as detectives helped solve this crime.

Don't linger on that, don't linger on how we got here.

'Nice job not reacting to the face slap,' I say.

'One learns to brace while walking into cold water.'

Ah. That's why they do it. So they can be cool while getting smacked in the face. That's some life planning.

I take a drink of coffee. Another silence threatens, and so I give myself a shake. I didn't start this conversation to linger on the guilt I didn't know Kallas was feeling, and I didn't start it for it to go nowhere.

'So you heard everything I said?'

'Yes, of course.'

Naturally, that's all she says. Deep breath. Come on, come on, spit it out you fugitive from reality.

'You know I… you know I think I might have infected the boss? DCI Taylor?'

'Yes, of course. I already wondered if that might have been part of your trouble. A lot of people close to others who died are blaming themselves, often wondering why they survived while others didn't.' A moment. That familiar, sympathetic look across the table. 'You are not alone. And DCI Taylor was a busy officer, he would have come across many hundreds of people in the community…'

'He was closest to –'

'It does not matter. It is impossible to know how and when and where the DCI became infected. Your guilt is understandable, Tom, but please accept that there is no one else who will share your need to appropriate blame in this way.'

I swallow. Having blundered into the conversation, I really wasn't expecting compassion. Certainly wasn't looking for it. On the other hand, what did I think she'd say?

Lower my eyes, swallow again. Don't cry, you fool. Now, come on, you started the conversation, and you didn't do it because you wanted to talk about Taylor.

'You heard the other thing I said?' I ask, although I don't actually manage to look at her.

A beat. The silence. She waits for me to lift my eyes. She reaches out and squeezes my hand.

'You said many things, Tom,' she says. 'We do not need to talk about them.'

She pauses. Maybe she doesn't pause. Maybe she just stops. Maybe that's all that there is.

What was I looking for anyway? *I love you too? I will tell Anders to return to Estonia, and you and I will be swimming naked together in icy waters by the weekend?*

'My husband is home. I have children. You and I need to work together, and neither of us is going anywhere. We should not talk of feelings, regardless of what they might be.' A beat. I stare at her like a hopeless fool, waiting to see if there's anything else. Waiting for the crumb to be thrown from the table.

There are no more crumbs, but she squeezes my hand again, everything said that had to be said, and then she elegantly drains her cup of coffee, nods at my cup for me to do the same, I obediently follow, and then together we get to our feet.

Well, I think *we should not talk of feelings, regardless of what they might be*, accompanied by the hand squeeze, more or less said *my husband is home, and I really need to make this work, but for sure, I want you to take me over the desk, and one day, hopefully, that will happen.*

And so we walk from the coffee shop back to the car, just as we're getting booked for parking on a yellow line. She shows the traffic warden her ID, the guy is about to make a disparaging remark but, as has been well documented, Kallas is gorgeous with an occasional killer smile, and she uses it now, and he smiles with her, gives me a more grudging nod, and as the rain begins to fall on another bleak and miserable afternoon in autumnal Glasgow, we get back into the car. I stick Bob on the CD player – the near-seventeen-minute majesty of *Murder Most Foul* – and off we head back out into traffic.

'I am not sure why this song exists,' says Kallas, eight minutes later.

* * *

1930hrs. On the button.

The guy who makes the sandwiches. A desk sergeant. The supervisor of the cleaners. Me. A constable I recognise, whose name I don't know. Five others whose identities and job titles are unknown to me. The politician, who must not have thought his more regular channel would offer the requisite anonymity. DCI Barnard, who once I helped on a nationwide fraud case. A face I recognise, to which I can attach neither name nor job title.

Thirteen in total, sitting in an anonymous room at Police Scotland HQ in Dalmarnock. Thought there'd be more, but on the other hand, there are three of these meetings a day. Used by our people from all over the west of Scotland.

That's who we are.

The sandwich guy is the main man. He's just one in a group, arranged around three desks pushed together, but he stands out. Natural authority. The little conversation that there is dies away, and all it took was one glance from him at the clock above the door.

'Thanks for coming,' he says.

He looks around the table, his eyes settle on me.

Harrison is in the café. Drinking coffee, looking through bullying and harassment figures that came out of the last station-wide staff survey. Waiting for me. Made sure I got here, heading back to the station to eat pizza together at our desks afterwards.

His hands open. I like this guy. Speaks as little as possible. If only everyone was like this.

I swallow. Nervous, which is strange. I'm not usually nervous. I've been here before. And literally here, sitting in this room, doing this. This thing.

'My name's Tom,' I say. Words up and out without any aforethought. It is after all, my name *is* Tom. How hard was that to say?

I pause. He looks at me.

You've come this far.

By Douglas Lindsay

The Barber, Barney Thomson

The Long Midnight of Barney Thomson
The Cutting Edge of Barney Thomson
A Prayer For Barney Thomson
The King Was In His Counting House
The Last Fish Supper
The Haunting of Barney Thomson
The Final Cut
Aye, Barney
Curse Of The Clown

The Barbershop 7 (Novels 1-7)

Other Barney Thomson

The Face of Death
The End of Days
Barney Thomson: Zombie Slayer
The Curse of Barney Thomson & Other Stories
Scenes From The Barbershop Floor

DS Hutton

The Unburied Dead
A Plague Of Crows
The Blood That Stains Your Hands
See That My Grave Is Kept Clean
In My Time Of Dying

DCI Jericho

We Are The Hanged Man
We Are Death

DI Westphall

Song of the Dead
Boy In the Well
The Art of Dying

Pereira & Bain

Cold Cuts
The Judas Flower

Stand Alone Novels

Lost in Juarez
Being For The Benefit Of Mr Kite!
A Room With No Natural Light
Ballad In Blue
These Are The Stories We Tell

Other

For The Most Part Uncontaminated
There Are Always Side Effects
Kids, And Why You Shouldn't Eat More Than One For Breakfast
Santa's Christmas Eve Blues
Cold September

Printed in Great Britain
by Amazon

48749043R00156